Goya's Ring
and The
Naked Maja Dancing

Richard L. Katz

PEGASUS BOOKS

Pegasus Books
3338 San Marino Ave
San Jose, CA 95127
www.pegasusbooks.net

First Edition: October 2015

Published in North America by Pegasus Books. For information, please contact Pegasus Books c/o Christopher Moebs, 3338 San Marino Ave, San Jose, CA 95127.

Library of Congress Cataloguing-In-Publication Data
Richard L. Katz
Goya's Ring and The Naked Maja Dancing/Richard L. Katz– 1st ed
p. cm.
Library of Congress Control Number: 2015952715

ISBN – 978-1-941859-39-1

1. FICTION / Thrillers / Historical. 2. FICTION / Action & Adventure. 3. FICTION / Historical. 4. ART / History / Romanticism. 5. HISTORY / Holocaust. 6. FICTION / Romance / Action & Adventure

10 9 8 7 6 5 4 3 2 1

Comments about *Goya's Ring and The Naked Maja Dancing* and requests for additional copies, book club rates and author speaking appearances may be addressed to Richard L. Katz or Pegasus Books c/o Christopher Moebs, 3338 San Marino Ave, San Jose, CA, 95127, or you can send your comments and requests via e-mail to cmoebs@pegasusbooks.net.

Also available as an eBook from Internet retailers and from Pegasus Books

Printed in the United States of America

For my fabulous children, Natasha Keel Katz Magee and Ariana Wendy Keel Katz, who had to endure my spontaneous stories I made up when I put them to bed as young children.

And in memory of my paternal grandparents and uncles whom I never had the opportunity to meet, because they were slaughtered in WWll by Nazi collaborators.

Inspired by a series of true events, *Goya's Ring* is an action adventure story that tells the tale of Alessandra Santana, a beautiful Spanish Art historian and amateur opera singer, on the trail of a priceless Goya masterpiece lost to the art world for 200 years and stolen by the Nazis. In her quest, she unexpectedly unlocks secrets of her own past as well as that of her client that ties them together.

Written in the style of a marriage between *Monuments Men*, *American Treasure* and *The Da Vinci Code,* the page-turning novel binds together the Spanish Inquisition with the Holocaust. A thrilling tale of intrigue, deceit and romance, *Goya's Ring* dives into the shadowy world of art collectors and museums, and finishes with a breathtaking twist.

GOYA'S RING
AND THE
NAKED MAJA DANCING

Goya's Ring and *The Naked Maja Dancing*

Prologue

Berlin, 1938

"Jew! We know you're in there."

Inside, Solomon Braverman stood to the side of the window and subtly pulled back the curtain. He had heard the knocks, but he was too frightened to answer. He knew what was coming.

Solomon's wife, Rifka, huddled behind him and peered outside. "Gestapo!"

Solomon placed his hand on her mouth and whispered, "We're not here."

The knocks grew louder. Heavy footsteps rumbled up the stairs.

"Jews," a new voice shouted. "It's time!"

Six-year-old Devorah and her teenage brother, Arthur, peeked out from their bedroom doors, terror in their eyes.

"Is it them, Papa?" Arthur asked a bit too loudly.

"Shhh!" his parents hushed him.

Devorah started to cry. Her mother smothered Devorah's face in her bosom. The muffled sobs continued. Solomon prayed the Nazis wouldn't hear them.

"We know you're in there," yet another voice shouted. "You have until tomorrow morning to gather your things. One suitcase per person. Be at the railroad station at 8:00 am, or we will burn your house down."

The sound of boots stomped away toward nearby houses.

Solomon ordered everyone into the living room.

"Children, I have been expecting something like this since last November, when Jewish homes and businesses in our neighborhood were burned and looted."

"Why would they do that?" Arthur asked.

"Because our neighbor, Herschel Grynszpan, killed the German Ambassador's Secretary to France," Solomon said.

"Why did Herschel kill someone, Papa?" Devorah asked.

"His family had been 'requested' to leave Germany'," Solomon explained, taking Devorah's hand in his. "Herschel, who was living in France at the time, decided to take revenge. He intended to kill the Ambassador but when he wasn't there, Herschel took his rage out on the poor secretary."

"But *we* didn't do anything wrong," Devorah's eyes pleaded, "did we?"

Solomon hugged his daughter.

"No, dear. It just seems that being God's chosen sometimes means we have to suffer more than others."

He faced his family.

"Stay here."

Solomon climbed into the attic and brought down a painting he had hidden there since Kristallnacht. He hung it on the wall.

"Arthur, get the camera and tripod. I want to take a picture of us together."

He suspected he wouldn't be seeing his children again for a long time. Perhaps never.

Arthur screwed the Leica camera on the tripod and set the self-timer. He hastened to join the rest of the family, who posed in front of the painting.

When the camera clicked, Solomon removed the painting from the wall, wrapped it in brown paper and tied a string around it.

"I'll be back before dark," he said as he hastened to leave.

Rifka blocked the door. "That painting has been in our family for one hundred thirty years."

She clutched his sleeve. "You can't sell it."

"I'm not selling it. I'm buying our children's future."

Solomon moved Rifka aside and headed for Prinz-Albrecht-Str-8, Gestapo headquarters. He'd have to hurry to get the film developed in time and get to the headquarters in time before they closed.

As he passed the Air Ministry, just a short block from the feared Gestapo building, Solomon hesitated. One week earlier, he had approached a low-level Nazi to arrange a meeting with Reinhard Heydrich, the head of the Gestapo.

"I have something his Excellency might be interested in."

The functionary had laughed.

"Jew, you have nothing he won't have in a few weeks."

But Solomon didn't give up. He knew that, while Hitler had been rejected twice from Vienna's Academy of Fine Arts, that hadn't stopped him from assuming the role as the ultimate art critic. And Solomon knew Hitler had a fondness for the works of old masters, dating up to the 19th century. The Goya in Solomon's arms dated back to around 1810 and had never been exhibited in public. He felt confident the painting would interest the Fuhrer. The question was how to gain access.

Arden Hagel, a friend and art dealer, provided the answer.

"You know that painting you have coveted for years?" Solomon asked.

"The *Naked Maja Dancing*?"

"I need to arrange an exchange?"

"I have many clients who would pay handsomely for such a treasure."

"Money is of no value to me now. I need to get my children out of the country."

Solomon had heard about the British Jewish Refugee Committee, which in response to the events of Kristallnacht, appealed to members of the British Parliament to allow Jewish children to immigrate to England. Parliament had agreed, and the first sealed trains left one week earlier. Solomon intended to get his children on the Kindertransport before it was too late.

"How can I be of assistance?" Hagel asked.

"Do you know anyone close to the Fuhrer who could act as a go between?"

"Perhaps," Hagel hesitated, "Hermann Goering. He's closest to Hitler, and he is also an ardent art collector."

"This is no time for jokes," Solomon responded.

"I do not joke about such matters."

"And just how are we going to get in to see the Reichmarshal?" Solomon asked.

"His brother, Albert, will arrange it. He hates the Nazis and uses his family connection to do what he can to help Jews."

\#

Solomon's heart beat faster as he entered Gestapo Headquarters. An appointment with the man who established the

Gestapo was intimidating to say the least, and the massive Nazi cross that filled the atrium made Solomon's knees knock.

"I have an appointment with his Excellency, Herr Goering," he stammered.

The uniformed guard pointed down the block.

"His offices are in the Air Ministry Building now."

The more he thought about it, the more he was sure his plan wouldn't work. *Why would Goering bother to allow his children to leave?* He could simply confiscate the painting and have "the "Jew" thrown in prison.

As Solomon approached the Air Ministry building, the winter air felt a bit colder. *You have nothing to lose,* he told himself. He tightened his coat, and resolute, he marched up the steps.

"Are you Solomon Braverman?" the guard asked.

"Yes," a surprised Solomon blurted.

How did they know? Were they going to arrest him?

"Is that the painting?"

The guard pointed to the package under Solomon's arm.

Solomon nodded.

"Leave it with me, and I will see that his Excellency gets it when he returns."

Solomon clutched the painting. "But I must see Herr Goering in person."

"I am afraid that is impossible. He won't be back for several days."

The guard reached for the painting. Solomon didn't have "several days."

"Does his Excellency know what it is I want?"

"The Reichmarshal only told me to accept the painting."

Solomon turned to leave. He had no idea what he was going to do, but leaving the painting was not an option.

Another guard blocked the doorway. He placed his rifle in front of him.

"You will not be allowed to leave the building with the painting," a voice said from behind. It sounded familiar.

Solomon turned to see a uniformed Hagel.

"Yes, that's right. I am a member of the SS."

Hagel snatched the package from under Solomon's arm and tore away the brown paper wrapping. His breath caught.

"Such a masterpiece! I am sure Herr Goering will be pleased."

Hagel nodded to the guard blocking the exit to move aside.

"Go home, Jew, and pack up your things," the first guard said and shoved Solomon toward the door. "Tomorrow, you will be taken to a new home."

"But my children," Solomon said, turning to face Hagel, "you must let them leave."

"It is not up to me," Hagel said. "It's his Excellency's decision, and he is very busy right now."

"Please, Arden. For old time's sake. Please ask."

Hagel stared at Solomon and nodded.

"If he happens to call, I will ask."

"Thank you. Thank you," Solomon muttered as he trudged out into darkening sky.

All was lost. Snow began to fall. He looked up at the sky.

"Why, God? Why always us?"

Chapter 1

Sixty-Five Years Later, New York City

In a large gallery in the Metropolitan Museum, a sign on an easel read, *Art and the Church*. Alessandra Santana, slim and stunning in her designer dress, looked around the room. A small crowd of elegantly dressed contributors sipped champagne. She dreaded such events. She was an art historian, not a fund raiser. She had pleaded with Seigfried to have someone else shepherd the group through the "members only" night.

Her boss was sympathetic but unyielding.

"But it is why I hired you. You know more about Spanish art than anyone, and this exhibit is full of Spanish artists. So please go out there and impress our patrons with the quality of our collections, as well as our expertise."

Alessandra tapped on a champagne flute to get the crowd's attention. The buzz quieted.

"Thank you all for coming this evening. Many of you may have seen the "Decadent Art" exhibit that ended a few months ago."

Alessandra scanned the crowd to get a head count. She continued in a slight Spanish accent that had been muted by her many years at Oxford.

"In that exhibition, we attempted to duplicate the German exhibit of the same name, whereby the Nazis tried to show the degenerate nature of modern art. This time, we have put together a show that attempts to deal with the Catholic Church's influence on art."

Many of the members appeared more interested in people-watching than the art hanging on the wall. She ignored their jaded looks and continued her lecture, pointing to the painting, *Portrait of a Lady*.

"In the sixteenth century, Spain's most famous painter was El Greco. He was born Domenikos Theotocopoulos, on the isle of Crete. He always signed his paintings in Greek characters. This painting is believed to be of his mistress, Jeronima de las Cuevas, a Jewish noblewoman.

Jews had been expelled from the country by then, so El Greco was brought before the inquisition for having relations with a Jew. Jeronima saved them both from the flames of the Inquisition by claiming to be a convert."

As Alessandra spoke, she noticed a man standing in back, who seemed to be intently listening. He stood out because he was at least a head above everyone else and because of what he was not wearing—no formal attire, no suit, no tie—just a leather Eisenhower jacket, jeans and tennis shoes. Inwardly she smiled. She thought she might as well direct her comments toward someone who really cared about the subject.

Alessandra glided to the next painting, *The Naked Maja* by Goya. The crowd moved with her. The Eisenhower jacket pushed up toward the front. He pulled a photo from his jacket and looked from it to the painting and back, as though comparing the two. Alessandra observed him as she spoke.

"*The Naked Maja* is on loan from the Museo del Prado. It is perhaps Goya's best known piece and, at the time, the most controversial."

To make sure Eisenhower jacket was still listening, she elevated the emotion in her voice.

"Sadly, as with El Greco two centuries before, the Inquisition summoned Goya to defend what was, in their view, a decadent work."

"Sounds like what the Nazis did," the Eisenhower jacket said.

The group turned their attention toward him.

"Yes. Exactly the point"," Alessandra nodded.

Suddenly, the crowd seemed more interested as they turned back to hear her response.

"'Degenerate art' was the term adopted by the Nazi regime in Germany to describe virtually all modern art. Such art was banned on the grounds that it was 'un-German' or 'Jewish-Bolshevist' in nature."

She addressed the entire crowd.

"How many of you came to our last exhibit?"

About half the crowd raised their hands, as did Eisenhower jacket.

"Then perhaps I should explain a little about what the Nazis attempted to do in 1937. The exhibition of Degenerate Art was mounted by the Nazis in Munich, accompanied by labels deriding the art. The idea was to educate the German people about the 'evils' of modern art, and especially its alleged Jewish/Bolshevik influences. The 'degenerate' art was surrounded by quotations from Hitler's speeches. It was supposed to inflame public opinion against this avant-garde art. Ironically, the 'degenerate' exhibition attracted five times as many visitors as the Nazi-approved 'Great German Art Exhibition' that opened in Munich at the same time",," Alessandra smiled. "Eventually, three million 'inflamed' visitors were 'educated.'

After the exhibit, paintings were sorted out for sale and sold in Switzerland at auction; some pieces were acquired by museums, others by private collectors. Nazi officials took many for their private use. Herman Goering took many valuable pieces, including a Van Gogh and a Cezanne."

"Didn't Goya also paint a *Clothed Maja?*" an older, grey haired man in the back shouted.

Alessandra stood on her toes to see who was speaking.

"Yes, but we are not sure it was the same woman as *The Naked Maja*. In fact, *The Naked Maja* is believed to be several women. The face is one, the body of one or more women."

"What about yet another Maja?" the Eisenhower jacket asked.

"What are you asking?"

"Didn't Goya paint another nude woman, but this time in a dancing mode?" the Eisenhower jacket said in a louder voice.

Who was this man? Why was he here? And how did he know?

"There were rumors of such a painting, but never confirmed."

Alessandra struggled to go on. She forced her eyes away from the casually dressed stranger.

"We need to move on, as time seems to be running short."

The tour passed more portraits, Goya's *Portrait of Leocadia Zorillo* and *The Executions of May Third 1808*. Alessandra paused at the *Zorillo* painting, but she said nothing. She studied the woman in the painting, standing next to her young daughter. She stole a glance at Leather Jacket, who hadn't moved from *The Naked Maja*. Alessandra moved on to the *Executions*.

"In *The Executions of May Third*, Goya exhibits his antipathy for war. You can see that the firing squad in the painting are not men, but massive, threatening shapes. At this time, Spain had been persuaded by Napoleon to join France in its war with England, which Goya bitterly opposed. Eventually, because of his antiwar beliefs, he moved to France and died there."

Leather Jacket had moved on to the *Zorillo* painting, then he approached. He raised his hand.

"You have a question?" Alessandra asked.

Jacket nodded.

"Do you have a name, sir?"

"David."

"Yes, David. Your question?"

"I've been doing some research and..."

A security guard strode toward Alessandra.

"I'm sorry folks, but we have to wrap up. Please follow me into the main gallery."

A few groans were emitted from the crowd. It seemed that David had gotten the donors' attention.

#

Seigfried Kleinermann, impeccably dressed, sat erect at his office desk. Unconsciously, he brushed a few stray hairs on his almost bald head." He opened his desk drawer and retrieved an envelope bearing the return address, "Yokahama Overseas Services, Ltd." He started to pull the letter out of the envelope when there was a knock on the door. He glanced at the monitor on his desk. Alessandra had already entered the main gallery.

Kleinermann quickly placed the letter back in the envelope, closed and locked the drawer. As he rose, he knocked over the sign reading, "Director of Art." He straightened it and shouted toward the door.

"I'm on my way."

#

Kleinermann was an imposing figure at the podium. Even at age 75, he maintained his posture and looked taller than his 5'9"— the same height as Alessandra, who stood nearby. His face was gaunt, but had that confident determined look of a man with a military background who was used to being in charge. He scanned the audience and spoke in a clipped, German accent.

"I hope you have enjoyed the tour with Ms. Santana. You see why we are so proud to have her here as our assistant curator and lecturer. Her knowledge of Spanish art and its place in history has been a great help to us in putting together this fine exhibit."

Kleinermann beamed as the audience enthusiastically applauded her. Alessandra forced a smile, clasped her hands together and bowed. As people started to leave, some came by to shake Alessandra's hand. With one eye on the person whose hand she was shaking, she searched the crowd for David. Just as the last guest was leaving, she finally spied him coming into the main gallery, a photo clutched in his hand.

"Another *Naked Maja?*" Alessandra asked.

David thrust the photo towards her.

Alessandra peered at the photo. Her eyes widened.

"Can you come with me? I need to get something from my office."

Without waiting for a response, she hurried away. David followed.

In her office, she peered through a magnifying glass at the photo. David looked over her shoulder. The photograph showed two adults who stood in front of a painting; a couch was nearby. Each adult embraced one child in front of them. It was difficult to see much detail in the painting, but Alessandra could make out a naked woman who appeared to be pirouetting, as if dancing.

The dancer wore some kind of pendant around her neck and the left hand was raised, showing a ring. The view of her body was from the side, so one could only see part of her breast and buttocks.

Alessandra lowered the glass.

"Where did you get this?"

"From my mother. It's a smaller copy of the only photo she has of her parents."

"And the painting?"

"The Nazis stole it."

David retrieved the photo from Alessandra. "So, was there another *Naked Maja?*"

"There are rumors." Alessandra hesitated. "How large is the original photo?"

"Eight by ten inches."

"Could you bring it here?"

"My mother won't let it out of the house."

David reached for his wallet, retrieved a business card and thrust it at her.

"You'll have to come and see for yourself."

Alessandra looked at the card. She shook her head.

"I normally don't go to stranger's homes."

"Even when they offer you the opportunity to locate a great artist's work?"

Alessandra smiled.

"Tell me you're not interested," David interrupted, "and I'll leave you alone."

"I…" Alessandra started to say.

David seized the card from her hands and scribbled on it. "Look," this is my mother's address. She's a widow and lives alone. Please reconsider. Bring an escort if you want. If you change your mind, call me and I'll arrange to meet you there."

After David left, Alessandra studied the card, "David Edlestein, CPA." *How dangerous could this be?* After two hundred years of rumors, there was finally evidence that there may have indeed been a third *Maja*. It was the opportunity of a lifetime, but she was gun-shy. Months earlier, she went hunting for a missing Picasso and ended up regretting it. She'd have to sleep on it, but she knew it would be a fitful sleep.

Alessandra tossed and turned all night. She just couldn't get the Picasso incident out of her head. As she had done many times before, she replayed the scene at JFK Airport. The clue was there somewhere…

\#

The 747 rolled to a stop in a secure part of the Airport. The Picasso painting sat safely in the belly of the plane, waiting for Alessandra to personally collect it on the runway.

Only one month earlier, she had flown to Paris to evaluate the recovered painting that had been stolen from the Pompidou Centre. She had given her assessment as to its authenticity, but the Centre wanted a second opinion. She was flying it back for her boss to personally evaluate.

Alessandra had done everything to assure the painting arrived undamaged. She supervised the packaging of the painting and accompanied it in an armored truck to Charles de Gaulle Airport. She watched it being loaded into the belly of the plane and made sure it was properly secured. She waited until the cargo compartment was closed, and only then did she agree to go aboard.

As soon as they landed in New York and the seat belt sign turned off, Alessandra rushed to the exit and waited while the ramp was pushed up to the plane. When the door opened, she was shocked to see a large entourage waiting for her. She spied TV cameras and what looked like members of the press.

Kleinermann had jumped the gun. Alessandra was taken aback. She knew the museum needed some good publicity for an upcoming fund raiser, but this was not the way to go about it. Nevertheless, she put on a smile and accepted the greeting of the Mayor of New York as he met her at the bottom of the ramp.

The Mayor, accompanied by Kleinermann, congratulated her in front of a stand of microphones and asked her to say a few words about the painting. Alessandra, however, intent on making sure the painting was safely removed from the cargo area, turned her attention to the belly of the plane.

The Mayor, apparently sensing her concern, pointed to a police escort who waited nearby.

"Don't worry. They will safely transport the painting back to the museum."

Alessandra then turned to Kleinermann who nodded. She gathered herself and faced the press.

"How did you confirm that the painting was authentic?" someone shouted.

Alessandra hesitated.

"I have not."

She paused as she saw the painting being loaded into a police van.

"Excuse me for a moment," she said and hastened over to the van driver. "Will you please see that it's taken directly to the restoration department of the Museum."

The officer nodded. "Those were our instructions from Mr. Kleinermann as well."

It took another half hour before she was finished with the press and was escorted in her own police vehicle back to the Museum. She hastened down to the restoration room where she saw Kleinermann and Bernard Von Herstellen, the museum's chief restorer, waiting by the container that housed the painting.

"We wanted you here before we opened the container," Kleinermann said.

He nodded to Von Herstellen to proceed. Von Herstellen eagerly pried away the boards. When he peeled away the wrapping from the frame, they all stared in shocked disbelief. The painting was gone! Only the frame remained.

Chapter 2

The alarm sounded at 6:00 am, but Alessandra was already in the shower. The water invigorated her. Having spent the entire night mulling over the lost Picasso, she was still no closer to figuring out what and where she'd gone wrong. Of one thing she was sure, the Picasso was on the plane when it took off, so someone on the plane had access to the belly of the plane or less likely, it got diverted somewhere after it left the airport.

In either case, she was placed on probation while the authorities investigated. The cloud of suspicion hung over her. He every move was now under scrutiny. With that hanging over her head, dare she embark on another adventure? As curious as she was about David's painting, there was no way she'd get involved without her boss' consent. And she wasn't sure she'd get it.

While Kleinermann had been supportive of her, she knew the Museum Board wanted her head. Many on the Board suspected she was involved with the theft. And who could blame them? After all, she had supervised every movement of the painting except the last one, and no one thought the police were involved. And even if she wasn't the culprit, "they needed a scapegoat," Kleinermann had told her.

"I said I'd resign if they fired you. We compromised on probation."

By the time she reached her office, Alessandra had decided she had to know if David's painting was real. What came after, she wasn't sure, but she was determined to follow the trail wherever it led. Three months of suspicious looks from the staff had taken their toll. She was always on edge, and sleepless nights didn't help. Short of the police finding the Picasso, regardless of the risks, she needed a diversion and maybe, just maybe, discovering a long lost treasure would gain her the redemption she desperately desired.

But she wouldn't tell Kleinermann her real reasons. To him, she'd argue the good publicity they'd get if the painting existed and they could locate it. Possibly the museum could get to display it, and finally it would raise the stature of the museum in the eyes of the art world. Kleinermann was always looking to elevate himself in the high society circles of New York.

#

Kleinermann reread the "Yokahama Overseas Services, Ltd." letter over and over. The amount the Japanese were willing to pay, while tempting, wasn't enough. He needed more money to complete an acquisition of his own that he had discovered in Argentina. Besides, he had no idea how to acquire the kind of art work they had in mind. There simply were no paintings of that magnitude available, at least not at the price they were willing to pay. He was about to call Mr. Yokahama when his phone buzzed.

"Ms. Santana is here to see you."

Without knocking, Alessandra poked her head in Kleinermann's door.

"Come in, my dear. That was an excellent tour you gave the other day."

He surreptitiously put the letter in his lap.

"Many of our donors called to compliment you."

Alessandra waved aside the flattery.

"I never got a chance to thank you for your support. It was generous of you to offer to quit on my behalf."

"The incident was unfortunate, but it's ridiculous to think you stole the painting."

"But some people do, so it's nice to have you on my side."

Alessandra smoothed her dress.

"Have you ever heard of a second Naked Maja?"

"By Goya?" Kleinermann asked.

"Yes."

"Only the one, The Clothed Maja."

Kleinermann pointed to the chair opposite his desk.

"Is there such a painting?"

"When I was a young art student in Barcelona, one of my professors told us there were rumors of another blasphemy."

"And you are telling me about this now because?" Kleinermann's voice trailed off.

"I may have a lead to find it, that is, if it was not destroyed by the Nazis."

"You have a lead?"

Alessandra sat in the chair and leaned over Kleinermann's desk.

"This man showed me a photo of a painting that fits the description. He says the Nazis stole it."

Kleinermann's eyes lit up.

"If such a painting was located by us, that would be a great coup for the Museum."

Alessandra nodded.

"And of course, it would do wonders to wipe away any doubts about the Picasso's mysterious disappearance." Kleinermann's eyes took on a mischievous glint.

"You want me to pursue this?"

Kleinermann nodded.

"You are not afraid to risk another incident?" Alessandra asked.

"The Board wouldn't like it, but if you could recover the painting, they wouldn't mind the good publicity. So, keep me advised."

Kleinermann let the letter slip to the floor as he came out from behind his desk.

"You are serious?"

Kleinermann put his arm around Alessandra in a fatherly-like embrace.

"My dear, from the look in your eyes, it is obvious that you had already decided to pursue it. So you might as well do it with the blessing of the Museum."

Chapter 3

Alessandra could hardly contain herself as she glided out of Kleinermann's office. The man had verified his reputation for risk which was one the reasons she had gone to work for the Museum in the first place. He was a legend in her field, and it was obvious from the first interview they shared a similar view of acquiring art. To Kleinermann, if there was a chance to acquire or at least be involved in acquiring a major work, his rule was to act first and ask questions later. She sprinted back to her office, calmed herself so as not to reveal her enthusiasm, and dialed David's number.

#

David paced outside his mother's apartment building. The light had gone and the air turned frosty. Occasionally, he blew into his hands to keep them warm. Trails of mist flowed from his mouth.

Fifteen minutes had passed and he was beginning to worry Alessandra might not show. She had sounded skeptical on the phone. He didn't blame her. But he was sure once she saw the larger photo and heard his mother's story, she'd sign on.

A taxi pulled up. Alessandra stepped out. She looked professional in her business suit, but out of place for the neighborhood, a working class section of the Bronx. David eagerly shook her hand. He was struck by its softness and the almost sensual way in which she returned the greeting. He watched as she looked around warily.

"Don't worry, the neighborhood's safe." He offered his arm.

Alessandra hesitantly slipped her arm into his. "No neighborhood is safe in New York."

"You've been seeing too many movies." David led the way to the elevator.

David knocked on the door to his mother's apartment.

Alessandra pointed to a small slanted oblong object on the door jamb. "What is it?"

"It's a mezuzah."

Alessandra arched an eyebrow.

"There's a small scroll inside with inscriptions from the bible. In Jewish homes, it's traditional to place the mezuzah on the doorpost of every room. It reminds us of our obligations to God." He banged on the door. "Mom, are you in there?"

"David?" A voice called out from inside.

"Yeah, mom."

"Don't you have your key?"

"Just wanted to be sure you were dressed." He touched his lips with two fingers and then touched the mezuzah.

Alessandra appeared perplexed.

"It's good luck," David said. "Keeping the tradition will grant long life for our children and us." He turned the key and opened the door. "We have company," he shouted.

Alessandra put two fingers to her lips and touched the mezuzah, then hastily crossed herself and followed David through the door.

Devorah Edlestein wore a smudged apron over a frayed housedress. Her gnarled hands feverishly diced some celery and carrots at the Formica kitchen counter. She barely looked up as Alessandra and David entered the room.

David ambled over and hugged her. She turned to face him. Her eyes sparkled as they lit on Alessandra.

"Alessandra, this is my amazing mom, Devorah Edlestein."

Devorah wiped her hands on her apron, and grasped both of Alessandra's hands in hers.

"Such a *shayna maidel*. So, you're from Spain?"

"Barcelona."

"Our ancestors originally came from Spain." Devorah reached out, "Come, let me take your coat."

As she reached for the coat, Devorah's eyes lingered on the cross dangling from Alessandra's neck.

"So, how long have you two known each other?"

"Mom! Alessandra's only here to help identify the painting."

David motioned for Alessandra to follow him.

"Do you mind?" Alessandra asked.

"It's a free country." Devorah wiped her hands on her apron and joined them in front of the photo hanging on a faded wall in the living room.

Alessandra peered at the photo. "Can we take it into the light?"

David looked at his mother who waved her hand as if to say, "Go ahead." David pulled down the photo and held it near the lamp next to the sheet covered couch.

Alessandra squinted, retrieved a small magnifying glass from her suit pocket and studied the photo. Her brow furrowed.

"Mrs. Edlestein, how long had the painting been in your family's possession?"

"Generations. That is, until the Nazis burned it?"

"You don't know for sure it was burned," David protested.

Devorah opened a drawer from a mahogany bureau and pulled out a sheaf of newspaper clippings. She thrust one of them at Alessandra. The headline blazed, *NAZIS BURN FAMOUS PAINTINGS*.

A photo below the headline depicted a bonfire with uniformed Nazis throwing paintings on the fire.

"After the war, gentile friends of our family sent the article to me," Devorah said. "There was a note."

"Mom, we have no proof ours was in that fire."

"They knew someone who saw it burn," Devorah said.

Alessandra's heart sunk. She turned to leave.

"Will you stay for dinner," Devorah asked.

Alessandra hesitated.

"Yes, please stay," David said.

Alessandra was about to politely say "no," but changed her mind. Perhaps she could learn more about the painting's history. Even if the painting couldn't be recovered, maybe she could still prove it once existed, which in itself would make history. "Okay, thank you. I am hungry."

During dinner, the conversation turned to Spain. "You know, if it wasn't for King Ferdinand, we wouldn't be here discussing the painting," Devorah said. "And I think he did the Jews a favor by the expulsion order."

Alessandra's eyes widened.

"I don't agree," David said. "He set the precedent that resulted in the Holocaust."

"Aha!" Devorah smiled. "And here we are."

"Mom, you don't really mean that Hitler also did us a favor."

"Look at it this way, without Ferdinand and Hitler there would be no Israel."

David turned toward Alessandra. "I can't believe I'm hearing these words from my mother."

Devorah stared at David. "And without World War II, the civil rights movement would not have happened until many years later; nor the feminist movement, nor the gay rights movements."

She fixed her eyes on Alessandra.

"In the end, all the bad things dictators did to the Jews, only made us stronger. We're survivors."

"Can we talk about the painting?" David asked.

"What painting? There is no painting." Devorah teared up. "Leave it be." She excused herself and left the room.

Alessandra gave David a quizzical look.

"My mother says these things because she tries to look on the bright side of things, but whenever I bring up the painting, she clams up. It's too painful to talk about because it bought her freedom, but not her parents."

"I don't understand."

David glanced toward his mother's bedroom. "I just wanted to make sure she closed the door."

He sat opposite Alessandra. "This is what I know. The painting's been in the family forever. How we got it, I don't know. But I do know how we lost it."

Alessandra nodded her head as if to say "go on."

"The whole family was in line at a railroad station in Berlin waiting to be taken to a concentration camp when, at the last moment, a German officer snatched Artie, that's my uncle, and my mom out of line. They were put on a train with other children and then taken to England."

"And the painting? Is there a connection?"

"My mother has a vague memory of her father talking about making a deal with a Nazi officer. The story goes, my grandfather traded the painting for his children's freedom."

Alessandra felt a cold chill. She knew many Nazis, particularly Hitler and Goering, went to great lengths to "collect" works of art. Both set up vast networks of agents to locate and confiscate art collections of prominent Jews. If the collections weren't taken outright, the Jews were allowed to leave Germany by "donating" their possessions. Some eighty thousand exit visas were obtained this way. Apparently, Devorah's family was one of them.

"What happened to your uncle?" Alessandra asked.

"He died during the War fighting for us."

Alessandra glanced back at the photo which had been rehung on the wall. "If it's burned, what is it you want from me?"

"I just don't believe the painting was burned. Why would they? Besides, I've read about other Jewish Holocaust survivors making claims for art work taken by the Nazis that they thought had been destroyed."

In fact, Alessandra knew of one such case that involved a museum in Hartford.

"Is there some way of checking to see if the painting was actually burned?" David asked.

"The Nazis kept meticulous records of everything," Alessandra said. "I can check with my sources, but even if it existed you may need more than just a photo to reclaim the painting."

"Such as?" David asked.

"If the painting is still in Germany a photo might be enough, but other countries have more strict requirements for making a claim. In that case, you would need something that tied your family to the painting. A witness. A letter. Something."

"Witnesses are probably dead. Any letters that would tie my family to the painting were left in Germany and certainly gone."

"Did your mother ever tell you the history of this painting?" Alessandra asked.

"Only what I already told you."

"Do you know if any of your ancestors was ever named Zorillo?"

David shrugged.

"Ask your mother." Alessandra lifted her coat from the rack. "And thank her for dinner. Call me when you know the answer."

For the next two Wednesdays, as per usual, David went to his mother's apartment for dinner and tried to get her to talk about the painting's history. "Mom, what can you tell me about the origins of this painting?"

"You should eat more vegetables."

David dished himself up some more string beans. "There, is that what you want?"

"I want only what is best for you."

"Then tell me about the painting."

"It's burned, just like my pot roast."

"You roast is fine, mom."

"Really? You like it." Devorah lifted the meat platter and started to dish up. "Here, have some more."

David threw down his cloth napkin. "Dammit mom. Why won't you talk about it?"

Devorah started to pick up the dishes from the table. "Will you come next week?"

David nodded.

"I like it when you come to dinner. Ever since Papa died, I don't like to cook just for myself."

The following week was more of the same.

"What if the painting wasn't burned?" David said. "Wouldn't you want to try and get it back?"

"That Alessandra is very nice. Too bad she's a *shiksa*."

"It's not that way with us. Strictly business."

"Next year you'll be forty-five. A forty-five year old man should be married and have *kinder* by now."

David smiled. "You mean you want grandchildren."

"So, is that so wrong?"

"I'll make a deal. Tell me about the painting and I'll get married and give you lots of grandkids."

"To a *shiksa*?"

"To anyone." David raised his voice. "Just tell me."

"If I knew, I would tell you." Devorah lowered her voice. "I was too young when I . . ." Devorah got up from the table. She leaned over and kissed David on top of the head. "I am sorry, I am no help."

"Does the name Zorillo mean anything?" An exasperated David asked.

She threw up her arms and walked into the kitchen.

David suspected his mother knew something but was holding back. However, it seemed clear she wasn't going to crack. He decided to see Alessandra in person and tell her he had come up empty. At least for now.

The next morning he was at the Museum at opening time. Something told him to check the "Art and the Church" exhibit again before contacting Alessandra. When he reached Goya's *Portrait of Leocadia Zorillo*, he realized why he felt compelled to revisit the exhibition. He took out his photo of *The Naked Maja Dancing*, and repeatedly compared the two. Was there a resemblance? He couldn't be sure.

He hurried to the information desk. "Can you tell me if Ms. Santana is in?" He handed the volunteer his card.

Without a word, the volunteer dialed his phone. "No answer. Want to leave a message?"

"Tell her I asked about the *Portrait of Leocadia Zorillo*," David said and left.

That evening he received a call from Alessandra. She was still at work.

"So, what's the Zorillo connection?" David asked.

"I don't have time to explain now. And I have a very busy schedule tomorrow, but I will take a lunch break. I like to leave the museum to feed the ducks at the Hernshead Boat Landing in Central Park. Can you meet me there at noon?"

"I'll bring sandwiches," David said.

The next day, David spied Alessandra, dressed professionally in high heels, hat and faux fur, as she threw bread crumbs at the ducks swimming in Central Park Lake. She looked his way and smiled. He held up the brown paper bag he was carrying and awkwardly smiled back.

As though for the first time, he was struck by her exotic model-like looks. How could he have not noticed before? Damn, she was beautiful.

She offered him some crumbs as he sat beside her and unwittingly stared before he caught himself. He took a few crumbs and threw them toward the ducks.

David adjusted his tie. "So, what's the connection?"

"After Goya's wife died, Leocadia Zorillo left her husband and moved in with Goya. Eventually, she moved to France to live with him and stayed until he died."

David nodded as if to say, "Go on." He took a bite of his sandwich.

"Goya is rumored to have painted her dancing naked while she was married. But because Goya had already been called before the inquisition once for painting *The Naked Maja*, he gave Leocadia the painting on the condition she would never show it in public. I believe she honored his wishes and it has stayed in her family all these years."

David excitedly turned to face Alessandra. "You think—"

Alessandra interrupted." What did your mother tell you about the name?"

David rose. "Nothing." He started to walk backwards. "She has a tendency to go senile on me at convenient times, but not today." He turned and quickened his pace. "This time she'll answer the question."

"Wait for me," Alessandra said as she hurried after David.

Chapter 4

David rang the bell to his mother's apartment. Without waiting for a response, he quickly inserted his key, kissed the mezuzah and marched inside. Alessandra, right behind, hesitated, crossed herself, kissed the mezuzah and rushed to keep up.

Devorah stood in the kitchen kneading dough. A tray of freshly cooked rugalach beckoned on the counter nearby.

"Zorillo. Are we descended from any Zorillos?" David asked, his voice rising.

Devorah peered over his shoulder at Alessandra, then nodded toward her son.

"I thought I taught him better manners." She looked back at David. "No kiss. Not even 'Hello, how are you?'" She shook her head. "Such a son."

"Come on Mom, answer the question."

"In the old country..." Devorah sighed, "his grandfather would have rapped his knuckles and sent him to his room without dinner. And if he wasn't so big, I would do it now."

"Mom! This is important."

Devorah wiped her hands on an already smudged apron. "It's about the painting, yes?"

David nodded.

She offered the tray of pastries toward Alessandra who plucked one and popped it into her mouth.

David reached for one, but Devorah pulled it away. She turned her head to the side and craned it toward David. He shrugged and kissed her on the cheek.

Devorah smiled. "Was that so hard?" She strolled over to the photo in the living room showing *The Naked Maja Dancing* in the background. Tears welled up. "Do you have any idea what the painting means?"

"Yeah, it means if we get it back, you'll stop worrying about every dime you spend."

"If it still exists," Alessandra interjected.

Devorah wagged a finger at the photo. "That painting is the reason you're here. My parents used it to barter a space on the Kindertransport that took us to England."

David fidgeted.

"Me only six and Artie fifteen. I cried for days. I was afraid I'd never see my parents again." Devorah cast her eyes downward. "I never did."

David put his arm around his mother and hugged her.

"Every time I look at this photo, I remember." Devorah gently removed David's arm. "I never forget."

"I know Mom. I'm sorry to—"

"What do you know? Safe here in America, never having to worry about the next knock on the door. You know nothing." Devorah glanced at Alessandra. "I'm sorry."

She turned her gaze to the window. "A wonderful country, this America."

Alessandra didn't know what to say. While she had heard of stories similar to Devorah's, this was the first time she had met a Holocaust survivor. It moved her deeply, but it was painful to watch. She touched Devorah on the shoulder. "Mrs. Edlestein—"

"Devorah. Call me Devorah."

"Devorah, it would help to know if your family name was once Zorillo. There may be a connection with the painting."

Devorah again pushed the tray of rugalach toward Alessandra who nodded and picked one. "Delicious," Alessandra said, "What are these?"

"Just some left over dough, nuts and raisins."

Devorah offered the tray again. "You like them?"

Alessandra shook her head. "I love them, but I shouldn't."

"Please, a skinny *maidel* like you needs to eat." Devorah pushed the tray closer.

"Mom!"

Alessandra hesitated.

Devorah waited.

Alessandra wrapped her thumb and forefinger gingerly around another rugalach and plopped it into her mouth.

"No Zorillos. Sorry."

"Mom. Are you sure?"

"The painting's burned so what's to get back?"

Since the last meeting Alessandra had done some checking. David was right. There were many stories like Devorah's where supposedly "burned" paintings had shown up after the war. "It's possible it wasn't."

Devorah looked quizzically at Alessandra.

"Can I see the newspaper clipping again?" Alessandra asked.

Devorah reached into the bureau drawer for the clipping. "Do you think there's really a chance the painting wasn't burned?"

"Before the War, Joseph Goebbels—he was Minister for Propaganda and Public Enlightenment-ordered the seizure of all art the German deemed 'degenerate.' The works were collected and assigned a registry number."

"What did they consider degenerate?" David asked.

"Anything Hitler did not like. And his dislikes included some of the most famous artists in the world; Paul Klee, Wassily Kandinsky, Edvard Munch, Marc Chagall and the most degenerate artist of all, my countryman Pablo Picasso."

"Were they burned?" Devorah asked.

"Some were. Though the Nazis hated this art, they realized their usefulness as a means of raising cash to finance their war machine. The most valuable pieces were auctioned off and others were distributed to four German dealers, who arranged for their sale on the international art market. But more than five thousand paintings and works of art deemed unsuitable for sale were destroyed in a bonfire in the courtyard of the Berlin central fire station as a fire department training exercise."

"Is this what our newspaper clipping documented?" David asked.

"I assume so. But that's not the end of the story. Some of those so called 'burned paintings' have shown up in collections since the war."

Alessandra pointed to the newspaper clipping. "This was taken in 1939, so if we can find any record of your painting's existence after that date, there is a chance it's in someone's collection."

"So, then we could make a claim." David said.

"Probably not without something more than the photo of the painting. If that is all you have, I don't think I can help."

"There's something you should know," Devorah said. "After the war broke out, my brother Artie joined the Navy and became a carrier pilot. In 1944 he was shot down over Palau in the Pacific." Devorah paused to catch her breath. "He was only twenty-one."

"Mother, will you please—"

"He had a ring," Devorah said.

"A ring?" David said.

Alessandra put her hand up as if to silence David.

"He promised one day to get back the painting. He told me that he had proof. Why didn't you tell me about this before?" David stammered.

"Before the Nazis came, my family would talk about this special ring that had been in our family for generations. It was as though we were blessed because of that ring. When my parents sent us off to England, they hid that ring on my brother. Artie later told me that it was connected to the painting. Until now there was no reason to tell anyone about it."

"What did the ring look like?" Alessandra asked.

Devorah marched over to the photo and pointed to her Mother's left hand.

Alessandra squinted at the photo, reached into her purse and pulled out a magnifying glass. "It looks interesting but I can't make out the fine details."

Devorah pointed to the "dancer's" hand in the painting. "And I think that may be the same ring that's on my mother's hand."

"*Mira nomás!*" Alessandra exclaimed. That ring would be all the proof they would need to reclaim the painting. But the photo wasn't clear enough to prove the rings were identical. They would need the original ring and then, if they were lucky enough to locate the painting, they could compare it with the ring on the dancer's hand.

"Where's the ring now?" David asked.

"With Artie. He never took it off."

"At the bottom of the ocean?" Alessandra asked dejectedly.

Devorah nodded.

Mierda!

Chapter 5

All the way home, Alessandra could hardly contain herself. The existence of *The Naked Maja Dancing* had been a rumor in the art world for years. Although it had never been exhibited in public, after Goya died, Leocadia had apparently bragged about its existence and must have shown it to some friends who later claimed to have seen the painting. But no art expert ever came forward to verify it. Therefore, the Nazis may not have realized the true value of the painting that had bought Devorah her freedom.

And now the ring. Even though they'd never see the actual ring again, they did have a photo and as such, it was an important discovery, a very important one. She remembered a ring had played a prominent role in another Goya painting, but which one? She knew she wouldn't sleep until that question was answered, and for that she'd need her resources back at the museum. So, late as it was, she directed the cab driver to "Take me to the Metropolitan Museum, please." It was time to burn the midnight oil.

Henry, the guard at the Museum was happy to have some company. Without asking, he brought her a mug of coffee, for which she was grateful. She thanked Henry and went to work.

First she pulled down every book she had on Goya. She was about to open one of the large tomes when she remembered that Google had downloaded all the Museums books as well as the New York Central Library's. It would be quicker if she searched on line. She plugged in her access code and in seconds, a complete bibliography of books on Goya popped up on her screen. Before searching for the ring she wanted to refamiliarize herself with the history of both *The Naked* and *Clothed Majas*.

She knew that art historians speculated that the face and body of the *Majas* were not the same woman. To Alessandra it didn't matter. The face was the key. It was the face that would shed light on Goya's secret, for surely he painted the face of someone he wanted to honor. But who that person was had remained a secret all these years.

Was the woman in *The Naked Maja Dancing* the same woman in all the *Majas*? Her spine tingled with the thought of discovering the name of the woman who posed for two (and perhaps three) of the world's most noted art works.

Alessandra's research revealed much of what she already knew. Goya had been appointed the King's painter in 1786 and the whole Court's painter three years later. In 1808, He was called before the Inquisition to explain his portrait of *The Naked Maja*. The inquisitors wanted to know who the model was and for whom he had painted the "obscene" picture. When he wouldn't reveal her name, the inquisitors decreed that he wouldn't be allowed to paint for the King or Court any longer. Thereafter he moved to a country villa where all of his subsequent work remained private or was done for a select audience of friends. The *Naked Maja Dancing* fit the history.

She flipped to a photo of *The Clothed Maja* and compared it to *The Naked Maja*. The structure and the model's position were the same in both. And while most historians believed Goya used a different model for each painting, Alessandra thought that could be explained by the fact they were painted a few years apart. The model had simply aged.

If Goya had painted another nude, a painting he knew would risk the inquisition's wrath, he must have either used the same model again or painted someone he could trust. Perhaps that person was one and the same. If they were, then it was possible Devorah and David were descendants of one of the most famous models who ever lived.

Alessandra reached into her briefcase and retrieved the photo of the family in front of *The Naked Maja Dancing*. Devorah, with great reluctance had agreed to allow the photo out of her possession, but only after Alessandra promised to make a duplicate as soon as possible and return the original.

She took the photo to the copying machine and tried to blow up the portion of the photo showing *The Naked Maja Dancing*. Unfortunately the photo was so small it became grainy when enlarged. There was not enough detail to tell much about the model. But at least Alessandra could see a resemblance to the models in the other *Majas*.

To be sure, she'd eventually need the original painting to compare, that is, if it still existed. While the chances of that were slim, it was not entirely hopeless. And then after that, persuading whoever owned the painting to return it would also be a difficult task, but perhaps if she could locate the *Dancing Maja*, she could convince the owner to at least let her inspect it. She realized the whole enterprise was probably a fool's errand, but now that her intellectual curiosity had been piqued, she couldn't quit until there was no hope of finding the painting.

Alessandra checked the clock, 2:00 am. She rubbed her eyes, stretched and quickened her research. The ring was her next project.

Since the pose of both known *Majas* had their hands behind their heads, if they were wearing rings, none were visible. Alessandra decided to check other Goya paintings. She decided initially to ignore any paintings of children or groups or any of Goya's anti-war paintings. She concentrated on portraits of women. *Goya: Images of Women,* a book written by a colleague, was her starting point. She fanned through the book. Hundreds of photos flickered by. This would take a while. With a sigh, she began at the beginning. Two hours later, she stopped at a familiar painting, *The Duchess of Alba*.

Goya was a known womanizer. He had painted numerous portraits of the Duchess, a very handsome woman and there were rumors of an affair. In one painting, the Duchess was portrayed in black mourning clothes (her husband had just died). Two rings were visible. Through her magnifying glass, Alessandra could make out the inscription on the rings, "Goya" on one and "Alba" on the other.

It was evident from the portrait that the Duchess was not the model for the Majas, but what of the rings? Alessandra closely examined the photo of *The Naked Maja Dancing*. The ring the naked woman was wearing appeared similar in design to the "Alba" ring, but again, the photo was much too small to make out much detail. Alessandra squinted. She tried desperately to read the inscription on Devorah's mother's ring. No luck. Would Devorah be able to describe the ring in more detail? Did it have mother of pearl as in the Alba painting? This would be another clue that could tie the third *Maja* to Goya. It was too late to call. She'd have to wait until morning. It was going to be another long restless night.

Chapter 6

Alessandra awoke five hours later. To her surprise she was still in her street clothes. She hadn't even remembered coming home. She rolled over and checked the clock. Not quite seven. Too early to call. She'd wait until sometime after seven.

She hastened to the bathroom, splashed water on her face. Mascara leaked down her face. She prided herself on her grooming and didn't like what she saw. A shower would fix that, but she couldn't put off the call to Devorah any longer. She had to know. Hopefully Devorah was awake. To her surprise, she was.

"Was there mother of pearl in your ring?"

"I'm not sure, but I remember there was an inscription on the ring."

"What did it say?"

"I can't remember," Devorah said. "But it might come to me."

"If I showed you a photo of another ring that I think may be similar, would it help?"

"Come. I'll make coffee."

Alessandra showered quickly and headed to Devorah's house.

#

"Yes, the ring looks similar," Devorah said as she peered at the photo of the Duchess, "but I can't be certain." And no, "Zorillo" was not the name on their ring. She thought it began with a 'W.' I think I remember a name like White. Something like that."

#

On the taxi ride back to her office, Alessandra considered the "W" and dismissed it. Surely it was a "Z." It had to be. Then it would all fit. She wanted it to fit. She'd be famous instead of infamous and it might finally clear her name. If only she could dredge the ocean bottom and come up with that ring.

Alessandra hastily climbed the steps to the Museum entrance. She usually met with Kleinermann at 10:00am on Fridays. She checked her watch. She was already an hour late. He would not be pleased as he ran on German time. He was always prompt and he expected the same from his staff. She should have called. She'd head for his office as soon as she could set her bag down and grab a cup of coffee.

The door to her office was ajar. Uh, oh, he's waiting. What excuse could she come up with? "With the rain and all, it was impossible to get a . . ."

Gregor Melnikov's smiling face greeted her as she flew into her office.

"*Buenos días,* Senorita." He put his arms around her and held her tight.

"I thought you were out of town."

"Change of plans." Gregor held her at arm's length. "Dinner tonight?"

Alessandra hesitated. She was anxious to share her news but was reluctant to do so until she did more research. She feared he would drag it out of her. He always got her to say things she never intended to share. "Too busy."

She pecked him on the lips and shoved him toward the door. "I'll cook."

Bastardo. Gregor was the best damn cook in Manhattan. At least the best non-professional cook. "What time?"

"Seven?"

"Make it eight," Alessandra said and closed the door behind him.

#

Shortly after the Picasso incident, Alessandra had given a pre-arranged speech at the U.N. about the problem of determining the provenance of stolen art. A mutual friend, Malcolm Spencer, had introduced Gregor after the speech. "Alessandra Santana, meet Gregor Melnikov, second attaché to the Ukrainian ambassador to the U.N."

Gregor was charming, urbane and smart. He also was ruggedly handsome. She was impressed that he worked at the U.N., but he was a bit vague about his duties. She didn't feel right to press him on it and anyway, a little mystery added to his charm. It also turned out they shared a lot of common interests, including ice climbing and a love of wine.

At dinner one evening she had suggested a small boutique wine from Spain. "It will go perfectly with the gambas."

"Delicious," Gregor had commented, "it was a fine accompaniment for the shrimp. Your father taught you well."

"How did you know?"

For a moment he hesitated, then smiled and pointed to the label on the bottle, *Bodegas de Santana*. "Simple."

"It could be someone else with the same name."

"Then I would have guessed wrong."

A week later, over a drink, she told him she liked to ice climb. When he volunteered his own love of the sport, she was surprised. "I suppose you like to scuba dive also."

"And ride," he grinned. "I was in the Ukrainian cavalry."

"You know I ride?" She asked.

"You have the bearing of a horsewoman." Gregor lifted his glass.

She clinked her glass with his. "And of course, you ski."

"Quite well I may say." Gregor grinned.

It was too creepy, but Alessandra was intrigued. At first. The ice incident changed everything. Now they were just good friends, at least as far as she was concerned. Yet, she had to acknowledge his obvious manliness and that he had an animal magnetism about him. However determined she was to avoid any hint she was interested in him romantically, whenever he was around, her pulse quickened. And this time was no exception. She couldn't wait to share her news about the *Maja*, that is, if her research panned out.

In the meantime, she had to tell Kleinermann why she was late. She dialed his office to let him know she was on the way there. He was out. She left a message for him to call and collapsed into her chair. Perhaps Kleinermann would not be too annoyed if he knew about her exciting news. On the other hand, what did she have? Without the ring, nothing.

If she could only get her hands on the ring. That would be almost as valuable as the painting. And if the painting was anywhere other than Germany, it would be the proof she needed to claim the painting for the family. But the ring was at the bottom of the ocean.

In any event she had to know if the original painting was still around. If it was, there was one place to start, the *Art Loss Register*. The Register was a London based organization whose members included Christie's, Sotheby's, insurance companies and art trade associations dedicated to the recovery of stolen art.

She searched her desk drawer for a card one of their agent's had given her the prior year at a convention. It wasn't anywhere to be found.

She was certain she had put it in the right hand drawer where she put all business cards. The stack seemed thinner than she remembered. Had she thrown some out and didn't remember? Perhaps she had mistakenly put the card in another drawer? She shuffled the mess in the second drawer and found a few more cards. They must have slipped between the cracks at the back of the top drawer. The Register card was at the bottom. She punched the number in.

The person answering the phone asked for details of the painting and its history.

Alessandra answered as best she could. "Perhaps I could fax you a photo and article."

"That would be helpful," the voice said. "And I think I know someone that may be able to shed some light on your problem. If I can locate him, where can you be reached?"

"I'm a guest curator at the Metropolitan Museum. He can call me directly." Alessandra repeated her private number. "Just tell him to say he's from the Register. I'll be here late."

She retrieved the already enlarged copy of *The Naked Maja Dancing* photo and faxed it along with the article to the Register. Now all she could do was wait.

Chapter 7

As she waited for the call, Alessandra busied herself with the design of a special showing of Spanish art. It was a project she had proposed long ago. The Board finally had reluctantly approved the show, providing she could put together a display of premier work at moderate cost. In addition to fees demanded by some of the art owners, there was security, insurance, advertising, brochures, guest lecturer fees, housing costs for the lecturers and finally shipping charges, which in the case of rare art was quite expensive. She'd tackle the costs later. First, she had to determine what painters belonged in the exhibit.

She studied the list of painters she thought might be included and immediately ran into a problem. Should El Greco be included? He was born Domenikos Theotocopoulos on the island of Crete, in Greece, but at age 26 he moved to Spain, where he lived out the rest of his life.

She needed Kleinermann's input. She checked the time, almost six o'clock. He'd be leaving soon. She hurried to his office. The door was slightly ajar. His Clipped German accent seeped through the opening.

"Twenty million now and the rest later. That's what I need." There was a pause and then, "better than the Picasso."

Alessandra sheepishly peeked her head around the door.

Kleinermann looked surprised. He put his hand over the phone. "Be with you in a moment. Do you mind closing the door and waiting outside?"

She nodded.

Kleinermann smiled wanly.

She closed the door and paced in his outer office while she waited. She wondered who he was talking to and what painting he'd been talking about. A few minutes later, an effusive Kleinermann opened his door.

"Now dear. How can I help you?"

"What's better than the Picasso? And which Picasso?"

"You heard?"

Alessandra chided herself for the outburst. It was none of her business and rude to have listened in, however unintentionally. "I couldn't help but overhear."

"Well, if you must know. I was talking with a major donor about a major acquisition we are thinking of acquiring. But it's not for publication as yet, so I would appreciate it if you would keep this between us." Kleinermann looked intently at her. "I can trust you, can't I?"

She nodded.

"Now, what is it you need?"

Alessandra outlined her dilemma.

"Surely you know my answer."

Indeed she did, but she still wanted confirmation. She was too new at this to risk making a mistake.

"And Picasso?" Alessandra asked. "His life was the opposite of El Greco's. Do we want someone who fled to France and died there in our 'Spanish Artists Exhibit'?"

"Have you forgotten Goya who also left Spain and died in France? Surely we have to include him. Besides, as Picasso was a director of the Prado, your former boss would be upset if you didn't include him."

Yes, he would as she already knew. Then why did she seek Kleinermann's approval? The "lost" Picasso incident had jarred her self-confidence. She needed his reassurance she was doing the right thing. She rebuked herself for her insecurity. It wasn't like her. Her father had raised her otherwise and would be disappointed if he knew. She thanked Kleinermann and excused herself.

Back in her office, she revised the preliminary list of artists. Satisfied, she leaned back and stretched. She checked her new cell phone/watch combination, a gift from a grateful Japanese executive for arranging a special tour of the Museum for some of his staff.

She had an hour to kill before her dinner date with Gregor, so she decided to program in a few numbers. Before she knew it, it was 7:15. If she left now she could make Gregor's with a few minutes to spare. Gregor hated it when she was late.

Just as she was about to walk out the door, her land line rang. It was Henry, the guard downstairs. "A gentleman is here from the Art Loss Register."

She checked her watch again. Hopefully this wouldn't take too long. "Send him up."

A swarthy, casually dressed, wiry looking man stood in her open doorway. He smiled slyly.

"*Buenos días*, Señorita Santana"

Alessandra collected herself. "*Buenos noches*, Mr.?"

He glanced at her watch. "They should have warned me that you were so—"

"Tall?" Alessandra said peering down on this unusually short man.

"Fine. *Guapa*."

Alessandra ignored the compliment. She extended a hand. "Alessandra Santana."

He caressed her hand in both of his. "Jorge Vieras. Graduate of NYU, the Sorbonne and former staff writer with the *LA Times*. And now, the only Puerto Rican journalist attached to Reuters and *Paris Match*. Personally recommended to you by the Art Loss Register."

"And just why did the Register send a Puerto Rican journalist?"

Jorge scanned the bookshelves and pulled down a book with his photo on the cover. "You are lucky I was in New York when they called. Normally I'm in Paris where I live." He placed the book in her hand.

Alessandra glanced at the title of the book, *Stolen Holocaust Art*. Alessandra felt embarrassed. "I should have recognized your name." She gestured for him to sit.

"Who remembers the author of an inconsequential book?"

"It wasn't inconsequential to me or the thousands of Jews who were victims of the Nazis." She eyed her watch. "I'm sorry but I have an appointment. Did you get the fax?"

He nodded. "What else do you know about the painting?"

"I know that Goya had a mistress named Leocadia Zorillo who was married at the time. She was a Jewess."

"The woman in the painting?"

"I believe so, but can't yet prove it. Leocadia had a daughter, Rosario who Goya adopted after Leocadia joined him in France."

"What does that have to do with the painting?"

"The family that owns the painting might be Rosario's descendants."

"If true, it would make for a very interesting story."

"Will you help?"

"That is why I'm here. But for such a painting never before seen in public by such an artist, I will want something in return."

Alessandra expected the services of anyone associated with the Register to be pro bono. She raised an eyebrow, not sure what to say.

"I want exclusive rights to the story."

"You know where the painting is?"

"Not yet. But I have my sources."

"I can't believe it's that easy."

"I didn't say it is easy. If it were, you would not have called the Register." Jorge smiled. "I have thousands of Nazi documents. Between them and my contacts I believe I can help, but sometimes a man has to eat. No?"

He reached across the desk. "A deal, Señorita?"

"Only the Edlesteins can talk to you about rights."

Alessandra's new watch beeped. She was late. Gregor would be furious. She grabbed her coat.

Jorge handed her his card. "When you get their consent, call me."

As she shut the lights, she wondered if the Edlesteins would want the publicity.

Chapter 8

Although Alessandra was almost an hour late, Gregor surprisingly said nothing. He smiled when she walked in and handed her a glass of white wine.

"*Na zdorovia.*" Alessandra clinked his glass.

"*Budmo,*" Gregor said. "*Na zdorovia* is for Russians, Ukrainians say *'budmo.*'" He raised his glass.

"*Budmo,* then." Alessandra took a sip. She rolled the wine around her mouth and smiled approvingly. "Superb. A Verdejo! It's our best white grape but it doesn't do well in the North. Is it from Rueda?"

Gregor nodded as he showed her the bottle.

Alessandra examined it. "An Angel Rodriguez Verdejo. The best of the best."

"Nothing less would do for the daughter of a great winemaker." Gregor led Alessandra to the dining room table. Two black tapers flickered on a black tablecloth set with two black napkins surrounded by silverware. A plate of Gambas al Ajillo sat on a stark white oval serving dish. The large shrimp were surrounded by fiery small chilli peppers alongside whole baked garlic bulbs. A plate of Stuffed Piquillo peppers sat nearby.

Alessandra settled into the chair he had pulled out. She inwardly was pleased. Even though she was a thoroughly modern woman she still enjoyed being treated like a lady.

Gregor always seemed to have a surprise for her and tonight was no different. She missed the tapas of her home country, but Gregor's were innovative and a good substitute. Though the shrimp were usually prepared with crushed garlic, she appreciated his attempt to be creative by using the whole bulb. And the Piquillo peppers were a special touch. "You know the pepper only grows in the north?"

Gregor nodded. "In Navarre."

He had done his research. She was pleased with the care and effort he had gone through, but she suspected he wanted something in return. And it wasn't sex. She had put a stop to that after Smuggler's Notch.

#

Smuggler's Notch, Vermont

Alessandra struggled up the frozen waterfall. It was late April. The ice bristled as it slowly thawed. They had decided to climb the *Blue Room* on the mountain's East side. It was a tricky Grade 3 climb, and the melting ice didn't help. The skis on her back also hindered the climb, creating the earmarks of a Grade 5, a climb she had never before tried.

Alessandra put the negative thoughts out her mind and studied her next move. *Mierda* she muttered as she almost lost her footing. *Concentrate!*

Gregor, his long blond hair hidden by a heavy wool cap, was just below. He had done many climbs such as this in his native Ukraine, but usually alone. Alessandra hinted in the last month that she would like to accompany him on one of these climbs, but until now he had always blown her off. This time, Alessandra insisted she was ready and persuaded him to take her along. She had desperately needed the diversion. But she hadn't reckoned with the melting ice and it concerned her that she might not have either the skill or experience to finish the climb. As her footing became less sure with each movement, she was beginning to regret her insistence.

She watched Gregor re-center his own skis. He looked up as if to see if she was okay. She gave him a thumbs up. He nodded, removed one of the ice anchors Alessandra had left for him, planted his ice axe and moved upwards toward her.

Alessandra measured her route to the summit. Ten minutes later she was just 100 yards from the top. She began to relax and enjoy the moment. Come on, she told herself, *pay attention.* You're not there yet.

She checked the rope that tethered her to Gregor, then swung her right axe and thrust it into the ice. She tugged to make sure she had a good hold, pulled the left axe free from its perch and planted it just ahead. She freed her left foot, ready to move it upward. Suddenly, her right foot slipped its hold. Only her hands grasping the leashes hanging from the axes stopped her, and probably Gregor as well, from dropping 1000 feet below. If she didn't get a toe hold quickly, she was sure the axes wouldn't hold in the soft ice and then her weight, slight as it was, would pull them both into oblivion.

She dug her right foot into the soft ice and pushed up. She slipped. Again she dangled in open air. She tried her left foot. The action pulled her right axe loose. Now only one axe stopped her from slipping off the wall. She struggled to replant the right axe. The movement tore the left axe loose. Alessandra hurtled toward the rocks hundreds of feet below.

Gregor's mountaineering instincts kicked in. He snatched a carabiner off his belt and snapped it into another ice anchor that Alessandra had left behind. A millisecond later Alessandra skidded by, just missing him.

With deft hands, Gregor slammed the rope through the spring clip on the carabiner. He braced himself and held onto the rope as it reached its 90-foot limit. The sudden jerk on the rope jarred Alessandra. She had momentarily stopped her fall. She waited for the inevitable, free falling and Gregor with her. But she wasn't ready to die.

She reached frantically for the ice wall to plant an axe before Gregor's hold gave way. She couldn't quite reach it. *Please don't let me die like this. Not now.* She had to know. *How? Who?*

A tug on the rope told her she was moving up. She craned to see Gregor, a strained look on his face as he hauled her ever upwards, the rope gliding through the carabiner attached to the ice anchor. Somehow he had done the impossible, at least for most people.

Alessandra swung toward the wall. She reached out again and nicked the ice. She swung away and then back, closer. An axe plant, then a toe hold. Then the other axe and toe. She pulled herself tight to the wall and gave a silent prayer of thanks.

"Are you okay?" Gregor shouted.

Alessandra took a deep breath. I can't move."

"Are you hurt?"

She was frozen with fear, but Alessandra knew she had to conquer her fears. There was no way Gregor could pull her to the top.

"Just out of breath." She had to get moving before the ice got any softer. She breathed deeply a few more times and started up. Soon she was parallel with Gregor.

"Let me lead," he said.

"Gladly."

Gregor checked the rope on Alessandra and then himself. "We'll have to make it over to Elephant's Head and summit there, okay?"

Alessandra nodded.

Alessandra waited until he was about fifty feet above her. She wanted to make sure the route he chose was safe. *Safe? What did that mean anymore? How much longer would her boss be able to protect her?*

"Climb!" The order came from above.

She had to stop thinking about that damn painting. She began her ascent. She cautiously planted each axe and pulled to make sure it would hold before she planted the next one. Twenty yards. So far so good. Soon fifty.

The sun glistened off the ice and they made their way to the top. Sweat poured out from under her cap and down her brow. They dare not dally. She checked to see how much father to safety and was relieved to see Gregor was near the top.

And then *craaack*! Her heart stopped. The sound could only mean one thing, the ice above had broken off! She braced for what was to come next. First, a thunderclap! And then the inevitable. An avalanche of snow and ice hurdled toward them. *Mierda, mierda!*

The avalanche roared down the mountain. Alessandra flattened herself to the wall. She felt the safety rope that tied her to Gregor go slack. Gregor blasted past her, his arms flailing at the wall trying to plant an axe. She tightened her grip on the axe leashes, dug her toes in deep and prayed they would hold her.

The full weight of Gregor's 200 hundred pound body jerked the rope taught. Miraculously, she stayed anchored to the wall. Then the rope went slack. She feared the worse. She peered down through the snow dust. Gregor was nowhere in sight. *Mi dia*. Her breathing increased. Was Gregor alive? If so, what could she do to help him? There was no way she could descend alone. She decided she had to clear the Blue Room area and try and make it over the summit and get help.

She took one last look down before starting. The dust had settled and she thought she spied Gregor's red parka. Somehow, Gregor had anchored himself.

He glanced up toward her and gave her the okay sign. Then he signaled her to start up again.

Alessandra struggled to gather herself. No time to think about what had just happened. She had to get to the top and quickly. Fear permeated her every move, but move she did. She chose a route that avoided the avalanche area and sooner than she had imagined, she was over the first ledge and able to walk on relatively flat ground. She waited for Gregor to join her.

They hiked through a stand of birch trees and toward the sheer ice wall they needed to climb to reach the top of Elephant's Head.

Giant ice stalactites hung from a nearby ledge. Gregor pointed to a path that skirted the stalactites. Soon he was on the next ice wall climbing as though nothing had happened. Alessandra admired his grace as he established the route. He waved her up. She put aside her fears and followed him up the wall.

Within minutes they had scaled the 100 foot ascent and were again on flat terrain. They could now hike their way to the top. Gregor set off walking at a fast pace.

Alessandra struggled to keep up. They had climbed 2500 feet from the base and although they were only at 3650 feet, the altitude change was affecting her.

Gregor stopped for a moment. "So, we had fun today. No?" Gregor grinned as he pulled her toward him.

"No. *We* didn't have fun." Alessandra pushed away and pummeled him softly. "*We* could have died."

"Is that not why we climb, to cheat death?" Gregor grabbed her arms, pinned them behind her, and planted a kiss. She wiggled to get free. He held the kiss. She gave in and kissed back. He released her. Tears welled in her eyes.

Gently, he brushed them away and pulled her hat off. Her long black hair fell to her shoulders. He made as if to kiss her again.

Alessandra turned away.

Gregor shrugged.

She reached into her backpack, retrieved a sandwich and held it out to him. "Hungry?"

He smiled and accepted the sandwich. She pulled out a bottle of water and drank deeply.

Gregor sat down on a nearby rock. "Are you going to join me?"

"Not hungry." Alessandra stared out at the horizon toward Mt. Stowe, but saw nothing. Her mind was back to the Picasso. *How had the Picasso disappeared?*

"We need to start down," Gregor's deep voice brought Alessandra back to the present.

Alessandra checked her watch, four o'clock. The sun would soon be setting. "Race you down." She stepped into her cross country skis and hastened toward the downslope.

Smuggler's Notch had pristine snow as it was not normally used by regular skiers. Even expert skiers found it challenging, which is exactly why Alessandra insisted on taking their skis. While she wasn't as good a mountaineer as Gregor, she had cross country skied all her life and could made telemark turns like a pro. And she intended to beat Gregor down the mountain.

As soon as they hit the downhill, Gregor surprised her and bolted ahead.

Together they carved "S" turns in the unbroken snow, as Alessandra struggled to catch up. But this part of the mountain was too steep to try catching up, particularly in the soft snow. So Alessandra bided her time, hoping Gregor would make a mistake.

In one treacherous section, Gregor snowplowed his way through a series of turns.

Seeing her opening, Alessandra executed three beautiful telemark turns, but just as she was about to pass him, he shortened his turns and took a more direct line.

Now he was twenty feet ahead and stayed there until they were a few hundred yards from the bottom. Gregor glanced back and smiled at her. When he turned around, a large tree loomed ahead. It was obvious his speed was too fast to make a turn and avoid the tree. He threw his body into the hill and began to tumble.

Over and over he tumbled, picking up speed as he went. His skis came off. He put out his hands and clawed at the snow. But he didn't slow.

Alessandra saw the tree was directly in his path. She raced ahead, got below Gregor and just as he was about to roll into the tree, she stopped, planted both poles and allowed him to topple into her. The force knocked her over and on top of him. They had stopped inches from disaster.

They lay there for a few moments. "You okay?" Alessandra asked.

Gregor nodded. "You?"

Alessandra touched herself all over. "*Si.*" She kissed him on the cheek, "See you at the bottom," and then she was off to ski the last bit of the hill.

Alessandra reached the parking lot, removed her pack, skis and parka, and tossed them in the back of a pickup truck.

She climbed into the driver's side and glanced down at the New York Daily News on the seat. The headline screamed, *RECOVERED PICASSO PAINTING MISSING, MET CURATOR SUSPECTED.* A photo of herself stared back at her. She tore the newspaper into shreds and littered the ground outside the truck with them.

Gregor reached the lot. After he removed his skis, he laid them in the back of the truck. He walked around to Alessandra's side, gave her a sideways glimpse, and picked up the strewn newspaper clippings. He stuffed them into his jacket pocket.

"This trip was supposed to get your mind off of it. Meanwhile, the museum hasn't fired you."

"Probation is just the first step. It's only a matter of time."

Gregor reached into the window and kissed her.

She gave him a perfunctory kiss back.

He reached for her.

She gently pushed him away. "I'm not in the mood."

"Get over it. You've been in a foul mood for weeks now."

"Can't we just be friends?"

Gregor shrugged. "Okay. So, we are friends."

He hopped into the passenger side. "Stop worrying. If you're innocent, I'm sure you'll be cleared."

If you're innocent? To her, any man who wanted to be in her life would support her. No questions asked and vice versa. That was the beginning of the end of any chance of an affair. But that comment alone didn't do it. It was after the ice climbing adventure that she began to notice some odd quirks about him. He was away a lot. And when she asked about it he seemed defensive. She was sure he was hiding something. That was his prerogative, but she wanted a man who was totally open about his life. She didn't want any mysteries about "her man." So she decided he wasn't "Mr. Right," but kept it to herself.

#

Gregor popped one of the stuffed peppers in his mouth. "Take a bite and see if you can tell what they're stuffed with."

She did as she was told. He'd soon let her know what he was after. "Mmm. Wonderful." She took a good swallow of the wine. "And the chevre goes perfectly with the wine."

A broad smile crossed Gregor's face. "You never did tell me how you got involved with the Metropolitan Museum and the Picasso."

He stood and retrieved a bottle of Fonseca port.

Ah, she wondered when he would ask about the Picasso. It seemed strange to her that he never directly asked about it before. He certainly knew about it because it was front page news for weeks and even had arranged the Smuggler's Notch climb because of it. Up to now she had passed off his lack of interest in her life as just typical male cluelessness. But that usually translated into a man loving to talk about himself. Gregor never did. In that sense he didn't fit any neat profile. She decided to stop trying to figure him out. "Where should I begin?"

Gregor placed two glasses on the dinner table.

"At the beginning. Where else?"

"Well. As with most girls, my father's influence played a great role in my life. But in my case, my mother died when I was very young so he was everything to me. He encouraged me to be a woman of the world. Part of that was to study the arts. And that included music and singing lessons. He had the grand idea I could become a great operatic soprano."

"You sing?" Gregor poured the port.

Alessandra cleared her throat and began to sing.

O terra, addio; addio, valle di pianti...
Sogno di gaudio che in dolor svanì.
A noi si schiude il ciel e l'alme erranti
Volano al raggio dell'interno dì.

Gregor applauded. "*Aida*. Very well done. Perhaps you're in the wrong profession."

"No, no. I love to sing, but I had stage fright, so I turned to my next love, art."

Gregor motioned for her to go on.

"After graduating from the High School for Art in San Fernando, the most prestigious art school in Spain, I went on to study at the Sorbonne. Eventually, I realized I couldn't paint very well, so it was on to Oxford for a graduate degree in Fine Arts. When I graduated, with a little help from my father, I got a job at the Prado as an assistant curator."

"It helps to have connections," Gregor said.

"*Si*, but at first I had resisted. I wanted to be my own woman and get a job by myself. I was very stubborn. My father argued all he was doing was opening a door that would ordinarily be closed to most people. It was still up to me to get the job. He was just doing the introductions. I looked my father in the eye and told him, 'Thank you, but I can arrange my own introductions.' I was very proud of myself."

Gregor laughed.

"Eventually, I got a call from Senór Alvarez, the Director of Art at the Prado. My father had ignored me and thank heavens he did. It is very difficult to turn down an offer for an interview from god. In my world, Alvarez was god and the Prado was heaven."

Gregor raised his glass, "To a human god and the kind of heaven I can believe in."

Alessandra smiled. "Five years later, Kleinermann called me. I had met him while he was visiting Madrid trying to get the Prado to release some paintings for an exhibit he wanted to arrange in New York. He told me he needed an expert in Western European art to replace someone who had died. The timing was right as I was ready to leave Spain and explore the world. New York sounded exciting."

"And the Picasso?"

"Ah, yes the infamous Picasso. Do you remember when *Nature Morte a la Charlotte* was stolen from the Pompidou Centre in Paris? It made international news."

Gregor shook his head. "I must have been climbing somewhere and out of touch."

"Well, anyway, Kleinermann was asked to value it for an insurance claim. The insurance company wanted an outsider. No one connected to the Pompidou or the French government. As the Art Director for a famous museum they assumed he was an expert in all kinds of paintings. But he didn't feel comfortable giving his evaluation without the help from someone like me who is an expert in Spanish art, so he asked me to assist. The next thing I knew, an agent of Lloyd's showed up at my office and asked if I would help to try and locate the painting?"

"So, of course you said yes," Gregor said.

"Actually, no. I told him I had no expertise in locating stolen art, but I knew someone who did. I offered to introduce them. But he wouldn't take no for answer. Kleinermann had told him I was the best. The next thing I knew, he had offered to pay me $500 an hour, and that Kleinermann had pre-approved the whole enterprise."

"Ah. Everyone has their price. So, you did it for the money," Gregor said.

"Not until he offered expenses, first class airfare and the best hotels," Alessandra said with a grin.

Gregor twirled a cigar in his left hand as he licked the wrapper. He leaned over to use the candle to light his "Churchill." The size of the cigar dwarfed Gregor's squarish face.

Gregor took a toke and extended the cigar toward her.

"I would have offered you your own, but this is my last."

Alessandra rolled the cigar under her nose and inhaled its aroma. Her eyes crinkled. It had been awhile since she had a true Cuban. She drained the last of her port, took a drag on the cigar, exhaled and continued.

"I can't tell you everything. People's lives are in danger. What I can tell you is that Maeko Kuroguchi, the daughter of Kenji Kuroguchi, a known Yakuza mob boss rumored to have dealt in stolen art, had been in Paris the day the painting was stolen. I knew from my contacts at Sotheby's that Kenji had been a frustrated bidder of impressionist artists at past auctions. It was just too much of a coincidence that the day the painting disappeared, his daughter 'happened' to be in Paris. There had to be a connection. So I contacted an Interpol agent whose name I had been given and suggested he search Maeko's apartment. Sure enough, there it was."

"I think I know the rest," Gregor said. He poured himself another glass of port. "But I don't remember reading of any arrests."

He offered to pour her another round.

Alessandra placed a hand over the top of her glass. He only knew what the news media had published. She wondered what he'd say if he truly knew.

"Maybe she had powerful friends."

"Too much publicity." Gregor offered as he began clearing the dishes.

Alessandra indicated she wanted another drag on the cigar.

"There must have been another reason." Gregor handed her the cigar.

Alessandra studied Gregor. "If I tell you, this can never be shared with anyone."

Gregor made like a zipper across his lips.

"I'm serious."

Gregor crossed his heart. "I promise."

Alessandra hesitated. Dare she tell him the real truth that the recovered painting was a forgery, painted by Elmyr de Hory, and the Pompidou knew it. De Hory was the greatest forger of his time. He was such a talented artist that had he not forged paintings, he would have been recognized on his own as one of the world's greatest artists. But he was so good at what he did, he fooled many experts in the art world. Indeed until she warned the Pompidou that the Picasso, in her opinion, was de Hory's work, they believed it was the work of the great Spanish painter.

But with headlines extolling the "exquisite police work of the Préfecture de Police" and the beaming face of the museum curator alongside the Mayor's, for the public to now find that a forgery of the original had been recovered, had all the trappings of a *Pink Panther* movie. The real question was, if the recovered painting came from the Museum, had the staff been duped from the beginning or did they knowingly exhibit a forgery and call it the real thing? Either way, it made for a great story and a plot even Hollywood could not have invented.

So, rather than risk making headlines, the museum re-hung the forgery in the gallery and proclaimed it to be the real thing. Then it quietly put in a claim for the insurance money, claiming that the "real" painting had in fact been stolen. Of course they had to reveal to the insurance company, that the painting now hanging in the Museum was a forgery and they hadn't recovered the "original" after all.

The insurance company, not being fools, was not ready to pay a claim where the "original," as proclaimed to the public by the Museum, was hanging back in the place from whence it was stolen. Moreover, absent proof the Museum ever had the "original" in the first place, Lloyds asserted that it owed nothing.

The Museum was in a bind. If they sued, they'd have to reveal they defrauded the public by hanging a known forgery in their gallery. Instead, they decided to get a second opinion of whether or not the recovered painting was indeed a forgery. And who better to get the opinion from than Alessandra's boss, Seigfried Kleinermann. Since Alessandra was already in Paris, she was entrusted to bring back the painting to the Metropolitan Museum for Kleinermann's inspection. But she was on strict orders not to tell Kleinermann of her opinion as they wanted a totally unbiased opinion from him.

And that's when her troubles began. The Museum insured the painting, from an insurer other than Lloyds, while it was in transit. When it went missing, the Museum put in a claim to the second insurer. As far as the world knew, the painting Alessandra was shepherding to the Met, was an original. And since it was not available for inspection, no one could prove otherwise.

Then the French pressured the Japanese not to prosecute Kenji or his daughter for fear of revealing the truth about the painting. The Japanese were delighted to comply because they didn't cherish the idea of prosecuting someone for stealing a forgery. Indeed, if as the Museum now claimed, the original painting hanging in the Museum was not a forgery, then how could they prove Kuroguchi stole anything? It would have been an international farce.

Gregor came over and took her in his arms. "Come on. It's just the two of us."

The wine had taken its toll. She desperately wanted to tell Gregor the true story. Through drooping eyes, she studied him closely. He looked so much like Sean Connery. For a moment she imagined herself a "Bond" girl. And a true "Bond" girl would reveal all and melt into his arms. Instead, she pushed him away and headed for the door. "Someday, maybe," she said as she closed the door behind her.

Chapter 9

Alessandra always felt exhilarated in Gregor's company and tonight had been no exception. He was erudite and engaging, but not his normal charming self. Even in her semi-inebriated state, she sensed something was amiss. He seemed to have an agenda. His questions, while appropriate for their relationship, seemed more than mere curiosity. Maybe it was his Ukrainian manner as he could be quite direct at times. But she didn't know what to make of it so she dismissed any negative thoughts about him. She still had enjoyed herself and the food, as usual, was delicious.

She hailed a taxi and as she rode through the lighted city, her thoughts turned to David. How was she going to convince him on the need to work with Jorge? Maybe the best way was to have Jorge do it himself. Yes, she'd call David in the morning and make arrangements for them to meet.

#

Two nights later, Alessandra, David and Jorge sat in Alessandra's office. Jorge explained, "I want exclusive rights to the history and search for the painting. In exchange, I'll assist in locating the Goya."

David questioned why they needed Jorge. "I hadn't even thought about selling the story. Besides, what's so special about you that we should give you an exclusive?"

"*Primero,* you need me because I have the contacts to find the painting. And *secundo,*" Jorge snatched his book on holocaust paintings from the shelf, "this is how I earn enough to help people like you find what is rightfully yours." He deposited the book in front of David.

"And if I won't sign this?" David pointed to a contract Jorge had placed on the table.

"Then it's *hasta la vista.*"

Jorge took his coat from the rack.

Alessandra had said little up to this point, but things weren't going as she had hoped. She blocked Jorge's exit. "Your book seems to indicate you are *simpatico* with holocaust victims, no?"

"*Si, muy simpatico.*"

"But you need to make a living?" David asked.

Jorge threw up his arms. "Journalists are usually not very rich people."

"Unless you write the *Da Vinci Code*, "Alessandra piped in.

"I'm afraid it is not my style," Jorge said. "I deal with facts, not fiction."

David picked up Jorge's book and flipped through the pages. The room was silent as he read. He put his finger on a passage and read out loud. *"The Nazis didn't just steal valuable works of art, they stole the history and soul of the families that owned them"* David looked at Jorge. "That is a very profound observation. Are you Jewish?"

"In my heart, yes, though my priest might object to that."

"*Si*, but if you confess, he will have to forgive," Alessandra said.

Jorge smiled.

David smiled as well and went back to flipping the pages. He turned to the "Introduction." After a few minutes, he again looked at Jorge.

"Very impressive. How were you able to get your hands on the French Secret Service's investigation of the confiscated art? Wasn't that classified?"

Jorge grinned. "When you are an investigator yourself, you try and think of who else might have gotten a copy of the report. I figured the French must have sent a copy to their liberators, the Americans and the British. Sure enough, I found a copy in the National Archives."

"And the Russians? Surely they didn't share their information with us."

"Not until recently. Now they want to be our friends. The State Department put pressure on them to reveal how much artwork the former USSR confiscated for themselves. The information is slowly leaking out, but we have a long way to go. I'm afraid I had to resort to the old fashioned method." Jorge rubbed fingers together to indicate "money." "But please understand, the information is limited. If your painting is in Russia, it may be very hard to trace and more importantly, to persuade them to give it back."

"You think it's in Russia?" Alessandra asked.

"It's a good possibility. The Soviet Army plundered many German museums and private collections."

"I see why Alessandra asked me to meet you. I'm impressed. Will you promise to let us see what you write before you publish it?" David extended his hand.

Jorge eagerly took David's hand in his own. "No *problema.*"

"And we can request changes?" Alessandra asked.

"*Sí*. Request all you want," Jorge said.

"Will you make them?" David asked.

"As long as it is only to correct inaccuracies." Jorge tapped his chest. "Jorge Vieras does not give up content." He shoved the contract toward David.

Alessandra snatched the paper from David's outstretched hand. She scribbled, *Before publishing I agree to allow David and Devorah Edlestein to approve the writing for authenticity.* "Please sign and I'll make a copy."

Jorge read it over and smiled. "You don't trust me *Amiga?*"

"Sign. Then I'll trust," Alessandra said.

Jorge signed. "Ah, women!"

He handed the contract to David, who read it over and then also signed.

Alessandra made a copy and returned the original to Jorge.

"Now that we're partners, can you tell me how you know where the painting is?" David asked.

"But I didn't say I knew where it is," Jorge protested.

"You didn't have to," Alessandra said.

"*Amiga, amiga*, you must have trust or this relationship will never work."

"We don't have a relationship, we have a business arrangement." Alessandra glared at Jorge. "*Comprendo?*"

"*Sí, sí.* No need to get upset."

"Well. Where is it?" David asked.

"I'm not really sure. But I have a good idea. As I said, we know the Russians confiscated *mucho* art from Germany. What we don't know is exactly what they took. But recently someone in the Hermitage got around to opening crates in their storage room and found hundreds of pieces that had been delivered by the Soviet Army to the museum. As incredible as it sounds, it's been sitting in unmarked crates, unopened for sixty years."

"And you think *The Maja Dancing* is there?" Alessandra asked.

He took a folded paper from his inside pocket and turned to David. "This is a list of the paintings that were uncrated only last year."

David ran his finger down the list. He stopped at *Portrait of a Nude.* David shook his head. "There are probably thousands of nude portraits."

He handed Alessandra the document.

She studied the paper. "You read the wrong entry." She pointed to *Portrait of a Nude Jewish Woman* at the bottom of the page.

David looked confused.

"You're wondering how they know the woman was Jewish?" Jorge asked.

"She's wearing a mezuzah?" David asked.

"*Exactamente,*" Jorge interjected

"But they don't say it's a Goya." David said.

"Outside of Spanish art experts, very few people know about the painting. And since it has never been seen in public it's unlikely the current owners know what they have. It will take a Goya expert to identify the painting.'

"And that's where we will need your services," Jorge said.

"And then what?" David interjected. "We ask and they just give it to us?"

"We will need to give them proof," Alessandra said. "But I can't go. You'll have to find someone else."

"Why?" David asked. "Is it because of the Picasso disappearance?"

"You know?" Alessandra asked.

David nodded.

"Everyone knows," Jorge added.

Alessandra locked eyes on David. "And you still want to do business with me?"

"Nobody in their right mind would steal a painting entrusted to them," David put his hand on her arm. "Especially if they'd be the prime suspect."

Alessandra clasped his hand. "Thank you for the support. But museums are very reluctant to deal with me now."

"The Hermitage and the Met exchange art all the time." Jorge glanced at David. "They'll trust her if the Met backs her."

He turned to Alessandra. "And the Met would love to get credit for recovering a painting lost for two hundred years. *Correcto?*"

"How reliable is this list?" Alessandra asked waving the paper.

"My source copied that list from the Director of the Hermitage's own private files. It is not a public document, but I must trust that my source copied the list correctly. If I'm wrong, I paid a lot of rubles for nothing."

Jorge put on his coat. "I trust the source. But without you to help us negotiate a deal and authenticate the painting, we stand no chance of getting the painting back."

"I'll talk to my boss. I cannot do this without his approval," Alessandra said. "When I know something, I'll call. *Está bien?*"

"*Bien.*"

Jorge took his leave.

David took Alessandra's hand. "If we get the painting back, my mother will bless you."

Alessandra went home that night in turmoil. The idea of locating a lost painting as important and valuable as *The Naked Maja Dancing* was enticing. And if successful, she just might be forgiven for the loss of the Picasso, maybe even a heroine.

But her instincts told her this was a bad idea. When she first agreed to help David, it had seemed a simple job-she'd make some calls, write a few letters and see what she could dig up. She hadn't known if she could locate the painting, but wanted to help. She never really thought it through. She assumed the painting would be in Germany. If so, the German authorities were anxious to show their repentance over past sins. They usually bent over backwards to return stolen or confiscated art. A mere photo of a painting indicating it belonged to a Holocaust family would probably be enough. Russia was a whole other matter.

No museum outside of Germany was going to return a painting as valuable as *The Naked Maja Dancing* based on a mere family photo. Some other indication of ownership would almost certainly be required. Obviously there would be no papers to prove ownership. That left the ring and that proof was lost when Artie's plane was shot down. So, regardless of what Kleinermann thought, finding the ring was Mission Impossible. She had to pass.

Early the next morning Alessandra telephoned David and asked him to meet her at 11:00 am in the museum's conference room. She wanted to tell him the bad news in person. First however, she searched out Kleinermann to tell him of her decision.

He was reading a journal when she gently knocked on his open door. He glanced up and smiled as she entered.

Alessandra came right to the point. "I decided not to work on locating the Goya."

Kleinermann looked surprised.

Alessandra laid out the problem.

"So you need the ring?" Kleinermann asked.

Alessandra nodded.

"Your resume said you've participated in marine archeological dives in the Med."

"Yes, but we weren't looking for just one small ring."

"Nevertheless, you found rings and objects even smaller."

Kleinermann got up from his desk and grasped Alessandra by her shoulders. "If you bring back that painting, it would be a great accomplishment. It also would go a long way with getting the Board off your back."

"Sigi, do you have any idea of the odds of finding that ring?"

"What do you have to lose? The museum will pick up the tab."

Kleinermann was being all too cavalier about this. He clearly didn't understand the difficulty of the task. She tried another tack.

"The painting may be in Russia. And you know how difficult they've been in returning lost Holocaust art."

"Russia? You think it's there?"

"Possibly at the Hermitage."

Kleinermann raised an eyebrow. "Yes, they can be difficult, but not impossible. When you find the ring, I'll deal with the Russians." He gently guided her to the door.

Alessandra stopped. "Why are you pushing this so hard?"

"I'm just looking out for your interests."

Alessandra knew protesting further would be to no avail. She had lost her bid for common sense, but she had no one to blame save herself. She had done too good a job on selling Kleinermann on the importance of the painting. It was obvious he was obsessed with acquiring it no matter the cost . . . or danger. But maybe he was right. If they could locate where David's uncle crashed his plane, they could minimize the search area, greatly increasing the odds of locating the ring. And if they found the plane, the ring had to be in it or at least somewhere near it.

But now she had to tell David that without the ring there would be no claim. Upon hearing that she was sure he'd have the same reservations as she. Somehow she'd have to sell him on the idea that diving for the ring was worth the effort . . .and risk. To do that she needed some information. She rushed back to her office and called Devorah.

#

At 11:00 am sharp, Alessandra hastened to the conference room. David was not there yet. She paced. Ten minutes and four hundred paces later, David burst into the room.

"Sorry, I'm late. Did your boss agree?" David asked.

"There is a problem."

"He said no?"

"We need the ring," Alessandra said.

"Are you nuts?" David tossed his jacket onto a chair. "It's at the bottom of the Pacific."

"Your mother says you're certified."

"Sure I'm certified. As an accountant. The 'C' in CPA means 'Certified,' as in Certified Public Accountant."

"You know what I mean."

"Yes and you're crazy." David put on his best Tony Soprano imitation. "Fuhget about it."

"If you want to restore your family's heritage you'll have to take a risk."

"I haven't dived in ten years."

"It's like riding a bike."

David motioned for Alessandra to sit. "Your pacing is making me nervous."

"And you're avoiding the subject." Alessandra said.

"I dove because my ex-wife liked it. I quit when she left me for a younger guy." David pulled out a chair and eased into it. "I never really liked it."

Alessandra sat opposite David. "Do you want to get the painting back or not."

"The Navy thinks my uncle's plane went down in about three hundred feet of water. Too deep."

Alessandra rose. "Then I guess it's over."

"Are you telling me that there's no other way to prove our ownership?"

"Unless you have a document from the Nazis, no."

"Dammit. I'm the only family my mother has left. If something happened to me, she'd blame herself."

David rose and put on his coat. "I want that painting back badly. But not at the risk of my life. Nobody dives to 300 feet. At least nobody sane. Thank you for trying."

Alessandra watched him walk out. He was right about one thing. It was deep. But was it too deep? And just how dangerous was it? Before she'd give up, she needed answers. Maybe Jorge would know someone. She searched her new phone/watch for Jorge's number. As she did, she scrolled over Gregor's number. Of course! If anyone had an answer, Mountain Man would. He seemed to know everything. She called the Ukrainian.

#

A few days later Alessandra barged through the outer doors of "Rose and Edlestein, Certified Public Accountants." She wheeled a luggage carrier with strange looking scuba gear attached.

A large black woman sat behind a glass window. She gave Alessandra a quizzical look. "Can I help you?"

"Would you tell Mr. Edlestein that Ms. Santana is here?"

"Do you have an appointment?"

Alessandra shook her head.

"Then I'm afraid - -"

Alessandra ignored her and opened the inner door. She peeked in. "Which way?"

The black woman jumped in front of Alessandra. "Ma'am. You can't come in here."

David opened his office door and stepped out. He gently nudged the black woman aside.

"Iris. It's alright." He glanced at the scuba gear. "Where the hell did you get that?"

"It took all my womanly guile to persuade the proprietor of the dive shop to lend it to me.

"What the hell is it?"

Alessandra's eyes sparkled. "Rebreathers! Heliox, trimix. Ever hear of them?"

"Yeah. They're exotic gas mixes for deep dives. They're for pros. I suppose now you're going to tell me you're a professional diver."

"Three hundred feet. You did say that's where the plane is?"

"And that's where it's staying," David said. "I appreciate your efforts, but I need to rebreathe here. I'm not risking my life with some dilettante female Jacques Cousteau."

Another man, mid 50s, tie askew, rambled into the reception area. Seeing Alessandra, he quickly straightened his tie and ran his hands over his hair. He watched, transfixed as Alessandra reached down and lifted her skirt part way, revealing a long scar on her right leg.

As she bent over, her hair came undone. She shook her long tresses and looked up.

David seemed mesmerized.

Alessandra pointed to the scar. "Ten years old. Fell off a horse."

"What does this—" David said

Alessandra interrupted. "Racing my father. He won. I would have gladly added two more scars if I could have beaten him."

"I'm sorry. But comparing riding horses to the danger of deep diving doesn't cut it."

Alessandra pulled up her skirt again, revealing a scar on her left shin. "Mountain climbing. Missed a foot placement rappelling. Bled all the way down to the valley floor."

"Okay. So, you're Jane Bond or Ms. Indiana Jones, but what do you know about deep water diving?"

"I've been diving since I was fifteen."

"But not with trimix or heliox."

"What I don't know, I'll learn. The dive shop promised to train us. If you're already certified, they said it will only take a month. And if we pass the course, I have been assured it's safe."

"Assuming you're right. I still can't go." David swept his hand in a circle. "See all these people? They depend on me."

Iris looked Alessandra up and down. "That's what we have a staff for."

"Will someone tell me what's going on here?" The tie askewed man asked.

"Alessandra," David gestured toward him, "meet my partner, Bob Rose."

Bob bowed deeply and swept his arms as a Count would greet a Queen.

Iris motioned toward the inner door. "I think we all need to talk." She looked back to the couple. "Please excuse us." She grabbed David's arm and pushed him toward his office. Bob trailed behind them, taking a final look at Alessandra who started to follow.

Iris blocked her. "Please have a seat."

As soon as all three were in the room, Iris slammed the door behind them. She glowered at David. "I don't know what's going on, but I do know that you haven't had a woman in your life in three years. And this woman is hot. So whatever it is she wants you to do, do it. And don't give me no damn lip."

"Is this about the Goya?" Bob asked.

David nodded.

"And you're worried about tax season?" Iris asked.

David shrugged. Before he could answer, there was a knock on the door and it opened.

Alessandra peered in. "I thought you said the painting meant a lot to your mother."

"Come on in," David said. "We were talking about you anyway."

Alessandra scanned the office. The walls of David's office were lined with photos of him surfing, sky diving, scuba diving, fishing, playing baseball, running track and getting a medal while standing on a swim platform. There were no professional plaques on the wall, but in one corner stood a case full of various trophies for baseball, track and swimming.

Bob pointed at the photos. "Tax season comes every year. And every year you find some way to avoid the crunch. Last year you claimed you had to go to a wedding in San Francisco. You stayed a month. Another time you said your ex-wife was dying of cancer and you had to be with her. She had a benign wart removed, but you stayed away for three weeks. And the year before that—"

"So, what's your point?"

"You hate being here in tax season." Bob smiled at Alessandra. "This is an opportunity that comes once in a lifetime. We'll deal with it. Go!"

David turned to Alessandra. "How the hell are we going to find a ring that's been gone for sixty years and probably covered in sand in three hundred feet of water?"

Alessandra noticed a small Greek statue on David's desk. "In our museum are artifacts we found from ancient Greek vessels. They include coins and yes, rings that are thousands of years old. When we found them, they were covered in sand and encrusted with god knows what. My boss thinks your ring will be a piece of cake."

"And you? What do you think?"

Alessandra smiled. "I think it's crazy and probably won't work."

"Good. Then we're in agreement."

Iris pointed outside.

They all looked at the window. Snow flurries floated by.

Iris whispered a bit too loudly in David's ear, "Would you rather be in here crunching numbers or diving off a beautiful island with . . ." She nodded toward Alessandra.

David slowly scanned the room, looking from one person to the next. He looked outside at the snow and then reached into his top drawer and pulled out a photo of his uncle Arthur in his flyboy uniform standing next to a plane. A tear welled in his eye.

"When do classes start?"

Chapter 10

Alessandra left David's office with mixed emotions. She realized that once again she had let her bravado get ahead of reality, something her father had warned her about. "You are impetuous, something I'm afraid is inherited from me. You need to be aware of it and try to conquer it, otherwise it will consume you."

She usually followed her father's advice, but Alessandra loved the rush she got when she spontaneously embarked on a new adventure. She loved the mystery of the unknown and the surprises around each corner. Of course she got into trouble from time to time, but even that was exciting as she worked her way out it. And here, she had done it again.

She hadn't put on a wet suit since she had graduated from University, some eight years earlier. And now she had committed to a dive "that even the most skilled scuba divers think is dangerous," a small detail the dive shop owner had warned her about, but she purposely failed to pass on to David. And for what? To look for an object the size of a barnacle that in all likelihood was buried in sand in a lagoon that could take months to explore. And then what? Even if lightning struck and they found the ring, would that be enough? If the painting truly was in Russia, regardless of Kleinermann's confidence, she knew it would be difficult to extract any "spoils of war" from that country. The Russians seemed to feel the art they took from Germany was a form of reparations for the terrible cost the Germans heaped on their citizenry. They wouldn't relinquish the painting easily.

Nevertheless, she had made her commitment and was determined to see it through, something else her father had preached. "Your word is your bond. A person's reputation depends on it. The Santanas honor their commitments at whatever the cost. Break it at your peril." She never had.

In any event, Alessandra was thrilled by the prospect of searching for two historically important pieces. Besides, even if they found nothing, she'd be diving in a world class scuba destination at the expense of the museum. Life was good.

She quickened her pace as she wheeled the tanks through downtown New York and ignored the stares as she did. Five blocks later, she entered the "Big Apple Dive Shop" and made arrangements to start classes.

Alessandra was thankful they could start the following week as she wanted to finish the course before her father's upcoming visit two months hence. That way, she could tell him she was fully trained and thereby circumvent an argument he would surely make against her enterprise. While she deemed herself the independent woman he had hoped to raise, she still sought his approval. She went to bed conjuring up arguments to counter his imagined objections. It was a sleepless night.

#

One month after completing the special diving classes, Alessandra nestled in a booth at an elegant New York eatery with her father Manuel by her side. A cheese trolley stood nearby. There were many partially empty wine glasses on the table and a plate of artisan cheeses.

Olive skinned and impeccably dressed, Manuel looked like the courtly don he was.

He handed Alessandra a small box. "*Feliz compleanos!* It's from Father Carlos and myself. He is sorry for missing your birthday. I almost had to cancel myself. We had some trouble with frost in the vineyards but he promised to send some church workers over to get it under control."

"How is Uncle Carlos?"

"He didn't feel up to traveling this far." Manuel pointed to the box. "Go ahead."

Alessandra tore at the paper covering the box and eagerly opened it. A small gold key gleamed inside. She looked at her father quizzically.

"I am afraid you will have to wait until you return home before using it. It opens something on our estate."

"That's not fair."

"It is what your uncle desires. He wants to be there when you use that key."

"But what is it to?"

Manuel took a sip of port. "So, what is this good news you couldn't wait to tell me about?"

"You're changing the subject."

"A father's prerogative."

"Can you at least give me a hint?"

Manuel shook his head and smiled.

"I'm sure whatever it is, it's worth waiting for." She slipped the key onto her necklace. "This way, I will be reminded every day to come home soon."

She touched her father's arm. "Papa, I'm going to find a priceless painting the world has never seen."

Manuel raised an eyebrow.

"Really, papa. I met this man, David Edlestein, who introduced me to his mother, Devorah, who has—"

"What about Gregor?"

"That's over. We're friends now. In fact it was Gregor's idea. Well, in any case we need to go to Palau to dive—"

Manuel smiled the smile of a father who has heard it all before.

"After your mother died, I tried to give you the best education, to train you to become anything you wanted in life; ballet lessons, singing lessons, even fencing lessons. But, It wasn't my idea to give you scuba lessons—"

Alessandra put a finger to his lips. "But you did."

"I found it very difficult to deny you anything. But that didn't mean I wasn't concerned. And I— "

Alessandra kissed her father. "No girl could ever want a better papa."

"And I didn't like it when you went off mountain climbing with Gregor. But at least he could protect you, so it gave me some comfort. Is he going?"

"No papa. I asked if he wanted to come, but as usual, he's off doing his own thing. But enough about Gregor. I'll be fine. I'm going with David."

"And this David, is he trained like Gregor?"

"Well, he's a CPA."

"A CPA?"

"An accountant."

"I see."

"Did I tell you we think the painting's in Russia. But they may not even know they have it."

"Such an important painting and they don't know they have it?"

Manuel sliced a piece of cheese and offered it to her.

"Just a few years ago, the Hermitage uncrated some works the Soviet Army had confiscated from Nazi Germany. They were not well documented. We hope ours is one of them."

"And you need to go diving in the ocean for this?"

Alessandra explained the need for the ring and how it ended up in the Palau Lagoon.

Manuel nodded. "Yes, yes. And if you find this painting? Then what?"

"Then I'll be famous. And maybe I won't be suspected anymore."

Manuel smiled wanly.

"You know all those lessons you paid for? Well, they're about to pay off. David and I have been training for a month to use some special equipment for the dive. I'm really excited."

"You make it seem very simple, *mi amor.*"

"You always told me there was nothing I couldn't achieve if I really wanted it badly enough."

"It seems you are about to put that statement to the test." Manuel, a worried look on his face, raised his glass.

Alessandra raised hers. "We leave tomorrow."

Manuel touched his glass to hers. "Be safe, my child. Uncle Carlos and I are anxious to have you use that key."

"Is he ill?"

He placed his hand on hers and squeezed. "Come home soon."

Chapter 11

Alessandra went back to her apartment with a heavy heart. The news about her uncle worried her. She fretted Carlos may be dying, but if he was, surely her father would have told her. Maybe he didn't want to overly alarm her. She was torn as to what to do. Should she go home to Spain and abandon the Palau dive? The paper sticking out of the fax machine made the decision for her.

She read the information over quickly and squelched an urge to shout out. It was everything she had hoped. Now for sure, they had to find that ring and it had to be before June when the typhoon season started. They only had a three month window. If she postponed the trip she wasn't sure if she could make alternative arrangements until the following year and who knows what could happen in the interim. No. It was now or never.

#

As she and David boarded the flight to Palau, Alessandra consoled her guilt about her uncle by resolving to go home as soon as she fulfilled her commitment to David. She took her seat looking forward to their adventure. Mentally, she went over the information they had received during their training.

They would need both nitrox and trimix to complete their dives safely. Nitrox mixes were hyperoxic in that they contained higher levels of oxygen than the 21% that existed in normal air. They were going to use Nitrox II which contained 36% oxygen and the rest nitrogen. The body had to eliminate excess nitrogen from a deep dive. Nitrox, because it had less nitrogen than normal air, reduced decompression times, which in turn meant longer bottom times. All that was good, as she anticipated they would need as much time as possible on the ocean floor to find an object as small as Artie's ring.

However, since they would be diving below 130 feet, they would have to switch to trimix which was a mixture of helium, nitrogen and oxygen. Trimix was essential for deep diving because helium had a lower narcotic effect than nitrogen. And at depths of 300' or more, getting disoriented could be fatal. Divers were known to have gone down when they should have gone up, apparently thinking they were headed for the surface. Almost all died as a result.

They were going to use a version of trimix which reduced the oxygen to 10%, the nitrogen to 20% and the rest helium. That mixture was chosen because someone named John Bennett had used that formula to safely dive to a depth of more than 1000 feet. His dive took nine and one-half hours to complete. And while it was interesting to know that a person could survive diving to such a depth, she wasn't comforted by it. What concerned her was that Bennett would not allow any member of his support team to go deeper than 300 feet, the expected depth of their own dive. He felt it was unsafe. So, no matter how many times their instructor told them it was safe as long as they strictly followed their dive plan, she didn't believe him.

She looked over at David who sat in the aisle seat, earphones on and eyes closed. He rocked his head in tune with the music. He seemed totally at ease with their mission. She stared at him for a while hoping he would open his eyes. When five minutes passed and he showed no signs of acknowledging her presence, she leaned over and turned up the volume on his head set. Puccini's *La Boheme* blared through.

David jumped up and stared at Alessandra. She turned down the volume.

"What was that all about?" David asked.

"Just needed some company."

David removed the earphones and twisted his pinky in an ear. "How often do you get to do this?"

"I've only done it once before. Assistant curators don't usually go on trips like this. But I think Sigi, Mr. Kleinermann, he likes the idea of discovering a painting lost to the art world."

"I hope we can make him happy." David removed his headphones. "Frankly, I don't have high expectations."

"Then why did you agree to come?"

"Let's see. I had a choice of working fifteen hour days staring at tax forms or diving with you."

"You don't care about the painting?"

"You and I both know this is a dangerous journey we're taking. There are so many things that could go wrong, I quit counting."

Alessandra nodded. "But in spite of that you came."

"Foolishly, yes. But I thought of my mother and uncle's escape from Germany. I thought of my grandmother going through the trouble of giving the ring and the photo to Artie for safekeeping. And I thought of Artie volunteering to fight in WW II. I couldn't let him lie on the bottom of the Pacific without trying to recover my family's treasure. He deserved at least that much, don't you think?"

"I'm glad you changed your mind."

David gently nodded.

Alessandra leaned toward David. "I did some research on Palau. Did you know that at one time it was a possession of my country?"

"And since they also financed Columbus' trip to America, they could have claimed us as well."

"Yes," Alessandra said, "at one time, we were the most important country on earth."

"Yeah, and on the same day Columbus set sail, the most important country on earth expelled its Jews."

"That was unfortunate," Alessandra said.

"Unfortunate?" David turned back to look Alessandra in the eye. "Not for the King. He financed Columbus' expedition with the property the Jews were forced to leave behind."

Alessandra lowered her voice. "I didn't know that."

"It took Spain until 1978 to lift the expulsion order. All those years it was illegal for practicing Jews to live in your country. But you're probably unaware of that also."

Alessandra put a hand on David's arm. "A lot of countries have been unduly cruel to your people. Isn't that why we're here?"

David turned away from her and replaced his head set. He closed his eyes.

Alessandra sat back in her seat and did the same. Minutes later she was startled as David softly sang the duet between Mimi and Rodolfo in the *La Boheme* opera.

Alessandra snapped on her headset, and frantically searched for the same channel. It was a part she knew well, having played the role of Mimi when her opera class staged a performance for the locals. She found the channel and happily sang along with David. He glanced at her and raised his voice as though caught in the emotion of the song.

A female flight attendant rushed over. "You have beautiful voices, but I'm afraid you might be disturbing the other passengers."

"Sorry," both David and Alessandra said simultaneously as they removed their headsets.

The woman sitting across the aisle from them said. "Oh, don't stop. We don't mind." She looked around for support.

"Yeah, it's a long flight," the male passenger behind said. "We could use the entertainment."

A few others nodded.

The flight attendant looked over the cabin. "Anyone mind?"

No one spoke up.

"Then I guess it's all right. But keep it low." She was about to leave when she suddenly turned and asked David, "Do you sing professionally?"

"Yes, every Friday night at La Scala."

"Really?"

Alessandra's eyes widened.

David grinned. "It's a restaurant in Little Italy. I moonlight at night as a singing waiter."

"Well I think you could sing in the real La Scala," the attendant said as she moved on to other passengers.

David turned to Alessandra. "Where did you learn to sing?"

"My father thought I should be taught everything so I would have choices later in life. I'm afraid this one was a failure."

Alessandra pulled back and examined David. "Ever since we met, I've been trying to figure out why you look familiar to me.

"And have you figured it out?'

"You look a little like. . ."

"Josh Groban," David interrupted.

"You've been told that before?"

David nodded.

"I would love to sing with him someday."

David smiled. "Maybe I can arrange it."

"You know him?"

"Our firm does the audit on his 'Find Your Light Foundation.'"

Alessandra looked impressed. "It's a nice fantasy but my voice would scare off a crow right now."

"I disagree. You have a marvelous voice."

Exactly what her voice coach, her father, her uncle and everyone she knew had said. But she had no desire to spend a lifetime on the road away from whatever family she might eventually have. The career she chose in the art world had been exciting and fulfilling and until the Picasso went missing, she had never regretted her decision. Since then, however, she had begun to question if she had chosen wisely.

She placed her earphones back on. She began to sing along with the music, a libretto from *Carmen*. David joined in at the appropriate moment.

She looked at him in a new light. She smiled, closed her eyes again and dreamt of the adventure before them. Five hours later she opened her eyes as the Captain announced their landing at Koror airport. She looked out to a visual feast of sapphire blue water surrounding a series of small coral islands. Her heart raced. No, she had chosen correctly. A life in the theater could never be this exciting.

#

After settling into their rooms, Alessandra called the dive boat Captain, Socrates. He had been in touch with the members of the Bent Prop Project whose mission was to search the jungles and waters of the Western Pacific for clues as to the remains of American soldiers who died during WW II.

"The Project Director gave me the coordinates of three sites that could be the resting place of the airplane. I've pre-scouted the area and taken depth readings. I'm afraid one of the sites may be too dangerous to dive." Socrates related.

"The currents?" Alessandra asked.

"Yes, and the depth. It also looks as though whatever is down there, is on a shelf that drops off into depths I couldn't read. Which means it's more than 600'. That's the limit of my gauge."

Alessandra was both pleased and concerned. Socrates had done his homework, but the one site concerned her. Perhaps they wouldn't have to dive that site. In any event, Socrates said he'd pick them up early the next morning at "6:00 am."

Neither Alessandra nor David could sleep. Jet lag and the anticipation of the next day kept both awake through most of the night. In the thin walls of their hotel, Alessandra could hear David rustling about. She tapped lightly on the wall. He soon knocked at her door. She wrapped a hotel robe around herself, slipped the chain off and held the door slightly ajar.

"Nervous?" he asked as he tugged his own terry cloth robe around himself.

She nodded. "Aren't you?"

"I was hoping you'd call this off. It's madness."

"It is, isn't it?" She opened the door fully and gestured for him to come in.

"After all the trouble my grandparents went through to see that my mother and uncle could one day lay claim to that painting, it would seem a sin if I didn't at least make an attempt to recover it. And it would be nice to say goodbye to an uncle I never knew. But I can't help but wonder if we're really up to it."

"If we follow the protocol, I'm sure we'll be all right."

David grasped her arm. "Why are *you* doing this? You have no reason to risk your life over a ring and a painting no one has ever seen and may not even exist."

Alessandra stared out the window. "I told myself it was to get redemption. Clear my name. But that's not it."

"Then what?" David asked.

"My father was right." Alessandra turned to him. "I'm a thrill seeker. I wonder if I'm here because I couldn't pass up the rush I get when the stakes are high and my life is on the line."

"Are the stakes high enough to risk your life?"

"In my world, it would be the equivalent of Carter discovering King Tut's tomb."

"I hope without the inscription and the curse." David said.

"'Death Shall Come on Swift Wings To Him Who Disturbs the Peace of the King.'" Alessandra said.

"Yes, that's it. And a few months after he discovered the tomb, poor Howard Carter was dead. I'll be happy just to survive these dives. But now at least I understand the stakes."

Alessandra noted the time. "1:00 am," She yawned. "Perhaps it's time to get some rest. We have a big day ahead of us."

"I wonder if my mother has any clue as to the importance of this painting."

David walked to the door. "We both know nothing may come of this, but I'm glad we came. I know years from now if I hadn't given it a shot, I would have regretted it. So, thank you for setting this up."

Alessandra gave him a peck on the cheek and closed the door behind him. She flopped on the bed and stared at the ceiling long after David had gone. She was too hyped to fall asleep. A vision of Leocadia posing for Goya twirled in her head. She imagined herself the object of Goya's brush and being immortalized in that way. It was the last vision she had before jet lag and exhaustion overcame her.

#

The groggy pair greeted Socrates at 6:00 am the next morning in the hotel dining room. The Captain was a short, burly man in his late fifties. His face had volcanic like creases along his cheeks and his teeth were browned from the constant cigarette he kept dangling from his lips. He had a no nonsense attitude and appeared to know his business as he gave a quick briefing over breakfast. He carefully went over the water and wind conditions, decompression stops and other rules to follow.

"This is going to be a long day. Late in the day, you may become fatigued in which case the danger increases. But follow my instructions and you will be fine. Okay?"

David gave a "thumbs up" sign and Alessandra nodded.

An hour later, they boarded the *Explorer Deuce*. On board, Socrates introduced Alessandra and David to Phillipe. "He's a half breed. Half native, half French. He will be your dive master and underwater guide."

Phillipe gave them a tour. The dive boat was 36' long and 14' feet wide, had benches along the sides, numerous dive tanks secured along the outside railing, its own compressor to refill the tanks and an open stern area leading to a dive platform on the back of the vessel. What differentiated this dive boat from most was the side scan radar and an ROV.

The curly haired Phillipe pointed to the Remote Operating Vehicle.

"We were going to use that to locate the plane but we've had problems at depth and are waiting for some parts to fix it. Hopefully, we'll get it operational in the next few days. Meanwhile relax. It will take an hour to get to the first site."

Alessandra welcomed the opportunity to catch up on her sleep. She stretched out on a bench and soon fell asleep. David was already out.

Alessandra and David awoke when the boat slowed.

Phillipe stood close by preparing the gear. He hooked up breathing apparatuses to the tanks and pressed the button on the mouthpieces to expel air. He turned toward Alessandra.

"I'm curious. If we do locate the plane, what do you expect to see?"

Alessandra had merely disclosed that they wanted to find David's uncle's last resting place. Nothing was mentioned about the ring as she was reluctant to disclose their real mission. She was formulating her answer when David spoke up.

"According to my mother, my uncle was something of a daredevil. He had volunteered to be one of the first to fly a Corsair from the deck of an aircraft carrier. At that time, the Navy considered it unsafe to take off and land on a carrier. My uncle proved the Navy wrong. During an attack on Japanese positions on Palau, my uncle's plane was reported to have been shot down. My mother will never rest until she sees proof he was in it."

"Assuming we get lucky and locate his plane, then what?" Phillipe asked.

"Maybe we can find some kind of artifact of his. I don't know." David said.

"In that case, you need to know some rules. Scavenging the area is strictly forbidden. Our license could be at stake if you remove anything."

Alessandra was well aware of the rules, but she and David decided that since Artie's ring belonged to the family, it didn't technically qualify as "scavenging." Even so, if they were fortunate enough to find the ring, they intended to conceal it.

"Don't worry, we know about the law and intend to obey it. I'm only here to verify my uncle's burying place."

As they prepared to dive, Alessandra noticed something was amiss with the dive tanks. She expected to see a hard plastic casing enclosing the various gas holding tanks. Instead she saw what appeared to be a Rube Goldberg rigged design.

"Are these rebreathers? I was expecting the latest equipment."

Socrates waved a dismissive hand. "Don't worry, these will do the trick. These have trimix gases just like the rebreathers. The only difference is I have to preprogram the depth and at one hundred feet you'll have to switch manually from the normal tank to the trimix. Phillipe here will take you on a training dive and you'll be fine."

Alessandra was nervous. They had learned on equipment that automatically adjusted for the depths they were about to dive. These would require an adjustment from the diver and considering their inexperience in diving to such depths, it worried her. David didn't seem concerned. Apparently their talk last night had pumped him up and he seemed anxious to get into the water.

Phillipe helped Alessandra and David put on their tanks, two in back and one in front.

Alessandra struggled to stand.

David lent her a hand, then he stepped onto the dive platform and took a giant stride into the water. Phillipe went next.

Alessandra gingerly inched her way to the platform making sure she didn't trip because of the fins on her feet and weight on her back. She looked at Phillipe who bobbed in the water below.

He signaled thumbs up.

Alessandra was surprised at the warmth of the water. She had been told it was 85° F at the surface year round but until she felt it, she didn't understand how warm that was. But because they were diving to a depth of 300 feet they wore dry suits with foamed-neoprene material. Where they were going, the temperature dropped to 48° F, so until they got below 150' their suits would be uncomfortably hot.

It took a while to clear her ears. At 10 feet, she hung on the guideline Socrates had lowered right after they anchored. David and Phillipe waited below her. She held her nose and blew. Still not cleared. She flayed out on her back in an attempt to equalize the pressure in her ears. This seemed to help and she slowly descended to the 30 foot line, but felt some pressure as she approached two atmospheres at 33 feet. Moving her jaw from side to side, the slight pain in her ears dissipated and she was able to continue. She knew from past experience that going to four atmospheres, or 100 feet would be no problem once she made it past the 33 foot barrier. What she didn't know was what would happen at 300 feet where the pressure was nine times greater than at the surface. During their training, they had only descended to 100 feet. She was beginning to doubt herself again.

At 100 feet, Phillipe pointed to his dive computer. He switched mouth pieces from the one attached to the front tank to the one attached to the rear ones. He signaled David and Alessandra who also switched.

As they descended further, the light thinned and soon they were forced to use their flashlights. At 300 feet the ambient light disappeared entirely. They swiveled their lights around in a wide arc. The beams covered only twenty feet of width and a distance of thirty feet. Alessandra realized that finding the plane was going to be much more difficult than anticipated.

Phillipe shone his light on Alessandra and then David.

They in turn pointed their lights at him.

He opened and closed his fist twice to signal "ten minutes." Even with the trimix, their bottom time was limited. Their training and pre-dive briefing emphasized that no extension would be tolerated. The risk was too great. They'd have to start their ascent no later than 10 minutes from now.

Both Alessandra and David made a circle with their thumb and index finger to signal their acknowledgment.

As they swung their lights over the bottom, Alessandra was shocked to see the ocean floor strewn with shipwrecks and parts of airplanes. The only hope of finding Artie's plane was to find its tail section protruding above the sand so they could read the markings on it. They were looking for plane "F-14" and hopefully the lettering was still intact.

Alessandra spotted a tail section. Excitedly she swam over. She could make out an "F," but the number was hard to read. She wiped away some algae. The number came into view. The upper half of the digit revealed a circle, obviously a "9." Disappointed, she continued the search.

She checked her air gauge. Low. She signaled Phillipe she was starting up early.

He gave her the "Okay" sign.

David, who was with Phillipe, signaled he was going up also. Using a decompression model they had learned at their "rebreather classes," they did three safety stops of two minutes each at 200', 150', and 125' before the "required" one at 100'. There they all switched the hose and mouthpiece back to the front tank.

At fifty feet, three tanks hung from the side of the *Explorer Deuce*. It was the pure oxygen promised by the Captain during their briefing. They would make one more decompression stop after this. The oxygen was meant to shorten the decompression time. They were forewarned to follow Phillipe's lead.

"When he stops, you stop."

No warning was necessary. They understood the dangers. It took thirty minutes before they all were back on board.

David hugged Alessandra as soon as they removed their equipment. "We did it. And no CNS."

Alessandra frowned. "We're not done yet. The fact we have no central nervous system symptoms doesn't mean there's no danger. There's still the problem of DCS."

"Yes, it is no time to celebrate. As you know, the more dives we do on the same day, the more dangerous it gets," Phillipe said. "Your bodies need time to expel the nitrogen, so she's right. Decompression sickness is always a danger."

"What about the weather. Are we okay this afternoon?" Alessandra asked.

Phillipe looked out over the horizon. "In the afternoon, the wind picks up and the currents get stronger, so surfacing will be more difficult."

After a refreshing drink of guava juice and some fruit, all four crowded around a chart in the wheelhouse. Black dots marked the map.

"There are only two more possible sites at approximately three hundred feet." Socrates pointed to a dot. "This one about thirty minutes from here and another one about a mile from there. If it's not in one of these two places, blame the Bent Prop Project."

At the second spot, they waited while Socrates used the sonar to scan the bottom for the best anchoring place. He frowned.

"This doesn't look promising. When I did my quick check before, I thought I spotted something that could be an airplane."

He motioned them over and pointed to a spot on the sonar. "See this. It probably is a plane, but it's too big to be yours. It looks more like a bomber." He checked his watch. "It's already 2 o'clock. If we dive here, after calculating surface time to clear the nitrogen, you won't have time to do the last dive."

"Then let's go where the best chances are," David said.

Alessandra nodded.

"Okay," Socrates said, "But I won't allow the dive if the currents are too strong. We won't know until we get there."

At 3:00 pm they arrived at the last site. Socrates dropped a float into the water. It slowly drifted south. He scanned the horizon. "It doesn't look like there's any weather coming in for a while, so if you go now, you should be all right. The current looks manageable."

Socrates did a last minute check of the tanks. "I've programmed these for three hundred twenty five feet so you have a little cushion. You'll have twenty minutes bottom time, but if you haven't located it in fifteen, come up."

Alessandra quickly jumped in.

David was about to go when Phillipe put a hand on his shoulder.

"I checked the sonar. There are many planes down there, some near that shelf the Captain warned you about. Be careful."

At two hundred feet, they could make out some shapes on the bottom. Again shipwrecks and airplanes, both Japanese and American loomed as they turned on their flashlights. Some planes were broken into pieces; tails, wings and cockpits were separated.

At three hundred feet, Phillipe signaled for them to check their computers and set their watches to count backwards. They had twenty minutes.

The terrain was slanted which meant that some wrecks were much lower than 300 feet. Alessandra spotted a few tail sections and explored them all. Each turned out be the wrong number. She saw David wipe away some coral from one plane section, then move on.

With 15 minutes to go, Alessandra spotted another tail of a plane closer to David. She pointed her light at it.

David swam toward the plane. His light illuminated a cockpit lying nearby.

She swam to catch up and noticed the markings as David scraped away crust on the side looking for the markings. It read "F-23."

With 6 minutes to go, Phillipe signaled for them to start up.

Alessandra started to ascend, when she spied another cockpit about twenty feet away.

She swam over and brushed off some sand from the cockpit. A skeleton seated in the plane stared at her. Tattered clothes were still on the body as well as boots. She figuratively shivered. As she turned away from the skeleton, she noted the tail section nearby.

She quickly floated to the side. No number was visible.

Alessandra checked her watch, one minute to go. What to do? How could she identify the plane? She looked back toward the body of the plane, and noted part of a number in front of the American star. She hurriedly scraped away the crust. "14" Appeared. No "F" could be made out, but Alessandra was certain this was it.

Alessandra felt a tug on her flipper. She turned to see David who floated above her.

He frantically pointed upward.

She shone her light on the airplane number.

He nodded but pointed to his depth gauge. It showed 330 feet. Again he signaled for her to come up, but she was too near victory.

She checked her watch, the zero blinked at her. Her gauge shows 335 feet.

Alessandra ignored David and slipped inside the opening of the cockpit. She delicately moved the skeleton aside. She searched under the seat. She checked her watch again. Another minute had passed. Too dangerous to dally. She signaled David who was hovering above that she was coming up.

Alessandra started to exit the plane but had second thoughts. She couldn't leave before one more check. She made a hasty calculation. She could spare another few minutes of bottom time if she took longer to decompress. All she had to do was reach the hanging oxygen tanks Socrates had promised and all would be fine.

She cringed as she poked gingerly at the skeleton. Its left leg disjointed from the rest of the bones. She shone her light down at the floor. A crusted circular object came into view. She grabbed for it and picked away some of the crust. Diamonds glinted in the light. She caught her breath and could feel her heart pound as she turned the ring over. Amazingly, the mother of pearl still shone. She could even make out the faint markings etched into the mother of pearl, "Weiss." It was just what she had expected from what she had learned just before leaving on the trip. She was holding Leocadia Zorillo's ring.

The real thing was far more beautiful than it appeared in David's photo. She caressed the nubby stones. To touch something Goya himself once owned and gave to his lover. *Asombroso* (amazing)! She unzipped the top of her suit. The cold water seeped in. She shivered but shook it off. She held the ring delicately in her fingers to drop inside her suit when the felt the plane shift.

Apparently her weight upset the delicate balance of the plane's resting place. She looked out of the cockpit. The plane was sliding toward the abyss. She scrambled to exit the plane. Just as she cleared the cockpit, there was a tug on her arm. David had come to help. The sudden jerk caused her to drop the ring. The precious treasure drifted toward the bottom. *Mierde!*

David gripped her arm tightly and pointed to his depth gauge. It showed "350 feet."

She shined her light downward. Thirty feet below, the ring glittered on the sand. The plane continued to slide off of the shelf. She tried to pull loose from David's hold, but felt herself being pulled toward the surface. She watched dejectedly as the ring disappeared from view.

Alessandra was furious as she was tugged upward toward the first decompression stop. But at 200', a pain in her abdomen jarred her back to reality. She had lingered too long. She realized the pain was the first sign of decompression sickness. She signaled David to stop. They were rising too rapidly.

She bit into her mouthpiece to deal with the pain. She also was freezing. In her haste to exit the plane, she forgot to close the zipper to her suit. The cold water was numbing. She wiggled free of David's grip and zipped up. Shortly, her body heat warmed the water and the stomach pain seemed to dissipate. She nodded to continue upward. At 125' it got worse. She began to breathe faster. She checked her gauge. She was sucking too much air. If she didn't control her breathing, she'd soon run out of air. At 100' the pain was excruciating. She convulsed. Her body shook violently. She took a big gulp of air. Nausea, tunnel vision and light headedness overwhelmed her. Then everything went black.

Chapter 12

David checked his depth gauge. 100'. His air gauge showed less than 500 psi. Low. Very low. The extra time on the bottom at a deeper depth than planned, had sapped precious air from his tank. He promptly switched mouthpieces to the front tank and again checked the air gauge. Barely enough to reach the spare oxygen tanks he expected to find at 50'.

David searched for Alessandra. Gone. She was there a moment ago. And Phillipe, gone also. What was happening? He looked below. Alessandra was slowly sinking out of sight. She didn't appear to be moving. Fear gripped him. He quickly dove toward her. He reached her at 130'. Her eyes were closed! But he could see her sucking air. He checked her tank. Only 100 psi. Almost out. He pressed a button on her jacket and slightly inflated the vest. Slowly she began to rise. At 100' he started to switch her mouthpiece from the back to the front tank, but noticed she had already done it. Suddenly she convulsed. DCS!

His heart pounded faster and he started sucking too much air. *Calm down*, he told himself. He had to get them to the decompression stop at 50'. She convulsed again and she appeared to have trouble getting air. He checked her air pressure. Zero!

He took a long pull on his air, removed his mouth piece and placed into her mouth. She opened her eyes and sucked in deeply. They would have to buddy breathe until they got to the spare oxygen tanks. His instinct was to rush her to the surface, but doing so would make the early stages of decompression sickness worse.

They ascended slowly and every ten feet or so David looked up trying to spot the tanks. The water was clear so he expected to see the tanks soon, but at 75', still nothing in sight. Had he miscalculated their location? He looked for the boat anchor line but it too had vanished. Stay calm, he told himself. He gripped Alessandra's arm tightly and continued upward.

At 50' David froze. Still no tanks in sight. He must have miscalculated and missed the boat? He did a 360°. No boat in sight. The currents must have pushed them away from the boat. He did have a wrist compass but wasn't sure he could use it correctly. He tried hard to remember the instructions.

What course had they taken from the boat to the plane? Foolishly, he hadn't checked when they first dove in. Now what? When they entered the water, the sun was behind the boat. Was that east or west? In the northern hemisphere he knew that would be west as it was midafternoon, but they were in the southern hemisphere now. Did that change things? Water down a drain flowed in the opposite direction but what about the sun? No, it had to be the same. The sun doesn't suddenly change its location when you cross the equator. They had to swim west. But wait, which way did the currents push them? When they jumped in they drifted under the boat, west. He put his left wrist on his right elbow and saw the needle point north. He turned the bezel on his watch compass to head east.

Although Alessandra had gone limp, she still appeared to be breathing. Good. But it meant David had to tow her. He struggled against the current as he pulled Alessandra with him.

Shadows appeared on the water. Clouds, or was the light beginning to fade? He checked his watch, 5:20. He had to hurry but swimming fast would use up more air. He hoped the boat would come into view soon as he was running out of energy as well as air.

David constantly checked on Alessandra as they swapped his air hose. So far, she was able to breathe. After ten minutes he was beginning to despair. Nothing in sight. Suddenly the light got better. Had the sun peeked out from behind a cloud? He squinted. Did he see a boat's shadow off in the distance? He held onto Alessandra and headed toward the shadow. All the while he checked his depth gauge so as to be sure to remain at 50'. As he neared the silhouette, it became obvious it was indeed the dive boat. But where the hell were the oxygen tanks? Socrates had forgotten the tanks. And where the hell was Phillipe?

He had to make a decision and fast. There was not enough air in his tank to last long enough to decompress either of them. They were originally scheduled to hang for thirty minutes at 50'. He calculated that the extra bottom time they had used required at least half again that much, forty-five minutes. He had to get them pure oxygen and there was only one way to do it. They ascended toward the boat. As they neared 15', David searched for the normal air hoses that every dive boat hangs over the side while divers are in the water. While it wouldn't be the pure oxygen they needed to decompress more rapidly, it would sustain them for awhile. The hoses appeared, hanging like the tentacles of an octopus. At least Socrates hadn't completely screwed up.

David thrust an air hose into Alessandra's mouth.

She sucked hard and opened her eyes. She grabbed his hand and nodded.

David removed her front tank and let it sink toward the bottom. He reached for one of the hanging air hoses and placed it into his mouth. Then he removed his front tank and hung it on Alessandra. He pointed below and flashed both hands five times, "50."

She nodded, let go of the hanging air hose, inserted the mouthpiece from David's tank, let some air out of her vest and slowly descended to 50'.

A splash overhead alerted David. Phillipe headed toward him with two tanks in hand. David pointed toward the surface and headed up. When he reached the top, David shouted at the Captain. "Get a hyperbaric chamber here. And fast."

"I've already called for help. The Palau search and rescue team are on the way. I'm sorry about the oxygen tanks, but the line snapped."

Phillipe popped to the surface. "I gave Alessandra a new tank. You better get back below."

David knew he had to get back to decompression depth. The longer he stayed on the surface the more dangerous it became.

Phillipe helped him put on a new tank, then David dove to join Alessandra. He calculated they would have to stay at 50' as long as the oxygen would last, leaving only enough to reach the surface. Hopefully by then, the chambers would have arrived and they could finish decompressing in them.

With five minutes of oxygen to spare, David signaled to Alessandra it was time to surface. Would the rescue party be there? As they neared the surface, David looked for signs of another boat. Nothing. No shadow, no profile. He glanced at Alessandra. Her body shook and her breathing became more agitated. This was bad as they were at a depth where the water was warm. If she was shaking at this depth, he feared the worst.

She closed her eyes. She was losing it.

He got hold of her and inflated her jacket a bit more. Gently, they popped to the surface.

The roar of a helicopter hovering above brought a sense of relief. They'd soon be in the portable hyperbaric chambers.

Phillipe waited at the side of the boat to help them aboard. David could see alarm in his face as he stared at Alessandra. David pulled off her mask. He pried her eyelids open. Her eyes looked vacant.

"Where are the chambers?" David shouted.

"They're in for repairs, but . . ."

David's heart sank. The roar of the helicopter drowned out the rest of Phillipe's words. David cupped his hands around his ears to indicate he couldn't hear.

Phillipe pointed to David, then to Alessandra and finally toward the helicopter.

"They'll fly you to Koror," he yelled. "There's a hospital there with a chamber."

David nodded.

Socrates and Phillipe lifted Alessandra out of the water.

Once on board, they hastily removed all her gear. She slumped to the deck.

David helped himself aboard but never took his eyes off of Alessandra. As he unbuckled his own equipment, he monitored Alessandra for signs of life. She never stirred. He checked her pulse. Faint. He grabbed a free oxygen tank, quickly attached an air hose and shoved it into her mouth. Instinctively she sucked at the mouthpiece. Her eyes remained shut.

Socrates signaled the helicopter to lower a line. A basket was lowered. They strapped Alessandra in it along with the oxygen tank by her side.

Socrates waved his hand in a circular motion.

The basket swayed as it lifted off the deck. Only meters from the 'copter, a strong gust of wind hit. The basket careened violently. The oxygen tank flew off almost taking Alessandra with it. The tank headed toward the boat deck.

The men on the boat scrambled for safety. The tank landed near Socrates, bounced once on the steel deck and flew into David. The full force of the nearly full, forty five pound, aluminum tank knocked him down . . . and out.

David woke up in the helicopter with excruciating pain in his chest. He tried touching his chest with his right arm but couldn't move it.

"I think you broke it," the medic sitting by his side said.

David grimaced. "My arm or my ribs?"

"Both."

David turned toward Alessandra. "How's she doing?"

The medic shrugged his shoulders. "Too soon to tell."

David's pain intensified. "Can I get something for the pain?"

"Sorry. We don't know how much your brain was compromised from the dive. Any narcotic could kill you. We'll have to wait until we can get you in a decompression tank."

David tried to concentrate his thoughts away from his own body. He craned his neck to see the ocean waves skimming just below the 'copter. What was the pilot doing? Was he unaware of the danger? David tapped the medic on his arm. He tried to sound calm. "Aren't we flying too low?"

"Sir. We are flying in an un-pressurized aircraft. After your deep dive, any altitude above sea level could kill you. Do not fear. The pilot is trained to fly low in such cases."

Of course! The whole idea was get them in a hyperbaric chamber which would artificially return them to the depth necessary for proper decompression. They had ascended far too rapidly which meant if they didn't get into a chamber soon, the nitrogen bubbles in their systems could be fatal. The quick ascent had allowed the nitrogen gas to expand before it had been eliminated from their bodies. And judging from her symptoms, Alessandra probably also had oxygen toxicity. Quick treatment was imperative. But in the meantime any altitude would worsen her condition. David was pleased the men in the helicopter knew their business.

He looked at Alessandra. She looked ashen. He wasn't sure she'd make it. She had risked her life over a damn ring. His ring! His painting! The ring meant nothing. The painting meant nothing. Her *life* meant something and he just wanted her to live.

David winced when the pilot made a sudden turn. He willed himself to reach out and hold Alessandra's hand. It felt cold. With his free arm, he tapped the medic.

"Can you check her pulse?"

The medic placed his hand on her wrist. He shook his head.

"What's wrong?" David asked.

The medic placed a portable defibrillator on Alessandra's chest and pushed a button. Her chest heaved but there was no sign of breathing. He hit the button again. Nothing. He crawled into the cockpit and whispered into the pilot's ear. He looked back at David.

"Sir, we'll get her there as soon as possible."

David couldn't believe it. He cursed himself for ever asking her to help locate the painting. He let out loud sobs.

Chapter 13

At the Belau Hospital, David watched the medics rush Alessandra inside. What was the use? She was gone and no known treatment could save her.

David was placed in a wheelchair and wheeled into the emergency room. A doctor was soon at his side.

"Where did they take Alessandra?" David asked.

"To the hyperbaric chamber," the doctor answered.

"But why? She's dead." David looked at the doctor. "Isn't she?"

The doctor shook his head. "We get many cases in here where there is no pulse, but when we get the diver back down to decompression depth, sometimes they revive."

There was hope after all.

The doctor told David his ribs and arm would have to wait for treatment until after they treated the decompression sickness. But in spite of the medic's concern, and much to David's relief, the doc did give him a shot for his pain.

The hyperbaric chamber was located in a separate wing of the Hospital. It was 24'x 9' and capable of treating up to four patients at a time. Apparently diving accidents were common in the area.

Alessandra's pale body, barely covered by a white sheet, was wheeled into the chamber and laid on a small bed.

A nurse placed her on pure oxygen.

David took a chair nearby with his own oxygen tank and waited.

Miraculously, within minutes Alessandra's body shook. She had begun breathing

David wiped away a tear and held her hand. He gently massaged it. David noticed some color slowly returning to her face and skin. Minutes later, she opened her eyes and touched David's arm.

"Did you . . ." She coughed. "Did you . . ." She pointed to the back of her ring finger. "Ring?"

David shook his head vigorously. "No, and we're not going back either. Do you realize . . ."

Alessandra closed her eyes and turned away.

David lowered his voice. ". . . we almost died."

Since David hadn't dived as deep as Alessandra, he was told he could leave the chamber in eight hours. And the shot had worked. The pain in his chest had diminished and miraculously, he was now able to move his arm freely. He touched his ribs. Still sore but getting better. He placed the oxygen mask over his mouth and lied down. Maybe he hadn't broken anything after all. It was a comforting thought as he fell into a deep sleep.

#

David awoke to a doctor checking his pulse. "How's the chest?"

David felt his ribs. "Sore."

"I've got good news. Nothing's broken. It's just a bruise."

David nodded toward Alessandra. "She going to be all right?"

"She stretched the limits of her dive profile and surfaced too fast."

"Yeah, I know. But will she make it?"

"It's very serious. We won't know for a while."

David became alarmed. "How long—"

The doctor placed his stethoscope on Alessandra's chest. "Our longest stay has been fourteen hours, but she may take longer." He rose and put a hand out to David. "Come on. It's time for you to leave."

David stayed close to the chamber. There was a small window he could look into to see if Alessandra awoke. For next few hours, she never moved. He took a break and went to the men's room. When he returned he noticed she had rolled over.

He tracked down the doctor who immediately entered the chamber to check on her. David watched as the doctor raised Alessandra's eyelids. Then he checked her pulse.

"Well?" David asked when the doctor exited the chamber.

"She's ready to be moved to Intensive Care, but she's not out to the woods yet." The doctor looked at David sympathetically.

"Go for a walk or something. We'll let you know when there's a change."

Good advice, David thought but he wasn't about to leave. He was told he could wait outside her room in ICU, but couldn't go in.

For the next eight hours he paced outside. Around midnight he got hungry and was just about to leave when he peeked into the window and to his amazement, he saw Alessandra suddenly sit up in her bed. They made eye contact. She smiled weakly. He gave her the thumbs up sign.

He rushed to the nurses' station and informed the duty nurse of the good news. She picked up the phone and dialed.

"The doctor's gone for the night. I've left a message for him."

David realized there was no more he could do, so he went to the ICU window to wave goodnight. Alessandra pointed to her ring finger. *The woman was possessed.* He shook his head from side to side. Alessandra turned away and lay back down.

David returned to his own hospital room and dialed Socrates who had asked to be informed of Alessandra's progress. He told Socrates the good news.

"Why did she break the rules?" Socrates asked.

David told him about the ring. "She was obsessed."

"This ring. Is it valuable?"

David pondered his answer. How much should he reveal? "To my family. It's been in our possession for more than two hundred years."

"Yes, yes. But what is it worth?"

More than you could possibly imagine. "It has historical significance, but that's all. To Alessandra it's worth a lot."

"Enough for her to risk her life?"

Where was this all going? "She's an historian. Maybe she fashions herself as a female Indiana Jones."

"In any case tell Ms. Jones I wish her a speedy recovery."

After he hung up, David pondered the phone call. He thought Socrates had pried a bit too much. But so what? The ring was gone and it was time to move on with his life. The task at hand was getting Alessandra well. He felt responsible for getting her into this mess. But angsting over it wouldn't get her better. He tried to focus on positive thoughts so he could get some sleep.

A few hours later he awoke to the blaring sound of a code blue alert. He felt a stab in the pit of his stomach. He grabbed a robe and rushed to the ICU. Alessandra was gone. With heart pounding, he hurried to the nurses' station. "What happened?"

"Cardiac arrest." A new face said.

"What?" David's voice quivered. "How?"

The nurse shrugged.

"Where'd they take her?"

"Her?"

David pointed to the hyperbaric chamber. "Yes, the woman that was in there."

"Oh, her. They moved her to a regular room, 5 B."

Thank god.

David found Alessandra asleep. He gently touched her hand. She didn't stir. He went back to his room, retrieved a pillow and a blanket and sat down beside her bed.

#

The next morning, Alessandra awoke to find David on the floor beside her asleep. A pillow lay on the floor nearby. Alessandra smiled. She rubbed her eyes and stretched. She felt a little sore, but otherwise seemed to be okay. She looked around and realized she was in a hospital. She tried remembering the events of the last few days, but wasn't even sure how long she'd been there. She had no memory of being brought in to a hospital. The last thing she remembered was dropping the ring. But wait, she vaguely recalled David helping her to the surface. And then another flash. The helicopter basket and clinging to its sides. Then nothing.

She watched David for any signs of life. He seemed to be in a deep sleep. He looked so vulnerable with his head back, mouth open and softly snoring.

She rose and shuffled over to him. She picked up the pillow and placed it under his head. She ran the back of her hand lightly along his face, then turned to leave.

"Are you all right?" David asked.

Alessandra turned back to him. "Physically I think so." She took his hand in hers.

"David, we almost had it. If only you had waited a few more seconds."

"In a few more seconds, we wouldn't be having this conversation."

"Without that ring the *Dancing Maja* is gone."

He sat up. "We've lived this long without it. We'll get by."

"It's your heritage."

"My heritage? It's a goddamn painting."

She fixed his eyes in hers. "It's more than that."

David helped Alessandra to her feet. "What are you talking about?"

"The woman in the painting is Leocadia Zorillo."

"Yeah, that was his mistress. So?"

"Before Leocadia joined Goya, she was married to a man named Weiss."

David looked puzzled.

"Remember your mother told us the ring had been passed down from a distant relative and it had an inscription on it that began with a "W."

David nodded.

"She also thought the full name was something like 'White.'"

David's eyes *widened*. "Weiss in German means White."

"*Exactamente!* And there's more. Leocadia had a daughter, Rosario. She took Rosario with her to join Goya in France. Goya later adopted Rosario." Alessandra moved toward the bed.

David waited.

"Rosario was just an infant when she went to live with Goya. When she showed talent as a painter, Goya wrote a friend in Paris and asked him to train her. When he wrote, he said, 'Treat her as though she were my own daughter.'"

"Well, since he had adopted her, she was technically his daughter," David said.

"Goya's wife was already dead when Rosario was conceived. I believe Goya was having an affair with Leocadia before, even while his wife was dying. The letter just confirms the obvious. She was Goya's natural child."

"Are you saying what I think you're saying?"

Alessandra nodded. "*Sí.* Goya is also your ancestor."

"You're mad."

Alessandra studied him. "When your mother told us the history of the ring and the 'W' engraved on it, I asked a friend at the Prado to do some research on Leocadia. Just before we left on this trip, he faxed me the information. I should have told you earlier, but you know I'm right. It all adds up."

"Well, it doesn't change anything. I'm not risking my life again," David held Alessandra by her shoulders, "or yours, for a painting."

"When you first contacted me, you thought you could make a claim for a valuable piece of art. That's all it was to you. But, now you know that painting is part of your heritage. And so is the ring. Goya risked his life to paint the woman he loved."

David stared at her.

"Because he would not tell the Inquisition the name of the woman who posed for *The Naked Maja*, Goya not only lost his title as the King's artist, but was threatened with death if he ever painted another nude." Alessandra rolled to her side.

"Nevertheless he painted Leocadia naked. That woman was your ancestor and that painting is not just another piece of art. It's an important piece of your history as well as mankind's. So, when I get out of here, I'm going back."

"You won't be able to dive for a while."

"Then, I'll wait."

#

A few days later, Alessandra was well enough to leave the Hospital. Neither spoke as he pushed her wheelchair outside. A taxi was waiting.

"Where are we going?" Alessandra asked.

"Russia." David helped her into the taxi.

"Without the ring, it's a waste of time." Alessandra turned away. She pouted all the way to the airport. When they arrived, she wouldn't budge.

"Are you coming?" David asked.

Alessandra folded her arms. "I'm staying until I get that ring."

"Okay, stay then." David opened the door of the taxi and waved the back of his hand at her. The ring on his finger glimmered in the sunlight. Her eyes widened.

She leapt out of the car and tugged at his hand. "*Caramba!*" She turned his finger as though on a spindle. "I was beginning to wonder if you had any cojones."

"Cojones, no. Brains, yes. Socrates helped me."

"Socrates?"

"They fixed the ROV. We used its robotic arm."

"And what about the no scavenging rule?" Alessandra said. "Wasn't he worried about his precious license?"

David rubbed his thumb and two forefingers together. She smiled knowingly.

David put the ring on her finger. "This belongs on a beautiful woman. I think that's what Goya had in mind."

Alessandra held the ring up toward the sun. "It's magnificent. Can I wear it? Really?"

David grinned.

Alessandra threw her arms around him. She looked deeply into his eyes, closed hers and planted a very wet kiss on him.

At first David seemed unsure how to respond.

She held the kiss.

He finally returned the kiss with equal passion. They remained locked in that embrace for a few moments. They broke. He stared into her eyes.

She lowered hers. There was an awkward silence.

"I need to call Kleinermann and tell him we're on our way to Russia."

"And we better alert Jorge as well."

Inside the terminal, David went to pick up their tickets. Alessandra checked her watch/cell phone. With the time difference, she didn't think Kleinermann would be in. She was right. She left a message on his voice mail. "We have the ring and are on our way to Russia. We'll be at the Hotel Astoria as prearranged."

Next, she dialed Jorge's cell phone and left a similar message. Not actually getting someone on the phone was frustrating. She had to share her excitement with somebody and since David hadn't returned, she called Gregor and woke him. Breathlessly, she related her adventures.

"Can you believe it? We actually found the ring and now we can prove the painting belongs to David's family."

"I am excited for you, my love. Call me when you have the painting."

Gregor's response wasn't quite what she had expected. He acted almost as if recovering the ring was a foregone conclusion. She brushed it off. Perhaps he was too drowsy to show much enthusiasm.

David flashed the tickets as she hung up. The Hermitage awaited. Soon they'd have the painting and she'd be redeemed. Maybe then Gregor would be excited for her.

Chapter 14

Gregor Melnikov put down the phone with mixed feelings. He should have shown more enthusiasm for her, but since he had her cell phone bugged months earlier, he had already been alerted to Alessandra's call to Kleinermann. So he had a hard time pretending her information was new. Next time he vowed to do better.

#

As a youth, Gregor was always the best athlete on his team. He caught the attention of government agents and was groomed to become an Olympic athlete. Unfortunately, while he excelled at ice hockey, football (or "soccer" as the Americans called it) and even gymnastics, he had not been good enough to make the Ukrainian Olympic team in any one particular sport. If they had had a triathlon of various sports, he would have been a lock. But he was also smart and movie star handsome in a rugged sort of way. So he caught the eye of a government spy agency and was enticed with promises that he could be the Ukrainian version of James Bond. Gregor bit.

He was groomed to use his good looks to ingratiate himself into the confidences of women. And he was very good at it. But he disliked the NKVD, so when the Soviet Union collapsed, he left the country and soon found satisfying work elsewhere.

Gregor had been on Alessandra's trail ever since the Picasso disappeared. His boss was determined to recover the painting and had personally selected Gregor for the task. Soon enough he had wormed his way into Alessandra's confidence. But she wouldn't sleep with him. In that regard, she was his first failure and that annoyed him. He looked upon "bedding" a woman as one of the perks of the job and she was denying him that perk. Someday, he would rectify that.

Gregor alerted his colleagues in St. Petersburg that she was on the way. They would keep him informed of her every move.

#

David and Alessandra arrived at the Hotel Astoria to find a message waiting from Kleinermann. *"I have arranged a meeting with an old colleague, Boris Stoyanovich, the museum curator. You are to meet with him tomorrow at 8:30 am in The Spanish Room which will be closed to the public for a short time. Wait for Boris in front of two paintings you will recognize."*

Alessandra reread the message. She was grateful that Sigi had eased their path, but was perplexed by the cryptic nature of his instructions. She spent the night imagining what paintings Kleinermann had in mind.

The Hermitage Museum is situated in the heart of St. Petersburg, on the banks of the River Neva. Alessandra and David were on their way to the New Hermitage, one of six imposing buildings that made up the complex.

As they approached the "Spanish Room," Alessandra's pulse quickened. If Jorge's information was correct she'd soon be face to face with an historical gem? But would they be able to pry *The Naked Maja Dancing* loose from the Hermitage's arms? Hopefully, Kleinermann's influence would help.

A red rope blocked the entrance to the doors of the Spanish Room.

"Señorita Santana and Señor Edlestein?" A guard asked.

"*Sí*," Alessandra said.

The guard removed the rope and pushed open the heavy doors.

They entered a vast dimly lit gallery. Alessandra adjusted her eyes. All the walls were bare except for two paintings at the far end of the room. Alessandra was stunned. She blinked. Were her eyes deceiving her? She rushed forward. Both *The Naked Maja* and *The Clothed Maja* hung side by side on the wall in front of her.

A sign underneath identified the paintings by name and artist. To the right of both paintings, a small sign in English, French and Russian proclaimed, *This space reserved for a newly discovered Goya.*

Alessandra gasped.

David came alongside. "What's wrong?"

"I thought they were still in the Prado."

David moved closer. "These are so much better than the photos. I hope our painting is their equal." He turned to Alessandra. "What does "Maja" mean?"

"It means a woman who has devoted her life to the pleasures of love," Alessandra said. She stepped back to admire the paintings. "Just imagine living in a world where even though you are the most revered painter in the country, you are threatened with death if you ever paint another naked woman."

"And that's why he made my ancestor promise never to exhibit it in public."

"Exactamente!"

A stocky, bespectacled man shuffled into the room. "I see you are surprised."

"Shocked would be more like it." The Prado rarely allowed these paintings to leave Madrid and when they did, it made international news. Why hadn't she heard about this exhibit? Perhaps she missed the news. "Mr. Stoyanovich?" Alessandra extended her hand.

"Call me Boris, please." He graciously kissed her extremity.

David extended his, which Boris ignored.

"I had to promise the Prado they would get the new Goya after our exhibit closes." Boris cracked a half smile.

"So you do have the *Maja Dancing*?" Alessandra said.

"We have a painting that I only recently realized was sitting in our cellars. We were unable to identify it until my good friend Seigfried called. He tells me you believe it's called *The Naked Maja Dancing*, a painting heretofore unknown to me."

"In Spain, there has always been rumors of its existence," Alessandra said. "If we could see it, perhaps - -"

"I will need to see your identification," Boris said. "Please."

Alessandra handed him her card. Boris nodded approvingly. "I've known Sigi for a very long time. We worked together in East Berlin while our two countries were close friends. But I haven't seen him since the wall came down."

Boris turned to David. "He tells me you claim to be the owner of the painting."

David pulled out the photo of his family posing in front of *The Naked Maja Dancing*. He held it up toward Boris.

"And what does this prove?" Boris asked.

"That's my grandmother." David pointed to a short, dark haired woman in the photo. "She's wearing the same ring as the woman in the painting."

Boris slipped a small magnifying glass from his pocket. "I'm afraid the photo is not detailed enough to tell me anything. Moreover, by itself it means nothing."

Alessandra pulled David aside and whispered into his ear. "That's what I feared. We're going to have to show him the ring."

She started to raise her hand, when David grabbed her arm.

"Suppose we can produce the same ring that's on the dancer's hand?" David said. "Then what? Will you accept that as evidence it's my family's painting and release it to us?"

"I'm afraid it is not that simple. Certain procedures will have to be followed. Do you have such a ring?"

"We can only know that when we see the painting," Alessandra said.

"Ah, Ms. Santana, I'm afraid I can't do that."

"Can't or won't?" David asked.

"Mr. Edlestein?" Boris asked. "You are Mr. Edlestein?"

David nodded.

"You are not in America. Here we make the rules." Boris pushed his wire rim glasses toward the end of his nose and peered over at David. "You understand?" He said with a hint of menace in his voice

David was about to speak. Alessandra cut him off. "Yes, we understand," she said. "What is it you require in order for us to make a proper claim for the painting?"

"The ring would be a good start," Boris said.

"A good start?" David exclaimed. "My family was slaughtered by the bastards that stole that painting. Just what evidence would you expect us to have? A receipt from Goya that he gave the painting to my ancestor?"

Again, Alessandra touched David on the arm. She raised her hand and flashed the ring.

"Very beautiful. But I will need to examine it closely to see that it is the real thing."

Alessandra slipped it from her finger and handed it to Boris.

Without inspecting it, he slipped it into his pocket.

David grabbed Boris' arm. "What are you doing?"

Boris nodded to the guard who had entered the room. The guard drew his revolver and approached.

David backed off. "You going to shoot me?"

"It is not wise to threaten a Russian official."

"He didn't threaten anyone," Alessandra said.

Boris pointed to David and spoke directly to the guard. "Arrest this man. He tried to beat me."

The guard grabbed David's arms and cuffed him.

"I don't believe this." David shouted.

"Take him downstairs while I consider his penalty," Boris said.

David tried to resist but the guard forcefully pushed him out of the door.

Once David was out of the room Boris took Alessandra by her arm.

She threw off his hand. "What is going on here?"

Boris gently steered her toward an exit.

"Where are you taking me?"

Boris said nothing. He guided Alessandra to an office. Once inside, he thrust some papers at her. "Fill out these forms. If all is in order and the ring is indeed the same as the one on the finger of the dancer, we will consider honoring Mr. Edlestein's claim."

"When?"

"In two weeks our exhibit will be finished. Then as promised, we will ship the painting to the Prado. You will have to negotiate with them as to the date they will return it to us. And only then—"

Alessandra interrupted. "We will expect the painting to be available at the end of your exhibit. The Prado has no right to show a painting they do not own."

"Even so, I did make a promise and—"

Alessandra interrupted him again. "I will deal with the Prado and I assure you they will not hold you to your promise." Alessandra hoped she still had some influence with her former employer. "Now, can we claim the painting in two weeks?"

"No. As you know, if we determine Mr. Edlestein's claim to be in order, we must ship the *Maja Dancing* back to its country of origin. You will have to accept delivery there."

In the heat of the confrontation, that detail had slipped Alessandra's mind. The protocol for the return of any Holocaust painting was for the holder to ship it to the country from where it was originally confiscated. "And which country is that?"

"We have yet to determine that. But I will consult our records and inform you accordingly. That is, if we approve your claim."

"And the ring?"

Boris removed the ring from his pocket. He flicked at a piece of coral crust that had formed around one of the diamonds. "Our experts will need to thoroughly clean this. If the ring is genuine you have nothing to fear, it will be returned in due time. On the other hand, if the ring is not as you say it is, Russian prisons are not known for their hospitality."

A shiver ran through Alessandra. What if the ring wasn't the real thing? "What do you intend to do with David?"

Boris looked sternly at her. "I had him arrested as a warning we will not tolerate American insolence. As long as he behaves, he will be allowed to go back to your hotel with you, but you will not be able to leave the country until we finish our inspection."

Boris extended his hand. "My driver will take you to your hotel."

"I've always wanted a matryoshka doll. Could your driver find us a place to buy one?"

"Of course."

#

After Alessandra left his office, Boris turned on the TV monitor. He watched as David joined Alessandra outside the Museum. David eluded her grasp and headed back inside.

Boris switched screens to the monitor outside his room. David was hastily marching down the corridor toward Boris' office. A guard stepped in front of David who attempted to shove him aside. In a flash, the guard threw David to the ground. Then, Alessandra came into view. She appeared to plead with the guard who stood pointing a gun at David. Boris shook his head, "Stupid Jew."

He switched off the monitor and dialed. "The situation is getting out of control. I have the ring. Now what?"

"Go through normal procedures," the voice at the other end, said. "I am sure the ring is genuine, but have your jewelry expert authenticate it. We may need that later. Have you located the painting?"

"We are still searching. You wouldn't believe the number of unopened crates buried in our cellars."

The voice was unsympathetic. "Your guests have a list of what's in your so called unopened crates, so someone in your employ knows what's in them. Perhaps you could find that person."

"You think we haven't looked?"

"I want the painting and that ring, so look again."

"And if I find it, I just can't release it. Someone will want the appropriate documentation."

"The photo and the ring are enough. You have your proof."

"You want us to turn over the painting to them?"

"Idiot!"

"But what about our client?" Boris asked.

"You mean, what about your money?"

"We are a poor country and they do not pay me like they do you."

"When this is over, you will be a very rich man."

Boris had already picked out the Dacha he wanted in the Crimea. "I will double my efforts to find the painting."

Chapter 15

On the way back to their hotel, David fumed as Alessandra filled him in on her conversation with Boris. While she spoke, the driver's eyes would periodically peer in the rear view mirror. David, concerned the driver could hear, decided to hold his tongue. He didn't relish the thought of languishing in a Russian prison.

Just before they reached the hotel, the driver pointed to an open air market. He pulled the car to the curb. "Boss say take you here."

Alessandra looked at David. "You interested in helping me pick out a doll?"

David leaned near Alessandra and whispered, "Why all of a sudden is Boris being so nice?"

"I asked him," Alessandra whispered back. "Besides we could use a diversion." She addressed the driver. "Thank you."

The driver turned around. "You must go hotel after. You understand."

David and Alessandra both nodded and excitedly fled the car.

The driver, now on foot, followed at a discreet distance.

David and Alessandra strolled by a stand of matryoshka dolls. Alessandra examined several. She chose one. "How much?"

The vendor pulled out an American fifty dollar bill and showed it to Alessandra. She was about to pay when the driver interrupted.

"You not buy these."

"Why not?" Alessandra asked.

"You want real matryoshka dolls. I show. Please to follow." The driver walked at a rapid pace until he came to a booth with a wizened old woman. "Here. Irina will give you real thing and at good price." He spoke in Russian to the woman.

The vendor nodded, lifted a multicolored doll and handed it to Alessandra. "One hundred Americanski dollar. Okay?"

David started to pull out some money, but the driver again intervened. He seemed to be very angry as he spoke to the woman.

She angrily gestured at the doll. She snatched the doll from Alessandra's hand and opened the bottom. Out came 18 other dolls, each smaller than the next. She placed them on a table side by side and then put her hands on her hips and posed Mussolini style.

The driver said something to her and then turned to David. "These good but I tell her you only can pay fifty dollar. She no like, but say okay."

David handed the vendor fifty dollars.

The vendor smiled. "Would you like box?"

"You speak English?" Alessandra asked.

"Of course. We get many American tourists. It good business to speak English." She picked up a box and thrust it toward Alessandra.

"What about those," David pointed to the 18 dolls on the table.

The vendor opened the box to reveal a colorful red doll similar to the ones on the table. "This is new one." She picked up the largest of the dolls on the table and pointed to some scratch marks. "Too many people touch."

The driver took the box and gave it to David. "Is okay. She not cheat you."

David opened the box and inspected the item. He removed all the nested dolls and counted, 18. Satisfied, he nodded and thanked the vendor.

He and Alessandra continued to stroll the street fair with the driver lagging behind, but always in sight. They admired a display of oil paintings, meandered around a clothing stand where David haggled over a sweatshirt but didn't buy. They admired the jewelry of one vendor who seemed to specialize in religious symbols. David picked up an ornate cross and held it up to Alessandra's neck.

"It's nice but I already have one." Alessandra pulled the cross out from under her sweater.

David lifted a mezuzah pendant to her neck. "What about equal time?"

Alessandra searched for a mirror. The vendor pointed to one hanging on a pole.

"It's lovely," Alessandra said as she twisted the mezuzah so it hung straight.

"We'll take it." David paid the vendor.

The vendor slipped the mezuzah off its chain and handed it to Alessandra. She in turn slid the mezuzah onto her silver chain to hang alongside the cross and the key her father had given her.

David pulled out a camera and focused it on Alessandra who smiled broadly. He couldn't help but admire how photogenic she looked. No, that wasn't it. It was her warmth that radiated through the lens. The more time he spent with her, the more he realized what a special woman this was; smart, gutsy, comfortable in her own skin. He snapped the photo and quickly checked the screen to see if he had captured what he felt. It was all there. He turned the camera around to show Alessandra.

"Your turn," she said as she snatched the camera from him.

David stood by the mezuzah vendor and posed. She snapped the photo and then asked the vendor to "Take one of us, please."

David awkwardly held Alessandra around her shoulder as the vendor took the picture, who then showed them the result. David's eyes revealed both his shyness and obvious affection for Alessandra. She had a playful look that said she understood exactly the effect she was having on him.

David searched for the driver who was nowhere to be seen. He nudged Alessandra. "Our tail appears to have disappeared. Is that good or bad?"

She shrugged. "Maybe they switched to someone we don't know."

"Or maybe Boris wants us to do something so he can arrest us. . . or at least me, on some trumped up charge."

"Then we should head back." Alessandra pointed to their hotel which was visible off in the distance. "But let's take our time." She put her arm through his and slowly they ambled through the market in the general direction of the hotel. Occasionally they would stop to see if anyone followed. They never noticed anyone suspicious.

Back at the hotel, the clerk handed David a small envelope. He tore it open. The ring dropped out along with a note. *The papers indicate your painting was taken from a castle near Berlin. This means we have to ship it back to Germany, the country of origin. If you would kindly call my office with an address in Berlin, you shall have your precious painting in two weeks.*

"We have to go to Germany," David said.

She quickly seized the note and read it. She beamed. "We'll have to notify Jorge. He'll want to photograph everything."

"Maybe we should hold off."

"Why?"

"After all the grief they gave me, something doesn't seem right."

Alessandra threw up her arms. "What do you suggest?"

David nodded toward the clerk. "Why don't we finish this conversation upstairs?"

David joined Alessandra in her room. He handed her the box with the matryoshka doll. "This is yours."

Alessandra fingered her mezuzah. "But you already gave me this."

David waved his hand dismissively. He twisted the bottom of the large doll and removed the remaining nested smaller ones. He stacked all 18 dolls side by side.

"It's like an onion. Peel away a layer and a smaller similar petal is right beneath. I think there's something amiss about this, but can't put my finger on it."

Alessandra lifted the smallest doll and looked at it admiringly. "The Russians have always been a very complex people and their art reflects it." She methodically reassembled the dolls into one piece. "But it all fits. They have a painting they removed from Germany. We can prove it belongs to you. Perhaps they are hoping to get some positive publicity out of this but in any case, we don't have a choice. They have the painting and unless you have another plan, we will have to go to Berlin to get it."

"I guess I'm being paranoid." David embraced Alessandra. "Thank you for all your help."

After David left her room, Alessandra called Gregor. There was no answer at his house so she tried his cell. He didn't pick up. Where was he? Just out or off somewhere mountain climbing? She left a message with the good news.

Kleinermann was next. He was in and elated by the news. "I'll make arrangements and while you're waiting in Germany, perhaps you could do a favor for me?"

"Of course," Alessandra said. "How can I help?"

"A friend of mine, Lothar Strumpkt runs the Altes Museum in Berlin and wants to make a special exhibit of religious paintings for the forty days of Lent. He called while you were recuperating in

Palau. He asked my advice on which Spanish artists he should showcase. I told him about you and he wondered if you could come and look over his collection. Now that you have two weeks to kill—"

Alessandra interrupted. She felt fortunate to have such a supportive boss and would do anything to please him. "It sounds interesting. Tell him I'll do it."

Lastly, Alessandra dialed Jorge in Paris. She related everything that had occurred to them and told him they'd be in Berlin shortly.

"It sounds too easy. I don't trust the Russkies."

"You and David both. And I can't say as I blame you. But the curator is a friend of my boss. I think he'll deliver."

"*Chica*, there's something you should know."

"What?"

"My contact in the Hermitage was recently found floating in the Neva river. They say he drowned, but he was an excellent swimmer and he didn't usually go swimming with his *pantalones* on."

Alessandra let out an audible exclamation.

"*Exactamente!* So, I hope you won't mind me wearing my skeptic's clothes when I show up." Jorge said. "As a journalist, they suit me better. See you in two weeks."

Chapter 16

A limo collected Alessandra and David at the Berlin International airport. Strumpkt, a squat, elderly well-dressed man introduced himself and climbed into the rear compartment with them. On the drive into the city, Strumpkt expressed enthusiasm about having Alessandra's expertise available for the upcoming exhibit. "It is so kind of Sigi to lend you to me for a few weeks."

Strumpkt turned to David. "And I understand you will shortly be reunited with a family treasure."

"One from which we should never have been parted," David bristled. It hadn't hit him until Strumpkt's heavy German accent insulted his ear. He was in the country that had slaughtered his family. And he was in the city where Kristallnacht kicked it all off. All the years of suppressing the hatred he felt toward this country suddenly surfaced.

"It's a new country now," Strumpkt pleasantly responded. "We acknowledge mistakes of the past and are trying to make amends."

"You mean like the Vice President of the free Democratic Party who compared the Israeli army to the Nazis?"

"Mr. Muelleman was roundly criticized for his speech."

"Yeah. And his party's membership rose dramatically amongst all those Jewish loving Germans," David fumed.

"I hope you will come to see a different side of Germany," Strumpkt replied.

David started to reply when Alessandra laid a gentle hand on his arm.

"David lost many members of his family here. I know he doesn't blame you for those deaths. And we appreciate all the efforts the current administration is making to return the property of - -"

David interrupted. "Yes. I'm sorry for going off like that. I had no right to sound angry with you. It's my first time in Germany and all the stories I've heard since I was a child....well, you understand."

Strumpkt nodded. "You aren't the first and won't be the last. So, your family is from here? Perhaps I could arrange for you to see your family home?"

"I have no idea of the address. Besides, I'm afraid it would be too painful. But I do appreciate the gesture."

David turned his attention to the landscape and tried to imagine what life must have been like when his grandparents lived here. But all he could envision were jack booted troops knocking on their door. He struggled to chase that thought from his mind.

No more was spoken until they arrived at the Kempinski Hotel. Strumpkt told Alessandra he would arrange for her to be picked up the next morning and taken to the museum. As for David, Strumpkt offered "the services of our driver to take you wherever you wish."

David declined. He had decided to learn more about his roots and he wanted to do it alone. So, for the next two weeks, he visited a series of landmarks connected to the Holocaust.

His first foray was to the rebuilt Neue Synagogue which had been desecrated by the Nazis during Kristallnacht and later destroyed by Allied bombs. The Synagogue had been turned into a museum with photographs of the holocaust prominently displayed. David felt something stir in him that had been dormant for years. Although Bar Mitzvahed at thirteen, as an adult he had abandoned formal religion and downplayed his Jewish birthright. The photographs of the Nazi atrocities appalled him but it motivated him to learn more.

He visited Sachsenhausen concentration camp where he learned 33,000 prisoners were forced to leave the camp and go on a death march as the Soviet army closed in on the German capital. Thousands died during that march.

Alessandra accompanied David to Wannsee, a suburb of Berlin to view the permanent exhibit of the House of the Wannsee Conference where in 1942, the Nazis met to plan the "Final Solution," to exterminate the entire Jewish population of Europe.

They viewed the initial exhibit, an overview of the historical background to antisemitism. It showed both the integration of Jews into German society and the rise of antisemitism.

The next series of rooms dealt with the frequently raised question as to how much the Germans knew about the genocide and the process of deporting Jews to the ghettos and extermination camps. It illustrated how forced labor was organized in the ghettos, how day-to-day existence was dominated by hunger, sickness and death. Finally, conditions in the concentration camps were described using photographs and documents.

Alessandra and David slowly strolled by the photographs of the camps. Emaciated Jews with armbands emblazoned with the Star of David looked like walking cadavers.

David stopped and studied the photos of the Nazi leaders which lined the walls of one room. He tried desperately to understand how normal looking men could have participated in such horrific acts.

They passed photos of the "shower" rooms. David couldn't help but imagine his grandparents being stripped naked and forced into the "showers." He could smell the stench and it sickened him. As they left the building, David teared up.

Alessandra touched David's arm.

"I can't believe this happened in the 20th Century."

She took out a handkerchief to wipe away her own tears.

"Unfortunately, man has been committing genocide for all too many centuries. And my ancestors have borne the brunt of much of it."

They went to a nearby Konditerei, sipped coffee, and ordered Bavarian pastries while they discussed the history of Jewish persecution. Two hours later, they had barely touched their pastries. When they left, they walked arm in arm comforting each other.

Each day when Alessandra left to work on the Museum exhibit, David continued his exploration of German/Jewish history. He visited the Jewish Museum, the Jewish Cemetery and discovered that Berlin was trying to make amends by encouraging Russian Jews to immigrate into the city so it could revive some of the community that once made Berlin a culturally diverse city. While he felt this was an encouraging sign, he was saddened to learn that only 20,000 Jews now lived in the city compared to more than 160,000 when the Nazis came to power. But he also learned that tens of thousands of Jews were applying for and receiving German passports. Perhaps it was time to forgive the entire German nation for the sins of the past. At least they were making an effort to make amends.

David tried to imagine how his grandparents had been taken from their home and how they must have suffered. He wondered what they were like. He had no idea because it was too painful for his mother to talk about them. So growing up, he had put them out of mind. But now that he was in the country of their birth. . . and death, he felt close to them.

At the end of the two weeks, David had decided he would never again avoid his Jewish heritage. Night after night, he and Alessandra talked into the wee hours about the importance of heritage, religious persecution, wars and the current state of the world. The more they shared in their vision of the world, the more he came to admire her. She was a special woman, at once independent and tough, as well as soft and passionate.

The subject of the painting came up time and time again because of its connection to the Inquisition and Goya's antiwar beliefs. They both realized *The Naked Maja Dancing* had taken on new meaning.

Jorge called and told them he had arranged a large three bedroom suite for all of them to stay in. "I want you each to be accessible so I can easily interview you both. And congratulations again on finding the painting. Frankly I'm still surprised the Russians gave it up so easily, but happy to see they want to join the world community. See you in a few days."

#

Alessandra and David happily moved into the luxurious suite. Afterwards, Alessandra arranged for a message in the Hotel spa.

David busied himself unpacking.

Later that morning, a porter wheeled Jorge's extensive luggage and equipment into the suite. He dismissed the porter and turned to his new roommates. "So what have you been up to these last few weeks?"

"I've been getting in touch with my heritage," David said.

Jorge slouched into the nearby chair. He waved his hand in a circle to signal David to continue.

David explained his rekindled interest in Holocaust history. "The last two weeks made me realize that I couldn't run away from my Judaism. Jews who thought they were integrated into German society were slaughtered along with persons whose only claim to Judaism was a distant Jewish relative. You can't - -," David paused as he noticed his interviewer nodding off.

Jorge, apparently jet lagged, closed his eyes and fell into a deep sleep.

David placed a pillow under Jorge's head and went to his own bedroom to take a nap.

They dined at the Paris Café. Cigarette smoke wafted from every table except theirs. The room was lined with photographs of pre-World War II life in Berlin, one of which graphically depicted a woman performing oral sex on a man who seemed detached from it all.

Alessandra pointed to the photograph. "If I did that to a man and he acted like that, I'd bite off his *cojones.*"

Jorge laughed. "Someone that disinterested wouldn't miss them."

The discussion turned to differences in mores between Europe and the United States.

"Perhaps the Germans had gotten too decadent," David offered. "Maybe, like Rome, they needed a cleansing and the Nazis provided it."

"Why do you Americans think sex is decadent?" Jorge asked. "In our culture it's the most natural thing."

"You obviously forgot the Inquisition," Alessandra interjected. "When Goya painted *The Naked Maja*, it was considered obscene."

"Well, I'm looking forward to seeing the sequel up close tomorrow," David said. "Just think, my ancestor was a porn queen."

Jorge raised his glass, "To Leocadia, a woman before her time."

They clinked glasses and for a few moments each of them retreated into the confines of their own thoughts.

To Jorge, the return of the painting to its rightful owner would be another notch in his quest to help and write about restoring lost Holocaust art to their Jewish owners. He felt good about his role in helping David. But he didn't really know anything about him. As soon as the painting was secured, he'd start the interviews. He was anxious to find out what made David tick. And Alessandra, this was one hot *chica*. He definitely wanted to get to know her better. Much better.

To David, the painting would put him face to face with a relative who was about to become legend. David never felt more "Jewish." Inadvertently, Leocadia had been responsible. He silently thanked her. And he was impressed with Alessandra. He had never met a woman with such a combination of looks, intelligence and spunk. But he immediately rejected any notion of romance. His mother would never approve and while she lived, he wasn't going to do anything to hurt her. As a Holocaust survivor she had suffered enough.

To Alessandra, *The Naked Maja Dancing* meant possible redemption, but her discussions with David had made her more aware of her own country's past anti-Semitism. As for David, whatever she was beginning to feel for him, she dismissed. It was going nowhere. She totally focused on the painting. The anticipation of getting her hands on such a historically important work was exhilarating.

The next morning they received the call that the painting would be delivered to David in his room sometime in the afternoon. They ordered lunch in the room so they wouldn't miss the delivery.

David and Jorge started a chess game in the living room of the suite. They were deeply immersed in the game when the telephone rang. Everyone jumped but Alessandra got there first.

"They're on the way up," she said.

David flipped over his king to indicate Jorge had won. He hastened to open the door and waited until he spied a well-dressed, white gloved man, accompanied by a uniformed guard, exit the elevator. The guard carried a large cardboard tube.

"David Edlestein?" The white gloved man said.

David nodded.

"My name is Walter Buchmeister. I work for Hasenkamp Internationale Transporte. I have a delivery for you." Walter removed one glove and held out a card.

David took the card and hardly glanced at it. "Come in please."

Buchmeister signaled for the guard to go ahead of him.

David introduced Alessandra and Jorge.

Walter handed David some papers. "Sign here, please."

David sat down to read the documents. "Looks in order," he said. "Do you mind if we check the tube before I sign?"

"Of course," Walter said.

Jorge and Alessandra crowded around the carton as David tore open the wrapping. He pulled a rolled up canvas out of the tube and unfurled it.

Jorge helped David hold it at arm's length.

"I can't believe it," David exulted.

"So, all is in order, ya?" Walter asked.

"Very much in order," David said as he signed the documents. David offered a tip, but Buchmeister waved him off.

"Thank you, but we cannot accept tips." Walter checked David's signature. "Congratulations."

David waited until the two men had closed the door behind them. "She's beautiful. She seems to admire the ring as she pirouettes."

David put the painting down and hugged Alessandra. He stared at the painting again. "Frankly, I never really believed we'd get it back. My heart's pounding. I just can't get over it."

He vigorously pumped Jorge's hand. "Thanks to you both. My mom will die."

"I hope there's time for a bath before the funeral?" Alessandra lifted the painting. "Do you mind if I have time with the painting alone?"

"Just don't drown her." David grinned. He pointed to his watch. "One hour before dinner reservations." He flopped onto the couch, his face beaming. "Tonight we celebrate."

Alessandra, carefully carried the painting and skipped into the bedroom.

"Before you get too excited, can we start the interview?" Jorge asked as he hit the "record" button on his video camera and took out a note pad. "You ready?"

David looked toward Alessandra's door. "Give me a moment to collect my thoughts."

Alessandra closed the door behind her and using pillows, propped the painting against the headboard. As she disrobed she studied the painting. Naked, except for the cross, the key, the mezuzah and ring, Alessandra decided to emulate the pose in the painting. She watched herself in a mirror and noticed her cross and key, which she promptly removed. She tried to imagine herself posing for the great artist.

Alessandra could feel her heart race. This was how Howard Carter must have felt when he discovered King Tut's tomb. She turned on the radio and searched for classical music. Fortuitously a gypsy melody played. She danced and twirled, reveling in the moment. She stared at the ring as Leocadia did in the painting. She stopped. Something was not quite right. She raised her left hand so it more closely resembled the painting. What was wrong? The ring! The ring in her hand and the one in the painting were different. She wasn't sure why, but they didn't quite match up.

She turned the ring in her hand. Was it fatter? Thinner? No, it was something else. She counted diamonds in the ring on her hand. Six. She counted the diamonds in the painting. Five! She counted again. Same result. She put a hand to her mouth to squelch a scream.

She headed for the door, realized she was naked and rushed to the bathroom. She wrapped a towel around her and barged into the salon.

"I think they're a little more formal than that in the restaurant." David said.

Alessandra grabbed David and Jorge, and pulled them into her bedroom. She pointed to the painting as she held up her left hand, fingering the ring. "Do you see a problem?"

David stared quizzically and shrugged. "She's right handed?"

Alessandra glared.

"Her nails aren't done?" Jorge offered.

"Count the diamonds," Alessandra said.

Jorge and David counted the stones in the painting. "Five," both said.

"Now count my ring."

"I don't believe it," David said. "That fucking Russian stole the ring and replaced it with a fake."

"He didn't have time." Alessandra said. "Besides, look at the crust on the ring. It's still there."

"Are you saying the painting's a fake?" David asked.

"Goya was meticulous with details," Alessandra said.

Jorge snatched the painting from the bed and turned it over. He turned to David. "What was the name of your grandparents?"

"Solomon and Rifka."

"Their last name."

"Braverman."

"The Germans were very efficient. When they took a painting from someone, they usually marked it with two letters matching the beginning of the victim's last name. This painting should have had a "BR" on it. He pointed to the back. "It doesn't."

David pounded his hand against the wall. "Damn. I knew it was too easy."

"Maybe I'm wrong and Goya miscounted," Alessandra said.

"Sure and maybe the Nazis missed marking this one," David said. "But I wonder how Boris didn't catch it either."

"Because he never had the ring until now and it's easy to miss. At first glance the rings look identical. And as for the markings on the back, unless you deal in lost Holocaust paintings you wouldn't necessarily know about it."

Alessandra sifted through her purse. "Anyway, there's a way to check its authenticity. I know an expert here in Berlin. He can date the oils and the canvas." She located her address book. "Hand me the phone, please."

Chapter 17

It was almost midnight before Gruber returned Alessandra's phone call. He insisted they come to his lab immediately. The sign in front said "Paul Gruber, Analytische Chemie." A slight, grizzled man, his black hair unkempt, greeted them at the door. The room was full of chemicals, magnifying glasses, electron microscopes, X-ray equipment and a laser based automated optical inspection (AOI) machine.

Alessandra handed Gruber *The Naked Maja Dancing*. With the tip of a scalpel he carefully removed a small paint sample from the bottom of the painting and placed it under the electron microscope. "When you described the painting and where it came from, I suspected it might be the work of Hans Schtiel." He peered into the microscope.

Alessandra, David and Jorge hovered nearby.

"Herr Schtiel was used extensively by the Nazis." Gruber twisted the dial. "Even some museums employed him."

"Why would a museum use a forger?" David asked.

"The Nazis ordered many works of art they considered decadent, to be destroyed. Some collectors hid the real paintings, and then turned over forgeries to be burned." Gruber stood away from the scope. "Obviously, if this is a forgery it was never burned."

"You think it's a forgery?" Alessandra asked.

"I need to do more tests. Preliminarily the paint samples seem consistent with those of paintings of the late 18th Century or early 19th Century as they might have been used in Spain. The pigments, cinnabar, red lake and charcoal black were traditional pigments. I see no anachronisms. But a good forger might be able to duplicate those paints."

"Really?" David said.

"Ever hear of Han Van Meegeren?"

"The Dutch forger?" Alessandra said.

"Van Meegeren mixed his own paints from raw materials such as lapis lazuli, white lead, indigo, and cinnabar. He used old formulas to ensure that they were authentic. He even made his own hair paintbrushes, similar to those artists at the time were known to have used. He then added phenol and formaldehyde to cause the paints to harden which made the paintings appear as if they were centuries old. After he completed the painting, he would bake it to dry it out, then roll the canvas over a drum to crackle it just a little. Finally, he'd wash it in black ink to fill in the cracks. He was so good even Goering bought one of Van Meegeren's 'Vermeers' from him."

"Van Meegeren was subsequently accused of being a Nazi collaborator for having done so," Jorge said. "The allies thought he had sold genuine Dutch cultural property to the Nazis."

"Exactly. But he was ultimately hailed as a hero," Gruber said. "In any event, if this is a forgery, we could check the canvas. The canvas can't easily be duplicated."

"Why not?" David asked.

"Unless he painted over an existing canvas, it's virtually impossible to buy a similar one 150 years later. The fibers used change over that time span," Alessandra said. "And I've never heard of any forger with the talent to make his own canvas." She turned to Gruber. "Have you?"

"No. Never. But we can only check by radiocarbon dating. For that I would need a few fibers and then I'd have to send it to a lab. I'm not equipped for it.'

"How long would that take," Alessandra asked.

"Weeks. And the test is not perfect. We can only come up with a range of dates."

"I don't have weeks to wait here." Jorge picked up the canvas. "And what if he did paint over? Then the carbon dating would only confirm that the canvas is authentic, right?"

"Correct. If the canvas is from the same period, the dating in that case would prove nothing."

"Can you check to see if there is a painting underneath?" Jorge asked.

Gruber lifted the canvas and placed on a table. He centered an overhead X-Ray machine directly above it. He moved away and flipped a switch. A computer nearby came to life. Soon an image appeared on the screen.

"There, you can see it," Jorge exclaimed.

Gruber adjusted the image. An outline of another painting under *The Naked Maja Dancing* came into clear focus.

"So, it's a forgery," David said.

"Nein. Many artists painted over their own work they were displeased with. All this tells us is the painter did not use a new canvas. If it's a forgery, the forger probably used a canvas from that same era. And if it's a true Goya, then obviously carbon dating would only confirm it was made in the proper time."

"So, what's next," David asked.

"I can do an X-ray diffraction test on the paints. That's how they discovered the forgery of Goya's *Portrait of a Woman.*"

"What will that reveal?" David asked.

"If there's white zinc paint, that was invented after Goya died, it's almost surely a forgery," Gruber said.

"What else can you do to check?" Jorge asked.

"We try and find other evidence of forgery. So I also recommend doing a Digital Authentication Statistical analysis," Gruber said. "We use a technique called wavelet decomposition. We break the picture into a collection of basic images called sub-bands. Then we analyze the sub-bands to determine textures. Each sub-band is assigned a frequency and we compare that frequency to known works by the artist. Each artist has his own signature frequency that is almost impossible to duplicate."

"How long will that take?" Jorge asked.

"Come back tomorrow night," Gruber said. "I will have the results for you then."

"What do we do if it's a forgery?" David asked in the taxi on the way back to the hotel.

"We find out where the original is." Jorge said.

David snapped at Jorge. "I thought you already did that when you told us it was in Russia."

"No, Señor Edlestein, I told you there was a painting in the Hermitage that *might* be your painting."

"Gentlemen," Alessandra said, "we have all had a long day. Let us see what Paul comes up with and then we can argue over what to do next."

#

The next night, the group reassembled at Gruber's studio.

"Come over here," Gruber said. "He pointed to split images on the computer screen.

"They look the same to me," David said.

"Me too," Jorge said.

"So, it's not a forgery?" Alessandra asked.

Gruber grinned.

"Why are you grinning?" David asked. "Is it because we are looking at an authentic painting of Goya?"

"The X-ray diffraction test showed clear evidence of white zinc paint," Gruber said.

"Then. . . "David pointed to the screen, "what does that mean?"

"On the left are the sub-bands from Hans Schtiel's known forgeries."

"And on the right?" Alessandra asked.

"Your painting!"

"So it is a forgery?" David asked.

"Ya. Definitely." Gruber went to the computer. He moved the mouse on the computer. Another screen popped up. "This screen shows Schtiel's frequencies on the left and Goya's on the right."

"They're pretty close," Jorge said.

"Ya. Schtiel was a very good forger and before we had these machines, he fooled many people."

"How did it end up in Russia?" Jorge asked.

"The Soviets raped this country of its art. We kept records of what they took. On my computer I have a record of every known work of art taken from our museums." Gruber moved the mouse again and a list of paintings appeared on the screen. "The original of this painting was once stored in the Kunsthalle Museum in Bremen, but your note indicates this forgery was taken from a castle near Berlin."

"Are you saying the original is still in Bremen?" David asked.

"No, it would have surfaced by now. I believe this may have been part of the collection taken from Schloss Karnzow in Kyritz. The Schloss was owned by Count Konigsmarck who lived there with his mistress. Wilken Von Alten, the director of the Kunsthalle Museum is known to have asked the Count to hide some of the museum's paintings so the Russians wouldn't get them. The Count hid them behind a false wall in the Castle, but the Soviets found them anyway and took them back to Russia. Apparently, unbeknownst to the soldiers, some of the paintings they removed were forgeries. I've heard rumors of an underground vault. But no one has been able to find the entrance to it."

Alessandra carefully rolled up *The Naked Maja Dancing* canvas and placed it in the tube. "How did the Soviets find the paintings if they were hidden?"

Gruber took off his white coat and washed his hands. "When the Red Army closed in, the Count, an ardent Nazi, decided to commit suicide and convinced his mistress to do likewise. He wanted to avoid being tortured into revealing the location of the paintings. Before he died, the Count must have told Von Alten where he was going to hide the collection. Based on this forgery, I believe the Count was concerned she wouldn't go along with his plan so he had some paintings forged and hid the real ones somewhere she wouldn't know about. In any event, they sailed out into the middle of the lake adjoining the Schloss and slit their wrists. But before doing so, the Count scuttled his yacht. He fell overboard and drowned. She had a sudden change of heart and was rescued just before the boat went under.

Since shortly after the Count died, Von Alten was killed in an allied bombing raid, she was the only one who could have revealed the whereabouts of the paintings. She must have snitched'."

"How do we find Karnzow Castle?" Jorge asked.

Gruber opened a file cabinet drawer, pulled out a map and laid it on his desk. He put his finger on "Kyritz." "It's approximately seventy five kilometers from here."

Chapter 18

The three adventurers took a taxi to the Berlin Airport where car rental agencies were open all evening. They rented a VW van and drove back to their hotel.

Alessandra had to check in with Kleinermann. She noted the time. "10:30 pm," 4:30 pm New York time. Kleinermann would still be in the office. She put in a call.

"I have bad news," Alessandra said when Kleinermann got on line.

"I know," Kleinermann said. "Gruber emailed me this morning. I was going to call you and tell you to come home after your lectures."

"We're not giving up yet. We're going to Kyritz."

"For what reason?"

"That's where the painting came from and we think it may still be there."

"Can I help?"

"Do you have any contacts at the Kunsthalle Museum?"

"I know the assistant curator, Jutta Bermann." Kleinermann said. "She trained under me while I was at the Alte Nationalgalerie."

"I need her phone number."

"I'll fax it to you when I find it."

While Alessandra spoke with Kleinermann, Jorge called Paris Match and had them rouse some research assistants. "I need to know who currently owns Karnzow Castle and see if you can locate a building plan."

By early morning Jorge had the information of ownership, but they were still working on the building plan. Kleinermann had faxed Jutta Bermann's home and cell phone numbers.

After breakfast, the group headed for Kyritz. David drove while Jorge slept in the back. Although she thought it was too early for Bermann to be at work, she called anyway and left a detailed message as to what she was looking for and asked for a call back. She left an identical message on Bermann's cell phone.

It took an hour to reach Kyritz, but they had difficulty finding the castle. It was not shown on their map and no edifice that fit the description of a castle graced the skyline.

They pulled into a gas station and asked directions. The attendant laughed at Alessandra's poor German and shook his head. She wrote down the name, "Castle Karnzow."

The attendant shrugged his shoulders.

David tried. "Wir suchen nach einem Schloss."

Alessandra raised an eyebrow.

"I learned a bit of German from my mom," David said.

The attendant nodded. "Ah, Schloss Karnzow. Ya, ya." He went inside and produced a local map. He pointed to a spot near a lake.

Ten minutes later, the rented Volkswagen drifted to a stop on the shores of a frozen lake across from Karnzow Castle. It was late morning in the middle of the March. Wisps of fog rose from the ice. David turned off the engine and rubbed his eyes.

Alessandra roused Jorge. She pointed to the bag on the seat beside him. "Do you have binoculars in there?"

Jorge reached inside the bag and handed Alessandra a small set of field glasses. She adjusted the lens and peered out the front window. In the few moments since they stopped, the windows had fogged. She wiped the window with her sleeve and peered again. Too blurry.

Alessandra trudged outside and focused the binoculars. Snowflakes fell gently on her.

The Castle, four stories high, came into sharp focus. It looked more like a large nineteenth century manor home than the storybook castle they had expected. The Castle was surrounded by barbed wire fences on all sides except lakeside. Workers were busy erecting scaffolding around the building. Guards patrolled the grounds.

Jorge and David blew on their hands as they came out of the car. Each took a turn looking through the glasses.

"You call that a castle?" Jorge said.

"Schloss means castle in German," Alessandra said. "Apparently, some schlosses are bigger than others."

Jorge snickered. "I think this Schloss has castle envy."

Alessandra smiled. "So, what did your assistants dig up on the current owner?"

"After the Count died, his mistress moved back to the Castle with her son from a former marriage. The Count left her everything. The son now owns the Castle and apparently is remodeling it into a conference center."

"I wonder if any of the paintings are still in there." David said.

"If Kleinermann's friend at the Kunstahlle picked up my message, we may soon know." Alessandra rubbed her arms. "Meanwhile, I'm freezing. Let's find a place to get coffee."

They located a bäckerei in the outskirts of Kyritz and were happy to find it had a warm fire glowing in a large hearth. A few cloth covered tables surrounded the fireplace. They found an empty table, removed their heavy coats and ordered "Kaffee."

"Und brötchen, bitte," David added.

In short order, the "Kaffee" and small dark rolls arrived with homemade butter and jam.

Jorge stood by the open hearth and rubbed his hands near the fire. "Even if we find that the painting is still in the midget Schloss, then what? We can't just walk in there, introduce ourselves and ask them to give it back."

Alessandra glanced around and moved her hand up and down. "Please lower your voice," she whispered, "they may understand English." She nodded toward the table next to theirs where three men spoke quietly and puffed away on foul smelling cigarettes. "If it's in the Castle I doubt they even know it. They wouldn't know what to give back." Alessandra said.

David joined Jorge by the fire. He turned his back to the fireplace and faced Alessandra. "Why don't you call the Kunstahlle again? Once we know what we're dealing with, we can formulate a plan."

Alessandra pointed to a sign, a picture of a mobile phone was circled with a red slash going through it. Underneath, in German was written, "Nicht aufruffen an der Mobiltelefon, danke sehr." She slipped on her coat and walked outside.

David turned to Jorge. "Standing by this fire, makes me a bit queasy."

"I don't blame you. If half my people were french fried in this country, I wouldn't stand anywhere near a fire."

"Or an oven," David said.

Alessandra smiled as she reentered the bäckerei. David and Jorge rejoined her at the table. "Besides *The Naked Maja Dancing*, they have never relocated a Van Gogh and a Gustav

Klimt. All three paintings were sent to the Castle at the same time as about twenty others. Every other painting has since been found. It's my guess that those paintings are still somewhere in that Castle."

"So, what do we do about it?" Jorge asked.

"First, it's unlikely they would even let us search the premises. We're nothing but a bunch of strangers and have no authority to do so," Alessandra said.

"I agree," David said.

"While I don't think anything will come of it, why don't we at least ask?" Jorge said.

"Because all we'd do is alert them to the fact they may have some very valuable art in their possession. That would give them time to find the painting and hide it. And we'd never know they found it," David said.

Jorge took a sip of his coffee. "Okay. Then what do you propose."

"I know it's nuts, but the only option I see is to break in and steal back my family's painting," David said.

Jorge coughed up a chunk of roll he had stuffed in his mouth. "Great idea."

"You have any other solution?" Alessandra asked.

"You're with me?" David said. "I was only half kidding."

Alessandra glared at him. "I don't think anyone here began this adventure to go home empty handed. And I certainly did not risk my life for that ring to give up now. This painting is too important." Alessandra held out her hand. "Can I have the car keys please?"

"After what happened here in Naziland, I have no desire to get arrested by the Gestapo," Jorge said

David stared at Jorge. "When we started on this adventure I never thought we'd get this far. And I never truly understood the risks we were taking diving to depths of 300 feet or more. But after what we've been through, the idea of abandoning the search at this point and thus ensuring my family's painting remains here in Germany…" David choked up "… is a nonstarter."

"I don't believe what I'm hearing," Jorge said.

"We are going to the Castle with or without you," Alessandra said. She again held out her hand signaling for the keys. "You in or out?"

Jorge threw up his arms.

David pointed toward the door. "After you."

#

They hid the van by a clump of trees near the frozen lake. David peered at the Castle through Jorge's binoculars. "There appears to be two guards. Maybe before we break in, we at least ask if they'll let us tour the Castle."

"And how exactly do we do that?" Jorge asked.

"Alessandra tells them she works for a museum and is interested in German architecture. They might just let us in," David responded.

"You forgot about the second part," Jorge said. "After they let us in, what do we say? 'Guten tag mein Nazis, we'd like to explore your poor imitation of a castle to find a painting you bastards stole from this gentleman's relatives. And if we find it, you of course wouldn't mind giving it back, would you? 'Nein, nein. Come right in and help yourselves.'"

"Okay," David said, "you made your point. But now what? Do we really go for it?"

"I don't know about you, but I don't have a plan that includes knocking off two guards," Jorge smirked. "Now, if we were in New York, maybe some of my Puerto Rican friends wouldn't mind trying, but - -"

Alessandra interrupted. "While you two are having fun, I have a plan."

She called Gregor's cell phone and to her surprise, he answered. "We have a problem and need your help."

"A problem? What kind of problem?"

"An ice problem," Alessandra said.

"Are you on a climb? I thought you were trying to find a painting."

"We think the painting is hidden in a guarded castle near Berlin. The only way to find it without alerting them to what they have is to break in. And to do that without being detected we have to either cross a frozen lake in back of the castle or swim under it.

Since there's no way of testing the stability of the ice, I think under is the best way. Will you help?"

There was a long pause.

"Well?" A frustrated Alessandra demanded.

"Well? It's not every day I am asked to break the law and expose myself to a German prison cell. Can I think about it for a moment?"

"How many moments?"

Another pause from Gregor.

"What happened to your sense of adventure...and your cojones?"

"Leave my cojones out of this. Just tell me what you need."

"There is one other thing. To increase our chances of not being caught, we should do the dive at night."

"Any other surprises?"

"How soon can you join us?"

"Give me twenty four hours. I'm in Switzerland right now on a climb. I'll call when I know the train schedule."

"Who was that?" David asked when Alessandra disconnected the call.

"I call him Mountain Man, my ice climbing friend. If anyone can figure out how to get us into that Castle, he can."

On the way back to Berlin, David slowed as the snow flurries intensified. He glanced at Alessandra. "You sure we want to do this?"

"You saw those workers? If they start excavating the Castle and find your painting, you can kiss that Goya adios. Anyway, we'll only be taking what is rightfully yours."

"Stealing a painting that belongs to you, that I understand," Jorge said. "But 'Ricans don't do ice."

Alessandra touched David's arm. "And you? Do you do ice?"

"Damn, woman, you frighten me."

Alessandra grinned. "Get in line."

David smiled. "How long's the line?"

"We've come too far to quit now. That painting is your . . . our destiny. It's calling to us. Now, do you do ice or not?"

David glanced at Alessandra. "You're not even supposed to dive yet."

"We would just be going a few feet under the ice. It's not like real diving."

"Rebreathers, deep sea diving and hyperbaric chambers. Now ice diving and breaking and entering." David turned the car onto the exit for Berlin. "You're a dangerous woman."

Alessandra smiled and touched David's arm affectionately.

"You're both loco." Jorge said. "But it's a great story."

Francisco Goya 1746-1824

Countess D'Alba

When Goya visited the Duchess' estate in 1796 to 1797, she was thirty-five years old, just widowed, and in the flower of her beauty. Goya's portrait has her pointing to the sand where the words, *solo Goya* (only Goya) are inscribed. The inscription had originally been covered, but during a cleaning of the painting in the 20th century, the words became revealed. Also, she wears rings inscribed "Alba" and "Goya."

Leocadia Zorillo Weiss

Leocadia was married to a jeweler, Isideo Weiss. Leocadia had an unhappy marriage with Isideo, and was separated from him in 1811. Her husband cited "illicit conduct" during the divorce proceedings. She had two children before the marriage dissolved, and bore a third, Rosario, in 1814 when she was 26. Isideo was not the father, and it has often been speculated that the child belonged to Goya. Leocadia lived with Goya after his first wife Josefa died in 1812 and in 1824 followed him to Provence and stayed with him until his death in 1828.

Rosario Weiss

Rosario was born in 1814, two years after the death of Goya's wife. At the time of her birth, her mother, Leocadia Zorillo Weiss was separated from her husband Isideo Weiss and living with Goya. So, even though she is named "Weiss," it is unlikely her father was Isideo. There is compelling evidence she was Goya's daughter. Her mother Leocadia Zorrillo Weiss lived with Goya from 1812 until he died. When Rosario was around 12-13 years old, Goya wrote a friend in Paris asking him to teach Rosario how to be a great painter. In that letter, he told his friend to "treat Rosario as though she was my own daughter."

Schloss Karnzow

In 1944, Count Konigsmarck, the owner of Castle (Schloss) Karnzow, was asked by the director of the Kunsthalle Museum in Bremen, to hide a collection of stolen Holocaust art in his castle fifty miles northwest of Berlin. All the best paintings were removed from their frames and stored behind a false wall. The Soviet army eventually found the paintings and took some of them back to the Hermitage museum where they remained until the 1990s. One of the paintings was a Goya.

The Clothed Maja
(*La maja vestida*) hangs side by side with *The Naked Maja* in the Prado museum. The paintings were first owned by Prime Minister Manuel de Godoy, who was known as an avid womanizer, and originally hung in his home in front of the *Naked Maja* in such a manner that the *Naked Maja* could be revealed at any time with the help of a pulley mechanism.

The Naked Maja
is the painting that caused the Spanish Inquisition to interrogate and ultimately threaten to punish Goya if he ever painted another nude woman.

Chapter 19

At the Ostbahnhof station in Berlin, Gregor watched from his compartment as Yvgeni Petrofski approached his train. He had known Yvgeni since they joined the organization together some fifteen years earlier. Yvgeni lugged a large duffel bag which he plopped down on the platform and waited.

Gregor hurried to meet his old friend who promptly wrapped him in a Russian bear hug.

"Everything you need is there," Yvgeni said.

"Yvgeni, you never change." Gregor lifted the duffel bag. "Always straight with the business."

"Be careful."

"If we were careful, we'd never do the things we do. Would we?"

Yvgeni nodded in agreement. "God be with you."

Gregor smiled at the irony of his friend's use of the word "God." "In the old days, you would have been thrown out of the party for saying that."

"In the old days, we didn't need God. The state took care of us. Now we need all the help we can get." Yvgeni turned to leave. "Your friend is waiting outside in a grey Volkswagen SUV."

Gregor hefted the heavy duffel bag along with his own and hurried toward the front of the station. He spotted Alessandra chatting with two men. He closed the gap until she turned, smiled and extended her hand. He dropped the bags, pulled her into his arms and tried to kiss her passionately. She turned away and politely pecked him on the cheek.

David appeared uncomfortable.

Gregor stepped back, and looked at Jorge, then David and back to Alessandra. "Did you get what I asked?"

"It's all in the truck." Alessandra pointed to David and Jorge in turn. "This is David and Jorge. Gentlemen meet the Ukrainian mountain man."

David and Jorge tried to shake Gregor's hand, but he waved them off. "Come men. We have planning to do."

At the hotel, Gregor asked to go directly to their suite. He had hardly put his luggage down when he turned to Alessandra. "Building plan. You have it?"

Jorge pointed to a set of blueprints on the coffee table. "We were unable to find the originals. This is the set of plans that were recently submitted for the remodel."

Gregor hastily scanned the plans. "It does not tell us much as to where the paintings might still be, but . . ." He ran his finger over the area marked "*kellar*." "If the painting is in that Schloss, there's a good chance it's hidden somewhere in the cellar behind some kind of false wall or hidden room."

"And how do we get in without being detected?" Jorge asked.

"I suspect some kind of alarm system is installed. But probably not on the higher floors. They wouldn't expect an intruder to climb that high." He pointed to a room on the third floor. "This is where we will try and enter." He turned to Jorge. "I understand you are a journalist."

Jorge nodded.

"You have interviewed many people. Yes?"

Again Jorge nodded.

"We will need a diversion." Gregor sat on the couch and patted the place next to him. Alessandra joined him. Gregor brushed his hand across her leg and left it there.

David winced.

Alessandra removed Gregor's hand and moved to one end of the couch.

"Here is my plan." Over the next few hours, Gregor explained each person's role. When necessary he would retrieve a piece of equipment from the bag Yvgeni had brought and explain its use. When he was done, he asked if everyone understood their assignment.

"I have a question," David said.

Gregor waited.

"Why should we trust your plan? Who are you?"

Alessandra said, "I told you, he knows what he's doing and is a good friend. That's why you should trust him."

Jorge pointed to the gear that had by now been laid out on the floor. "How come you know so much about this? You a professional thief?"

Gregor laughed but said nothing.

"Well, are you?" David asked.

Gregor looked at Alessandra whose face indicated she too wanted an answer. "Before the breakup of the Soviet Union, I was in the Soviet Army where I received assault training."

Jorge smiled. "I don't want to know who you assaulted."

Gregor turned to Alessandra. "Were you able to get the scuba gear?"

"It's in the back of the van."

"Good. We go tomorrow night."

"Why so soon. Don't we need to practice or something?" Jorge asked.

Gregor walked to the window. He pulled open the curtains and pointed to a sliver of a moon. "In two days, that will be gone. We need the light."

Chapter 20

A few nights later, Jorge flicked off the running lights on the VW and drifted to a stop near some trees across the lake from Schloss Karnzow. They all wore white jump suits but Gregor, Alessandra and David had dry skin diving suits underneath. As they exited the van, they put on night vision goggles.

Gregor opened the rear doors. Scuba tanks and other dive gear filled the trunk. From under the pile, he pulled out three ice saws and three underwater flashlights.

"Remember, cut at a forty-five degree angle" Gregor handed a saw each to David and Jorge. "We don't want the ice falling in. We leave no trace. Okay?"

Jorge and David nodded. The three of them carefully moved onto the ice.

Gregor traced a circle in the ice with the edge of his blade. "Cut here."

David and Jorge, standing at opposite ends of the circle, began to cut a large man-sized hole. Gregor moved off a few hundred feet and started to cut a second, smaller hole.

Alessandra stayed on shore. In case of trouble, she was to signal with two short bursts of red light from a multi colored flashlight. The red color was chosen because of its relatively short light beam. Hopefully, it wouldn't be seen on the other side of the lake.

She worried the sound of the saws would reverberate across the lake, so she kept a close watch on the Castle grounds. Shortly, she spied two guards patrolling the side of the Castle facing the lake. They seemed to stop and look in the direction of where the sounds were coming from. She turned on her flashlight and gave it two short bursts in the direction of the men on the ice.

Gregor turned toward her. At first there was no reaction. She turned the light on herself and hit the ground. Gregor whistled softly and all three men followed her lead. The men covered their heads with white hoods and put their gear under their bodies.

A searchlight swept over the ice toward them. It was about to pass over their prone shapes when it paused. No one budged. The light lingered and then moved on. They started to rise when the light swept back their way. Quickly, they dropped back to the ice again. The light swept past. They waited.

Gregor turned his attention toward Alessandra.

She got up on one knee and trained her binoculars on the Castle grounds. She saw the guards light cigarettes and break out flasks. The wind kicked up and the snow fell more heavily. She had a hard time focusing through the drifts. She thought she saw a door to the Castle open and the two guards move inside. She waited a while longer to make sure there was no outside activity. This time she signaled the men with blue light. "All Okay."

It took ten minutes to cut both holes. The men headed back toward the VW.

Alessandra moved the scuba gear onto the ice. She waited there for the men to return from the car.

Gregor and David each retrieved a waterproof bag from the trunk and stuffed their white suits into it. They then folded that bag into waterproof fanny packs.

Gregor grabbed another waterproof bag into which he had placed their climbing gear. He unzipped it and checked the ropes, special climbing shoes and other equipment. Satisfied, he lugged it to the large hole where David and Alessandra waited.

All three put on their scuba tanks and mouthpieces. Goggles were pushed up on their foreheads.

Meanwhile, Jorge lashed the ice cutting tools together, dangled them on a rope and dropped the batch into the hole. Gregor dropped in after them. He shined a flashlight underwater up toward the hole.

David plunged in next followed by Alessandra.

Underwater, Gregor tied the rope holding the ice cutting tools to his belt.

Alessandra swam back to the hole and popped her head out. She removed her mouthpiece and called after Jorge. "It might be a good idea to stop and buy some cigarettes and whiskey. They seem to enjoy both."

Jorge signaled the thumbs up sign and headed for the van.

#

Underwater, Gregor led, followed by Alessandra and then David. The lake was shallow at first but deepened as they swam toward the Castle. The bottom was muddy with some occasional grasses.

Halfway to their target, Gregor spied a sunken yacht. He signaled the others with his flashlight but kept moving toward the Castle. The heavy equipment slowed their progress. Gregor checked his watch. Five minutes behind time. The plan was to be under the ice near the back of the Castle in twenty minutes. By then, Jorge was to have diverted the attention of the guards to allow the swimmers to emerge from the ice without detection. Gregor signaled the others to hurry.

As they neared the other shore, they passed over a car, a tractor and a barge. The bottom became shallow again and soon they were able to stand.

Gregor shined his light up at the ice. He pulled the ice cutting gear to him.

David positioned himself with his feet on the bottom and steadied Gregor.

Alessandra checked her watch. She signaled with four fingers, "four minutes."

#

Jorge pulled up near the side of the Castle's gate and stopped. He opened the hood of the vehicle and removed the cable from the battery. He placed a rubber washer over the battery pole, and reconnected the cable. He went back to car and tried to restart it. Nothing. Good.

He closed the hood and sloshed through snow. A sign in German directed anyone visiting to push the button near the gate. Jorge pushed and waited. He rubbed his hands together to keep warm. A guard approached

Jorge spoke in broken German. "My car went kaput. Can you help me?"

"Where did you come from?" The guard asked in perfect English.

"Berlin. I'm on the way to Ruppen. I got lost in the snow and then my van stopped. I may just need a boost."

"Where is your car?"

Jorge pointed down the road.

The gate swung open. The guard pointed ahead. "You go ahead. I follow."

The two pushed through the snow to the VW. Jorge pulled out a pint of schnapps and took a swig. He offered the bottle to the guard.

The guard eagerly snatched the bottle and took a large gulp.

Jorge lit a cigarette and offered one to the guard.

"Danke," the guard said. He turned his cigarette toward Jorge's lighter and lit up. He took a drag. "American?"

Jorge nodded and extended his hand. "Luis," he said, using his middle name, figuring if they asked for ID, he could always say he favored his middle name.

The guard grasped Jorge's hand. "My name is Eckhard."

"I live in Paris," Jorge said.

"A nice city Paris. Come we go to the car and see what we have."

At the truck Jorge opened the driver's side door and handed Eckhard the keys.

Eckhard sat behind the wheel and cranked. Nothing. He slipped out to the front. Jorge opened the hood. Eckhard shined his flashlight inside.

"Let me help," Jorge said. He took the light from Eckhard who peered inside the engine compartment.

Eckhard reached for the cable to the battery.

Jorge moved the light away.

"Shine the light over here?" Eckhard said, obviously annoyed.

Jorge moved the light toward the battery and then let it slip from his finger. It rolled under the truck.

"*Dumbkopf.*"

"Sorry," Jorge said and crawled under the truck. He quickly unscrewed the head of the flashlight and coughed loudly as he smashed the bulb on a protruding bolt under the truck. He screwed the head back on and pushed himself out from under the truck. He waved the light and stood up. "I found it."

Eckhard snatched the light out of Jorge's hand and tried to turn it on. "*Scheisse!* We will have to go back and get another torch. Come. Bring der schnapps."

#

Gregor slid the newly cut ice away and popped his head out of the hole. No guards in sight. He dropped his scuba gear on the lake bottom under the hole and lifted himself out. He checked again. Still no danger. He signaled for the others to follow.

Alessandra followed Gregor's lead and left the ice cutting tools along with her scuba gear underwater. David did likewise but kept his goggles which he put in a bag and handed it to Gregor. The two of them carefully shoved the newly cut ice back over the opening.

Gregor dumped the climbing gear bag onto the beach. They each removed their dive suits and put on black climbing clothes and then the white suits over them. Finally, they slipped on their special climbing shoes. They hid the bag behind a clump of trees. Gregor then tossed several ropes over his shoulder and they headed for the Castle.

A light shone in a ground floor room, but the window was too high to see in. A radio blared in German. David boosted Gregor up. One guard sat at a kitchen table drinking coffee. Gregor climbed down and together they surveyed the grounds.

Gregor tried to open a nearby door, but it was locked. He stood back from the door and looked up. He pointed to a top floor window that was slightly ajar. A down spout hugged the Castle wall close to the window.

Gregor slipped off his white suit and covered it with snow. He pulled on the down spout. It held. He clipped the ropes to a carabiner hanging from his belt and started to climb. His black suited body blended into the Castle wall.

Half way up, the spout loosened and came away from the wall. Gregor grabbed for a handhold on a seam in the wall and removed the pressure from the spout. He dangled with one hand as he reached for a wedge bolt to put into the mortar. The spout swayed and clanked against the side of the wall.

The radio inside the guard room went silent. Alessandra and David flattened themselves against the wall.

Gregor found a crack in the mortar and jammed in the bolt. He attached a carabiner to the bolt and slipped the rope through it and then through a figure eight device on his belt. He pulled on the rope. The bolt held. He let go of the down spout and dangled from the carabiner. His feet found a toe hold.

The kitchen window flew open and a guard popped his head out. He shined a light on the beach and along the grounds. The light stopped a few feet from Alessandra and David. The guard said something in German and then closed the window.

Gregor calculated he had about ten feet to go. His hands searched for a hold along the wall. He tested one to see if it would break loose. It held. Now the toe hold. He found one and pushed himself higher. Again. Another hand hold, then a toe hold. Then again. He was almost there. He reached for the window sill. Ice! His hand slipped and Gregor tumbled toward the ground. With a jerk he slammed against the wall. The bolt had held. A stabbing pain shot through him. He felt for his hip. Blood. The climbing suit was torn and he couldn't move his left leg.

Alessandra shined her light on Gregor. He pointed to his leg and dropped one end of the rope to the ground. She grabbed it immediately and lowered him down.

"It hurts when I move my leg," Gregor said when he was on the ground.

Alessandra felt for a break. "You may have just bruised a nerve." She packed some snow around the wound.

"We'll have to cancel," David said.

Alessandra glared at David. She scanned the wall. "I think I can make it to the attic."

"It's too dangerous," David said.

Gregor sat up. "Climbing ice, that is dangerous. This is piece of cake for her." He grabbed Alessandra's arm. "When you reach the bolt, put in another for safety. David will help belay you and then I'll help belay him. If I can't join you, I'll keep guard here and wait. And be careful of the window sill. Ice."

In a blink, Alessandra was on the wall ready to climb. Gregor stopped her. He pointed to her white suit. She quickly shed it and buried it next to his. Now clad only in her black climbing suit and back pack, she looked at David and nodded. He held the safety rope taught as he belayed her toward the upper window.

Alessandra reached the wedge bolt. She slid another bolt into a crack in the mortar and tested it to see if it would hold. Good. Then like a spider, she headed for the icy sill. Hand hold, toe hold, lift. Hand hold, toe hold, lift. The window was inches away. A strong wind kicked up. She clung harder to the wall. With the wind masking the noise, she tapped a bolt into a crack in the mortar, attached a three step etrier to the bolt and carefully placed a foot in one of its loops. She tested it to see if it would hold her weight. The bolt moved but held.

She reached the sill and slipped a grappling hook under the slightly open window and then secured a rope to the hook. With her free hand, she tried lifting the window. It wouldn't budge. She placed as much of her hand as she could under the opening and pushed hard. *Nada.* She tried again. The window creaked but wouldn't yield. Frozen in place. *Mierde.*

Chapter 21

Again, Alessandra tried to pry the window open. It wouldn't budge. She found a pocket knife from her backpack and scraped between the window frame and casing. Ice chipped away. She slipped the knife inside a pant pocket, then hit the window frame with the palm of her hand. More ice fell away. She tried to lift the window once more. It creaked and moved up a few inches.

She hesitated to see if anyone inside reacted to the sound. Hearing nothing, she gauged the opening. It was too small for most people, but she thought she might squeeze through.

Head first, she wiggled her way up to her buttocks, but there she stalled, hanging head first inside the room. She tried to turn, but was unable to. A moment of panic seized her. She tried to push back out, but couldn't. She was stuck.

Alessandra stretched out her arms and was able to place her palms squarely on the floor. She arched her back and pushed as hard as she could. The window groaned and moved up just enough to allow Alessandra to squeeze the rest of her body through the opening. Using her arms as a brace, she gently rolled onto the floor.

Alessandra turned on her flashlight. A torn fabric couch stood in the middle of the room, a leather chair was against a wall and assorted chairs and tables were strewn around. She plopped onto the couch for a few minutes to rest. She checked her watch. No time to waste.

She returned to the window. With both hands free she was able to nudge the window up a bit more, just enough for David to fit. She leaned out the window, attached a small climbing pulley to the grappling hook, slipped the rope through and dropped it to the ground.

Gregor attached a harness and the rope to David and belayed him up. Awkwardly, David inched toward the open window. He used Alessandra's wedge bolts as handholds to help relieve the weight.

Near the top, Alessandra reached over the window and held out a hand. David lunged for it, lost his footing and slipped half way down the wall before Gregor yanked the rope and stopped the fall. David slammed hard against the wall with a dull thud.

Alessandra heard footsteps coming up toward her. She signaled David to stay put and tiptoed toward the door. The footsteps stopped just outside the room. She reached into her pack for the ice axe and planted herself ready to attack. She took a silent deep breath and waited.

The door handle jiggled, but the door didn't open. The voices and footsteps moved away. She relaxed. Then suddenly the door slammed open almost pushing her into the wall. A flashlight shone around. Alessandra held her breath.

Someone came into the room. He seemed to move toward the window. She quietly pushed the door away from her and raised the axe.

"Just a cat," Jorge's distinctive voice called out. He shined his light toward Alessandra, then himself. He put his index finger to his lips.

"Ya, nothing here either," a voice said from a nearby room.

Jorge closed the door behind him.

Footsteps went down the stairs. She lowered the axe and let out a sigh of relief. She slipped the ice axe into her backpack, composed herself and hurried to the window.

David had managed to climb within a few feet of the opening. She held out her hand and helped him squirm through the opening. She signaled to Gregor.

He nodded. Slowly he hoisted himself up toward the window. Periodically, he stopped to massage his calf.

Alessandra anxiously waited for Gregor to reach the window. When he did, she extended her hand which he waved away. He was able to propel his body partly through the opening, but his backpack got stuck.

Alessandra tugged on the window which grudgingly gave ground. David grabbed Gregor by his shoulders and yanked. Together they thumped to the floor.

#

Inside the guard room, Jorge admired a photo of Eckhard's daughter. He shuddered when he heard the thud above. The other guard who had introduced himself as "Nieman," rose and hastened to the window. He trained his flashlight upward just in time to see Gregor's legs disappear into the attic.

"Anything?" Eckhard asked in German.

"Just the wind rattling the windows," Nieman said in English and returned to the table.

"When the snow lets up, we'll go and fix the car, ya?" Eckhard said.

"I'm in no rush." Jorge said.

#

Gregor pulled the blueprints of the Castle from his backpack. Alessandra and David crowded around him.

Gregor pointed to the door on the left. "There's a dumbwaiter through that door. Maybe we can use it."

They picked their way carefully through the furniture until they came to the door. It groaned as it opened.

Gregor checked his diagram. He pointed his light to the left wall of the room. No dumbwaiter. He shined the light around the room. Nothing.

"What now?" Alessandra asked.

Gregor studied the wallpaper on the walls. "It should be here," he said as he ran his hand along the left wall. He stopped midway, took out a pocket knife and scraped at the wallpaper. The edges of the dumbwaiter shaft appeared. He repeated the process until the whole frame of the shaft was visible.

He tore the rest of the paper and exposed the door covering the shaft. He pulled up on the door handle and after some effort he was able to raise it. He leaned into the open space and shined his light around.

A frayed rope, dangling from a pulley, led to a dumbwaiter car. Gregor pulled on the rope and the car rumbled upwards. He stopped and pulled more slowly so as not to make so much noise. The sound abated.

#

Inside the guard room, a radio blared the music from *Tristan und Isolde*. Jorge and Nieman played chess.

The rumble of the dumbwaiter burbled into their space. Nieman titled his head toward the sound.

Jorge tried to keep a poker face. He walked to the radio and turned up the volume. "It's my favorite of all Wagner's operas."

Eckhard, who had been in the toilet, opened the bathroom door and the sound of flushing echoed into the room.

Nieman listened a bit longer and then refocused his attention to the chess board.

#

When the dumbwaiter car reached the top. Gregor attached a new rope to it and threaded it through the pulley. He pointed to Alessandra to get in. "This leads to the kitchen next to the guard room. The cellar is just below. Look down there for any signs of a false wall or trap door." He pointed to the diagram. "The stairs here at the end of the hall should lead to the cellar. Wait for David there."

Alessandra slipped inside. Slowly Gregor lowered her to the bottom. He retrieved the car and signaled for David.

"You're obviously better at this than me." David said. "I'll lower you."

"It's too small for me. Besides, my leg is throbbing. I'm not sure I could curl it up to get inside. You go."

David reluctantly nodded. He scrunched himself in. The car rattled its way to the ground. He could hear the music from the radio and hoped it drowned out the sound.

David turned on his flashlight and peered into the kitchen. He searched for the stairs he had seen on the blueprint. His light caught a glimpse of a banister. He wriggled free of the car and headed for the stairwell.

Alessandra was nowhere to be seen but he could see a light coming from the bottom of the stairs. He hurried toward the light.

At the bottom step, David slipped. He tried to catch himself by holding onto the wall, but his body was ahead of his feet and he fell forward.

Alessandra lunged and caught him just before he hit ground. Together they tumbled to the cement floor. Their flashlights thudded to the ground after them.

For a moment he lay on top of her, the indirect lighting from their flashlights cast a shadow on her face. "You all right?" David asked.

She nodded. "You?"

David smiled and ran his fingers over Alessandra's cheeks.

"We have work to do," Alessandra said as she gently pushed David away.

David ran his hand along the wall feeling for any crack that might reveal a hidden door. Everything looked and felt normal.

Alessandra pointed to a space between adjoining concrete slabs on the floor. She removed her ice axe and pried a slab loose.

David helped lift it up. He shined his light into the empty space. Stairs led to a corridor.

Alessandra hugged David and whispered. "This must be it."

David returned the embrace. "We still have to find the painting." He signaled for her to go first. He followed behind and replaced the slab after him.

They found themselves in a tunnel that appeared to lead under the Castle. Water seeped from the walls and dampened the floor. Alessandra balanced herself with one hand on the wall as they inched along until they came to a heavy latched metal door that blocked their way. Alessandra turned the latch, but couldn't open it.

David put his shoulder to the door. It flew open and David stumbled into the open air.

#

Eckhard peeked outside the guard house window. "The snow stopped. We should go to your car."

"I'll go ahead while you two get your coats," Jorge said.

Jorge casually sauntered out of the Castle door. He closed it behind him and rushed to the car. He popped the hood, loosened the battery cable enough so he could slip off the rubber washer he had placed there before. He left the cable loose enough so it wouldn't make contact with the battery pole.

Jorge waited for the two guards to arrive. When he saw them coming, he checked his watch. Too soon! He needed to delay them another ten minutes at least.

Eckhard dropped a tool kit by the side of the car. He peered under the hood of the car as Nieman trained the flashlight inside. Eckhard rattled the lead to the battery. He reached into his tool kit, grabbed a wrench and tightened the bolt on the battery cable. He signaled Jorge to get in and start the car.

Jorge nodded. He walked to the driver's side, slipped and flung the keys into a snow bank. They sunk out of sight. "I'm such a klutz," Jorge said as he brushed himself off. "Can I borrow the light?"

"I'll help you," an exasperated Eckhard said.

#

Outside the Castle, bushes blocked David's way. He pushed through and Alessandra followed closely behind. They found themselves on the beach side of the Castle.

Alessandra shined her light up to the window where they had left Gregor. She turned the light off and on three times signaling him to come down.

Gregor came to the window and removed the pulley and bolts near the window. He hung onto the rope attached to the grappling hook and eased himself down. When he reached ground, he jerked on the hook. It flew off the window sill and hit the soft sand on the beach.

"We couldn't find anything. It's time to go," David said.

"Not so fast," Alessandra said. "My instincts tell me it's here."

Gregor checked his watch. "We only have five minutes."

"Maybe there's another building on the grounds where it's hidden." David shined his light around the grounds and stopped as it showed the outline of an ice house off to the side of the Castle. The three of them hustled toward it.

David easily opened the door and ducked inside. Metal lined the walls, but there was no vault or signs of a hidden room.

David surveyed the area around the perimeter of the ice house. His light glinted off a large round valve. Before David could say anything Gregor ran to the valve. He strained as he twisted. David grabbed the other side and together they turned. It popped open, revealing a large dark metal shaft that lead to the lake.

Gregor trained his light down the shaft.

"What do you see?" Alessandra asked.

"Nothing," Gregor said. "Maybe it was used as a method of getting water to and from the ice house." He backed away. "Sorry, but no vault."

They could hear an engine start and then a horn sound.

"We have to go," Gregor said. "Now!"

They scrambled to the beach and found the tree where they had hidden their bags. David pulled out his mask and put on his dry suit as Gregor and Alessandra lifted the ice out of the hole they had carved.

David jumped in and found the scuba gear. He lifted one tank at a time to a waiting Gregor. David stayed in the water as he put his own scuba gear on.

"Hurry, the guards will be back soon," Gregor said.

As soon as their gear was on, Alessandra and Gregor plunged into the opening. Gregor pulled the ice back over them and they headed to the other side of the lake.

David led the way. He searched for the car, tractor and barge he had spotted on the way to the Castle. As they reached each relic, he searched for the next to help guide them back to the other side of the lake.

They came to the sunken yacht. David shined his light down and saw Alessandra below, heading to the boat. David dove after her with Gregor close behind.

David caught up. He grabbed her flipper and pulled her to him. He wagged his finger side to side to remind her she wasn't ready to dive that deep yet. He pointed upward. She shook her head violently and pointed down. He shook his head from side to side. She made a square with her hands. He shrugged his shoulders. Alessandra pointed her ring finger.

The painting. The Count must have hidden the painting in the boat he scuttled. David pointed to himself and then down toward the yacht. He motioned for her to head for the ice hole near the van. She nodded. Gregor handed her the bag he was carrying and headed down with David.

At eighty feet, David and Gregor reached the forty foot yacht. "Count Konigsmarck" was plainly written on the stern of the boat. David gestured to Gregor who swam over and made the thumbs up sign.

They hurried to the top deck. A stairwell led below. They followed it down. Gregor pointed to an aft room and then himself. David nodded and headed for a forward room.

A small bunk bed took up most of the space in the forward stateroom. David looked under the bed. He pulled out the drawers. Nothing. He turned and joined Gregor in the other stateroom.

Gregor had opened both doors to a large closet. He pointed to the safe inside. Gregor turned the handle. No go. He studied the dial, then put his ear next to it and slowly spun it. He pulled away and put his hands up near his ears and shook his head. He checked his air gauge and showed it to David. Dangerously low.

David pointed up. He inflated his vest and drifted toward the surface. Gregor followed.

At twenty feet, they did a quick decompression stop and then headed toward a light shining from the ice hole.

At the hole Alessandra, wrapped in a blanket and Jorge welcomed them. Together they helped remove the scuba gear.

"We have to go back." Gregor said.

"You crazy?" Jorge said.

"We found a vault," David said.

Alessandra leapt to her feet. "I knew it."

"But we can't open it," David said.

Gregor reached into his fanny pack and pulled out a small plastic bag. "Semtex."

"The stuff they used to bring down the Pan Am flight over Lockerbie?" Jorge asked.

Gregor smiled.

"You are full of surprises," Jorge said.

"Won't that destroy the contents inside?" David asked.

"I'm just going to use just enough to blow the hinges off."

"Why didn't you do it while we were there?"

"Not enough air left." Gregor headed for the van. He hefted two new oxygen tanks. He looked at David. "You coming?"

"My mother will never believe this," David said as he followed Gregor to the ice. "Won't the water damage the painting?"

Gregor slipped into the ice hole. "I'm betting that if the paintings are there, the Count placed whatever is in the vault in waterproof bags." He stuck the breathing apparatus into his mouth and went under.

"You're both loco," Jorge said.

Alessandra put her arms around David. "Be careful."

"You sound just like my mother."

#

Across the lake, Eckhard put down his night vision binoculars and turned away from the window.

Nieman waited by the telephone, his hand resting on the receiver. He looked to Eckhard.

Eckhard shook his head. "*Noch nicht* (not yet)."

Chapter 22

David held his light on the safe as Gregor stuffed Semtex along the seams. Gregor then placed six feet of waterproof fuse into the Semtex which he calculated would give them two minutes to swim to a safe spot. He attached a pull ring ignitor to the fuse and signaled David to swim up the stairs. Gregor pulled the ring and followed.

At the top of the stairs, Gregor's air tank caught the top of the jamb. He backed down and tried again. He ticked off the time he had left. Maybe ten more seconds before the Semtex would blow. Frantically, he swam as low as he could into the opening. Part way through, an eruption rocked the boat. *Shit!* He'd miscalculated.

The surge blasted Gregor hard against the roof of the cabin and knocked out his mouthpiece. He became dizzy and dropped his flashlight. Inadvertently, he gulped in lake water and gagged. As he gasped for air, he swallowed more water. Slowly, he sank to the floor of the room. He sat here for a moment and tried to clear his head. He was disoriented and drowning.

Gregor flailed for the loose air hose but couldn't find it in the darkness. He groped behind in an attempt to find the connecting point of the hose but couldn't reach far enough. He had injured his arm and was slowly losing consciousness. He had to find his way out of the boat in the darkness or he was finished.

#

A safe distance from the yacht, David nervously waited for Gregor. The huge blast jarred him. Debris exploded out of the boat. *Oh, my god.*

As soon as the last of the rubble cleared the doorway, David headed back to the stairs. He found Gregor lying on the steps. He shined his light into Gregor eyes. Dilated. It was clear Gregor was dazed. Where was his mouthpiece? Bubbles burbled from the air hose floating behind him.

David snatched the mouthpiece and shoved it into Gregor's mouth. Gregor gulped for air. David lifted him out of the doorway. He slightly inflated both vests and towed Gregor up toward the surface. At twenty feet, he stopped and checked to make sure Gregor was still breathing.

Gregor's eyes brightened. He started to move toward the light coming out of the ice hole, but David restrained him.

David flashed five fingers and touched his watch. They needed at least five minutes of decompression time.

Gregor nodded toward the boat.

David pointed to his watch again and flashed four fingers. He let air out of his vest and headed down.

The Semtex had done its job. The vault's door lay on the floor. Inside were two black waterproof bags. *Gregor was right!* David hefted them up, resisting the temptation to open them. Excited, his breathing markedly increased. He turned toward the exit anxious to see what he had found. He pushed the bags ahead of him and kicked hard. As he tried to clear the room, he got careless. He didn't check his surroundings and missed a sharp piece of metal protruding from the vault. His suit snagged on the shard which pierced it and dug into his side. He pulled at the fragment and tore a silver dollar size hole in the jacket, but he was loose.

Blood spilled into the water as David swam toward the ice hole. His breathing increased even more. He had to calm down and control himself. He wasn't home free yet.

At twenty feet, David stopped again to decompress. He began to shiver as cold water seeped into his suit. Five minutes were going to seem like an eternity.

#

Jorge waited at the hole as Gregor popped up.

"Where's David?" Jorge asked.

Gregor put his hands over his ears. "I can't hear very well. The explosion almost knocked me out."

"David? Where's David?" Jorge shouted.

Gregor pointed down. "He went back to see if the Semtex did its job."

Minutes went by before they spotted a light coming back toward the hole. David popped his head out. He pushed the two bags toward Jorge.

"Ay, ay, ay!" Jorge snatched the sacks.

"My ass is freezing," David chattered. "I need to get warm."

Alessandra came onto the ice and helped David to the van. She shouted at Jorge. "Start the van and put the heater up full on."

Gregor dragged the scuba gear across the snow and threw it into the back of the van. Jorge was right behind with the bags. Jorge started to unzip one of the bags. Gregor pushed him toward the front of the van.

"Not now," Gregor said. "Do as Alessandra asked. We need to get out of here and fast."

#

Inside the guard room Eckhard trained his infrared binoculars across the lake. He smiled as he turned toward Nieman. *"Jetzt."*

Nieman lifted the telephone and dialed.

Chapter 23

Gregor tossed Alessandra three large beach towels from the rear of the van and jumped in front with Jorge. "Move it."

With only the moonlight to guide him, Jorge inched his way toward the main road back to Berlin. David trembled in the back with Alessandra alongside.

"You need to get those wet clothes off," Alessandra said.

David struggled to get free of his neoprene suit. She helped him undress. She used her handkerchief to wipe away the blood and then patted him down with the towels. David shivered. She felt his forehead and touched his chest.

"You're hypothermic. We need to get your body heat up. And quick." She started to strip. Gregor turned around.

"Eyes front please," Alessandra said.

With a grunt Gregor turned to the front.

Alessandra completed her strip act and snuggled in next to David as she pulled the towels around them.

Gregor turned around again. "Is this necessary?"

"Skin to skin is the fastest way to raise his body temperature," Alessandra snapped. "You want to do it?"

Once they hit the main road, Jorge turned on his lights and sped up. Except for the sound of David's teeth chattering, they drove in silence. As they rode, Alessandra massaged David's limbs.

Ten minutes out, Jorge slowed the van. He glanced at Gregor. "Are we safe enough now to check the bags?"

Gregor pointed to a side road. "Pull in there."

When the van came to a stop, Gregor and Jorge hurried to the rear. Jorge held a bag as Gregor unzipped it. Inside were two three-foot tubes sealed at each end by wax. He opened the other bag and pulled out a larger tube sealed in the same way. He used a knife and popped the wax out of each tube.

Jorge shook the large tube and a painting slipped out. Gregor did the same for the other tubes. Together, they carefully unfurled them.

Alessandra peered over the back seat and shined her light on the paintings. One by one, Gregor held the paintings under the light. Alessandra let out a soft whistle.

"Ay, ay, ay," Jorge said. "Jackpot! The three missing paintings."

In a trembling voice, David asked. "Is the real *Maja* one of them?"

Jorge and Gregor lifted *The Naked Maja Dancing*. Alessandra trained her light on the ring and counted. "Six." She flipped the painting over. The letters "BR" were clearly visible on the bottom right corner of the painting.

"Bingo!" Jorge exclaimed.

Alessandra kissed David gently on the lips. He wrapped his arms around her and held her tight. She snuggled her face against his, then wrapped the towels tightly around them.

They drove slowly through the snow drifts. Periodically, Gregor peered into the back. A look of angst crossed his face every time he saw Alessandra stroke David's face.

Two hours later they neared the hotel. David had stopped shaking.

"Are you alright now?" Alessandra asked.

"Very." David smiled.

"I mean are you warm?"

"Very."

Alessandra blushed. She pushed away and wrapped the towel around her. "You've a long drive ahead."

"Come with us," David said.

"I can't. I committed to do the lectures for the Museum." Alessandra handed David his white jump suit. "I'll see you in a few days." She dropped the towel and slipped a sweater over her naked torso.

David stared transfixed. "I need to cut my dive suit more often."

She smiled and demurely looked down.

He lifted her face to his. "Thank you for saving my life."

She kissed him hard on the lips. "Thank you for saving mine."

The van stopped a block from the hotel. Gregor and Alessandra leapt out.

Gregor leaned back inside the van. "I'll see you back in the States."

"And I'll see you guys in Paris," Alessandra said. She patted one of the tubes. "Take good care of her."

"What do we do with the other two paintings?" David asked.

Jorge jumped in the driver's side and started the car. "The Art Loss Register has an office in Cologne." He pulled out his cell phone and turned it on. "We'll call them after we leave Germany." He looked at David. "Now hop in and get some rest. We have a long night ahead."

Chapter 24

Gregor accompanied Alessandra to her room at the Bristol Hotel. She unlocked the door, placed her bag inside and turned to face Gregor. "I appreciate your help. We couldn't have done it without you."

Gregor moved to go inside, but she blocked him. He seemed taken aback.

"I'm tired and want to sleep. . . alone!"

"What do you see in him?"

"What are you talking about?"

"He's not much of a man. And he's a Jew."

She resisted the urge to slap him. "Stop it."

"After your lectures, you could come with me. I've a great climb planned."

"I'm tired of climbing mountains."

Gregor tried to kiss her full on, but she pulled away. He smiled ruefully, started to say something, then turned, hefted his bag and sauntered down the hall.

Gregor's cell phone vibrated. He flipped it open and listened. Without a word he closed the phone and hurried out of the Hotel. A black BMW M3 coupe pull to the curb.

Gregor peered in. He sniffed as he jumped in. "Smells brand new." He touched the smooth leather seats. "Been moonlighting?"

Yvgeni smiled. "Bond isn't the only spy to drive cool autos." He gunned the car and it lurched away from the curb.

"We monitored the Castle's phones," Yvgeni said as he sped toward the Autobahn. "After you left, they called the police with a description of the van. Somehow they know the van's on the way to Paris. If they find the van, they were told to make an arrest and take them back to the Kyritz station." He handed Gregor a map. "Maybe we can get there first."

"I have Jorge's cell phone number," Gregor said.

"I'm sure they're monitoring his messages."

"Then we better hurry because if his cell phone is on, it won't take them long to triangulate the van's location."

#

David tilted the seat back and tried to sleep, but couldn't. The excitement of the day and anticipation of bringing home *The Naked Maja Dancing* was too much to put out of his mind. And then there was Alessandra. She was unlike any woman he had known although admittedly, that was not a large number. Nevertheless, any moron could see she was unique. Beautiful, fearless and smart was alone enough to make a man's pulse quicken, but she had grace also.

And the woman had transformed his life. A few weeks ago he was a *nebish* CPA and now he imagined himself a Jewish James Bond. He felt invigorated and alive as never before. They had only parted for five minutes and already he missed her presence. Paris couldn't come soon enough.

Jorge looked over at David. "You must be thinking of the *Señorita.*"

David ignored him and tuned on a classical radio station. A Bellini opera blared into the car. David sang along.

"Now I know you're thinking of the *Señorita.*"

David sang louder. *"Suoni la tromba e intrepido—."*

Suddenly, red and white lights flashed behind them. David shot up and turned around. "Oh, shit!"

Jorge checked the rear view mirror. "Ay, ay, ay." He pulled over and pasted on a smile.

Two armed Polezei approached the van. *"Aussteigen, bitte,"* one of them said to Jorge.

"What did he say," David asked.

"He wants us to get out of the car," Jorge said. "Let me do the talking." He faced the nearest officer, put a blank look on his face and shrugged. "We don't speak German."

A beam of light hit Jorge between the eyes. "Out of the auto and keep your hands where we can see them," a voice said in English.

David opened his door, raised his trembling hands and stepped out. The lights from the police car revealed an officer holding a pistol aimed directly at him. Before he could take another step, a vice-like grip spun him around and slammed him up against the van. His legs were kicked apart and expert hands frisked his body. He was spun around again. A light blinded him.

"Where are you coming from?"

"Berlin," Jorge shouted.

Out of the corner of his eye, David could see Jorge on the other side of the van with his hands up. He watched as the other officer opened the tailgate of the van and shined his light around.

"Markus, look what we have here," the other cop said.

"Keep your hands up," the officer called Markus said as he meandered over to the rear of the van. He let out a laugh and shined his light in David's direction. "And why would you need scuba tanks in Berlin?"

"We were bored and wanted to go for a dive in your sewers," Jorge said.

"*Hey Bruno, it looks like we have a comedian,*" Markus said in German.

"You take care of the comedian while I check the bag here," his cohort replied.

Markus herded David to Jorge's side of the van. He reverted to English. "You may put down your hands now."

Both Jorge and David did as they were told.

Markus punched Jorge in the side. "I was speaking to your friend here."

Jorge doubled over in pain. He grinned at David. "I told you to let me do the talking," he gasped.

Bruno held the three tubes up to Jorge. "Perhaps this is what you went swimming for, ya?" He unfurled one of the paintings.

"No, no. They came with the rental," Jorge said. "You know, decorations for the walls of the van."

Markus hit Jorge with the butt of his gun. "You think Germans are dumb, ya?"

"I think we need to speak to the American Ambassador," David said.

"I think perhaps we go to the Kyritz prison, ya?" Bruno said.

#

As David and Jorge were placed in the police car, Gregor and Yvgeni rolled by. They pulled over a few hundred kilometers up the road and waited. When the police car passed them, Yvgeni pulled out and followed at a discreet distance. An hour later they stopped short of the police station and watched as David and Jorge were escorted inside.

Gregor waited a few minutes, then left the car and peered through the open doors into the station. When he was sure the lobby was clear, he stepped inside and approached the duty officer. *"I need to see your commander,"* he said in German.

"And you are?" The officer asked.

Gregor handed him his ID.

The Duty Officer looked it over carefully. "Wait here," he said and strode into his boss' office. Shortly the Duty Officer strolled out. "The Captain will see you."

#

David, Jorge and an interrogator sat around a table in a spare room furnished with a blackboard, a TV and a phone.

"I want to call the Embassy," David said.

"Being an American citizen won't help you," the interrogator said.

"We did nothing wrong," Jorge said.

The interrogator calmly moved to the TV and turned it on.

Blurry images of three people crawling out of the ice hole filled the screen. Other scenes showed the break in, David and Alessandra in the cellar, and Gregor's descent from the attic window. As the scene of their return to the ice played, David blurted, "The painting belonged to my family."

"So you admit you stole the paintings?" the interrogator asked.

"We admit nada," Jorge said.

"Jorge, they've got us breaking in on video tape, and the paintings are in our car." David turned to the interrogator. "So what do we have to do to get out of here?"

"Tell us who else is on that video tape."

And if we tell you, will you let us go?" David asked.

"That is up to my Captain."

"We found these paintings in the lake," Jorge said. "You don't even know who they belong to. We didn't steal them!"

The phone rang. "Ya. Ya. I'll be right there," the interrogator said into the phone. "Excuse me gentlemen," he replaced the receiver. "Please no swimming while I am gone." He laughed.

Hours passed before the Interrogator returned. He had a sly smile on his face.

"It seems you have friends in high places," the Interrogator said.

"We're free to go?" Jorge asked.

"There is one small detail," the Interrogator said. He placed a sheaf of legal documents on the desk in front of David.

David sat and flipped through them. "You want me to give up all rights to the painting?"

"It's the only way the executors of the Castle estate will not press charges."

"And if I don't sign?"

"Then you will be prosecuted, along with your friend."

David looked over at Jorge as if to ask "What do I do?"

Jorge faced the Interrogator and pointed to the ceiling. "We need to talk alone and in private?"

The Interrogator nodded. He lifted the phone, shouted some instructions. "We turned off the monitors. Knock when you are ready to talk." He left the room.

"Is that painting worth going to jail for?" Jorge asked.

"You trust him?"

"Whatever else you may think of the Germans, they tend to keep their word. They won't listen. So answer my question. Is it worth it?"

"Alessandra thinks it's worth dying for."

"And you, do you think it's worth dying for?"

"It's easy for you to say. You got your story. In fact you got a better story. Me, I don't have my painting."

"Is this about the painting or Alessandra?" Jorge pulled a chair next to David.

David looked away.

"Don't worry about her," Jorge said. "She'll do fine. But do you think your mother would want you rotting in a German prison over that painting?"

"It's not just any painting. It's my heritage." David glared at Jorge. "That painting saved her life once - -" David rose and paced the room.

"And it can save both of our asses now if you give it up."

David turned back. "One month ago, before we risked our lives to find that painting, the old David would have agreed. Now," he hesitated, "it's not that simple." He wasn't the old David anymore.

#

Gregor sat across from the police Captain. "Thank you for calling the executors. I suppose you will be returning the paintings to the Castle?"

The Captain poured schnapps into shot glasses. "You said you found them on a boat at the bottom of the lake?"

"Yes."

"And I suppose you had a good reason to be diving in a frozen lake in the middle of the night."

"Interpol operations are top secret," Gregor grinned as he clinked glasses with the Captain.

"Yes, I thought as much." The Captain plunked into his thick leather chair. "But under the circumstances, the executors will have to wait. I think it would be wise to first determine who owns the paintings. And just why were they on that boat?" He downed his shot glass. "Yes, yes, Colonel Melnikov, a lot of detective work awaits us."

Gregor rose to leave. "Thank you again for your cooperation."

The Captain accompanied Gregor to the door. "Perhaps you could be of some further assistance."

Gregor waited.

"Before we release your friends, I think perhaps it would be wise to determine just what we have here." The Captain smiled. "You agree?"

Gregor reluctantly nodded.

"Then in addition to the paintings' provenance, I would like to know if they are genuine or not," the Captain said. "And of course, we should also know how valuable they are. I wouldn't be doing my job otherwise. You agree?"

Gregor again nodded. "How can I help?"

"You said your field of expertise is art, ya?"

Gregor nodded.

"And you have worked with many museums?"

Gregor nodded again.

"Then perhaps you can recommend someone who can evaluate the paintings for us."

Gregor smiled and put his arm around the Captain. "You have come to just the right man."

Chapter 25

Alessandra stood at the podium of the lecture hall at the Berlin University of the Arts. She could see the audience applauding, but her mind was elsewhere. She anxiously awaited the call from David saying they had arrived safely in Paris. Perhaps he had called while she was giving her lecture. She waited until the applause died down, thanked the University President for allowing her to share her views of the current state of art in Spain, and quickly left the stage.

On the way out of the building Alessandra checked her cell phone/watch for an alert. Nothing. Perhaps they left a message at the Hotel. She hailed a cab.

During the taxi ride back to her hotel, she checked her watch again. No messages. If there were none at the hotel, she'd try calling Jorge's phone. The ride seemed interminable and was made worse as the driver wanted to practice his English.

"Yes, I'm enjoying the city. And yes, it's beautiful and would you please hurry." When they finally arrived, she hurried to the desk.

"Yes, there is a message," the clerk said.

Finally! "Can I have it please," Alessandra said.

"No need, as the gentleman who left the message is waiting here in the lobby." The clerk pointed to a uniformed German policeman.

Alessandra was near panic. Her first instinct was to run. The path to the front door was open. Keep calm she told herself. Act casual. "Thank you, but I left something outside. I'll be right back."

She prayed no one would notice her shaking. She moved toward the revolving door when she spied another officer standing outside. She turned around to see if there was a back way out. She froze as she almost knocked over the formerly seated officer. He was so close she could smell the bratwurst on his breath.

"*Fraülein* Santana?"

"Ye...s." It took all her effort to keep her knees from playing a bongo tune on each other.

"Allow me to introduce myself. I'm Sergeant Bruno Lutz with the Kyritz regional police." He handed her a card. "And this is

Officer Markus Perlmutter." He pointed to his colleague who had just come through the revolving door carrying three tubes.

Perlmutter held out his free hand. "A pleasure." He bowed.

Alessandra was at a loss as to what to say. She took his hand and nodded, all the while trying desperately to remain calm.

"We need your assistance." Perlmutter pointed to the elevator. "Perhaps we could discuss this in your room."

"May I know what this is about?" Alessandra asked, attempting without success to keep her eyes off of the familiar looking tubes in Perlmutter's hand.

"Yes, yes of course," Lutz said. "I can understand your concern, but you should know your name was given to us by a Mr. Melnikov. He assured us you would cooperate."

The bastard gave me away.

"Do I have a choice?"

Perlmutter pointed to the elevator again. "We will explain, but not here."

As they waited for the elevator, Alessandra fumed. How could Gregor do this to her? Did they go easy on him in order to capture her? They must have checked with the French police and found her out. That damn missing Picasso would follow her to her grave. She was sure whatever story she concocted, they wouldn't believe her. And what could she say anyway? After all, they did break in to the Castle.

"We understand you are a European art expert with a particular interest in Spanish art," Lutz said as they entered the elevator.

"I'm sure if you called the Metropolitan Museum in New York, my boss would clear all this up." Alessandra wasn't sure what Kleinermann would say, but he was her only hope.

The elevator reached her floor. "No need, we had someone monitor your lecture today and we are quite satisfied you are the one we are looking for," Perlmutter said. He pointed to the door. "*Bitte.*"

Inside her suite, Lutz motioned for her to sit. With the help of Perlmutter, he opened the tubes and unfurled the paintings. "What can you tell us about these?"

Alessandra heart stopped. Her worst fears were realized as she stared at the three paintings she had left with Jorge and David. "I didn't steal them," Alessandra said.

"Of course not," Lutz laughed. "The real thieves are waiting comfortably in their cells. We just need you to evaluate the paintings and if you can, tell us their history."

"History?" Alessandra asked.

"Ya. Who is the painter? Who might have owned it?" Lutz said.

"Don't you know who owned it?" Alessandra asked.

"We are very sensitive about art in Germany. We know many paintings were confiscated by the Gestapo." Lutz said. "We know that still today there are many paintings in the hands of people who are not their rightful owners. So, before we return them to those who claim ownership, we want to make sure."

Alessandra didn't know if she should feel relief or concern. "And what will happen to the thieves?"

"As soon as we know what we have here, they will be released on the condition they give up any claim to the paintings," Perlmutter said.

David would not do that easily, not after all they've been through. "They won't be prosecuted?"

Perlmutter shrugged. "The Castle owners don't want publicity."

Alessandra feigned surprise. "They were taken from a castle?"

Lutz glared at Perlmutter. He turned to Alessandra. "Where they came from is of no moment. We just need to know what we have here. Can you help?"

Alessandra glanced at the closet. She had an idea. "Can you leave the paintings with me? I will need to study them for a while."

"Ya, ya. Take your time," Lutz said. "We will wait here." He moved to the couch.

"That would be too distracting. I need to concentrate and to do that, I need to be alone. Can you please wait outside while I inspect them?"

Lutz looked at Perlmutter who said. "We will be very quiet."

"I'm sure you will," Alessandra said. "But just having two policemen here will be a distraction. I won't be long."

Perlmutter shrugged. "Okay. But we will be just outside the door."

Alessandra closed the door behind them and rushed to the clothes closet. She found the tube with the phony Hermitage Goya and quickly removed it. She exchanged tubes with the real *Naked Maja Dancing* and searched for a hiding place.

She rolled the real Goya tube under her bed and checked her watch. A message waited. How had she missed the call? It must have been when she was in the elevator. She'd check it after the police left.

She needed to kill some more time. Alessandra laid Klimt's *Beechwood* flat, kept a knee on one corner and a hand on another corner to keep it from refurling. She studied the painting and then repeated the action with the Van Gogh painting. She realized this was a special moment and wished she had more time to study *The Olive Trees* as it had not been seen in public since WW II.

She checked her watch again. A few more minutes and she'd open the door. But what if they searched her room? She stared at the closet. She grabbed Van Gogh's *The Olive Trees* and scooted into the bedroom. She crawled under the bed, retrieved the tube with *The Naked Maja Dancing* inside, then opened the closet and tried to stuff the tube into the sleeve of her coat. But it promptly fell out.

She needed something and noticed her scarf draped over the coat. This time, she threaded the painting up the sleeve of her coat and then jammed the scarf after it. The painting held, but a small portion was visible through the unbuttoned coat. She buttoned the top few buttons and closed the closet. Not the best hiding place, but under the circumstances, it would have to do.

Satisfied, she took a deep breath, grabbed the phony *Maja*, refurled the Klimt, retubed it and opened the front door.

"Have you finished?" Lutz asked.

Alessandra thrust the phony Goya tube at him. "This painting is definitely in Goya's style. No one has ever seen this particular work before, but he is rumored to have painted one just like it. As for the others," she held out two more tubes. "This one," she pointed to her left hand, "is called *Beechwood*. It once belonged to a Jew, Ferdinand Bloch-Bauer. And the other is Van Gogh's *Olive Trees*. It was taken from another Jew, Max Silberberg." She was grateful to Jorge for having filled her in on the provenance of the paintings. "What the Nazis did with them, I don't know."

"Do you know if the Goya was ever confiscated by the Nazis?"

If she told them the whole story and gave them David's name, would they truly return the painting to him? Something about Lutz and Perlmutter made her uneasy. And even if they did give David the painting, they'd only be giving him the forgery which he would recognize instantly. Would David then inadvertently give her away by saying something? Better to remain silent. "I don't know."

"Thank you for your help." Lutz said. "What do we owe you for this?"

"A thank you is enough."

"You wouldn't happen to know their value?" Perlmutter asked.

"Tens of millions."

"Perhaps more?" Lutz asked.

The paintings were in fact priceless but she knew that answer would not satisfy the detectives. Alessandra stifled a smirk. "Perhaps."

Both men smiled, bowed and quietly exited.

Alessandra closed the door after them and silently exulted. She had outsmarted *los bastardos*. She opened the closet and reached for her coat. She slipped the scarf from the sleeve and the painting dropped to the floor. She started to remove *The Naked Maja Dancing* when there was a loud knock on her door. Frantically, she closed the closet and answered the knock.

"Where is the other painting?" Perlmutter asked.

"What are you talking about?" Alessandra asked trying to keep her voice calm and eyes away from the closet.

"The Van Gogh. You forgot to give it to us."

The Olive Trees? "Are you sure I didn't give it to you?"

Perlmutter pushed his way into the room. He flashed an empty tube. "I am sure."

What had she done with it? Her eyes skimmed the room. Had she put it in the closet? She couldn't let them in there. "It has to be here somewhere."

Perlmutter put his hand on the closet door. "I will help you look."

"I must have left it in the bedroom," Alessandra said. "Let's start there."

Perlmutter hesitated.

Alessandra started for the bedroom. "You coming?"

Perlmutter surveyed the living room area and then followed her.

Peeking out from under the bed was one end of the furled up painting. Alessandra kneeled down and sheepishly handed it to Perlmutter. "Somehow, it must have fallen out of the tube and rolled under there."

Perlmutter gave her an "I bet" look. "Thank you again for your services."

When he closed the door after himself, Alessandra sunk into the couch. What could happen next? Her watch beeped. She had forgotten the message. She hurriedly dialed voice mail.

Chapter 26

Alessandra listened to her messages. Apparently, Gregor had called her the day before and left a message alerting her to the arrest and what was then the impending police visit to her hotel. Damn cell phone companies. How difficult could it be to deliver messages in real time? Jorge and David were in jail. She wanted to call but was warned not to because Gregor was sure Jorge's cell phone was monitored.

How did Gregor know about their plight? Was he caught also? Too many questions, but no real way to find out what had happened.

She desperately wanted to contact David. Now that he had understood the painting was worth fighting for, she feared he wouldn't easily give up his rights to it. She laid down, closed her eyes, and envisioned David in jail. If only she could send a signal that it was okay to give up the painting. It wasn't worth a long prison sentence.

#

It was the first time in his life David had spent a night in any kind of prison. The guards were generally courteous and the other prisoners left them alone, but it wasn't a pleasant experience. Going to the toilet in plain view of the world and being confined to a 10'x10' space was humiliating and disorienting. He wasn't anxious to repeat the experience.

Nevertheless, he wasn't quite ready to give up the painting just to obtain his freedom as Jorge had badgered him to do late into the evening. "You never had the painting before, so you won't miss what you never had."

"I also never dove in 300 feet of water before or visited a concentration camp. And I never had my uncle's ring before. But most of all, I didn't know the importance of that painting to my family's history."

"You still have the ring and regardless of who owns the painting, they can't take away your history."

"It's not just about me or my family now. Alessandra risked everything for this painting as well."

Jorge smirked. "So, this is about the *señorita*?"

"I don't know if I could face her if I gave up the painting without a fight." David realized that might mean spending time in a real German prison. The visit to Wannsee and Sachsenhausen concentration camp were too vivid in his mind to consider that a viable option. Nevertheless, he did owe an obligation to Alessandra. If he gave up now, what did she risk her life for? Would she forgive him?

All night he wrestled with the right thing to do. By the time dawn finally filtered into his cell, he had formulated a plan.

David shook Jorge who had finally conked out sometime after midnight.

"What's up man?"

"We're getting out of here."

"I hope you not doing this for me." Jorge rubbed his eyes. "I was just testing you."

"Because of you, I got to at least see my family's heritage and we did recover a ring that connects my family to Goya as much as the painting itself." David seized the bars of the cell with both hands. "Those bastards can keep the fucking painting."

Secretly David intended to get the painting back. He wasn't sure how just yet, but an appeal to world sympathy was part of the plan and he had just the person to get him access to the media next to him in his cell.

A few hours later they were on their way to Paris. As Jorge drove, David worked on a plan to get Alessandra and the Metropolitan Museum involved. After all, they financed the trip and were obviously anxious to get their hands on the painting. But until he worked out the details, he wasn't ready to face her. He wanted to be sure the rationalization for his actions were persuasive.

#

On the last day of her lectures, Alessandra came back to the hotel to find a cryptic note from David. *Proceed as planned to the original rendezvous point. Will explain all there.*

They apparently were out of jail. Maybe there was something to the occult. She called the concierge. "When is the next train to Paris?"

Chapter 27

Alessandra pulled back the curtains of an ornate suite in one the finest hotels in Paris. She was greeted by a spectacular view of the Paris Opera House. Fresh fruit, flowers and a bottle of champagne decorated the living room table. Kleinermann had outdone himself. She was pleased she would be able to repay his faith and kindness by bringing home the *Dancing Maja*.

She luxuriated in the view. It was raining, but that was Paris in the winter. Alessandra couldn't wait to surprise David and Jorge with the painting. She imagined them waiting in Jorge's apartment for news of her arrival and wondered what story they would tell her and what she in turn would reveal. Maybe she'd let them stew for a while. She dialed Jorge's apartment. No answer. "*Hola.* I'm at the Ambassador in room 214. Please call when you get this."

Alessandra hung her coat in the closet and looked around for a safe hiding place for the brown tube with the Goya inside. Nothing stood out. She decided what worked once could again. She slipped the tube up her coat sleeve and stuffed a scarf up after it.

She flipped open her suitcase and started to unpack but was interrupted by a knock on the door. Alessandra flew to the door. Jorge stood there smiling.

"Where's David?"

"What? No hello? No how are you? My, my, for a well brought up Spanish woman, that's a bit rude."

"*Hola. ¿Cómo está?*"

"Don't ask," Alessandra grinned.

"We lost the painting."

"You did what?" Alessandra did her best to act surprised.

"Yeah, someone tipped off the police." Jorge pushed his way into her room. "They grabbed us just outside Berlin but they kindly agreed to let us go if we gave up any claim to the painting."

"Seems as though you had no choice."

"That's what I told David, but he's too embarrassed to face you."

Jorge opened the bar. "Mind?" He lifted a bottle of scotch and without waiting for her reply poured himself a double. "I left him at my apartment."

Alessandra returned to unpacking and tried not to sound too disappointed. "Apparently he's not answering your telephone."

"How well do you know Gregor?" Jorge asked.

Alessandra opened a drawer and threw in some blouses. "I thought I knew him, but now I'm not so sure."

"So, you suspect him also?"

Alessandra meandered to the closet. She retrieved the painting and thrust the tube at Jorge. "Would you mind keeping this at your apartment until we leave? I'm afraid to leave it here."

Jorge took the tube. "You didn't answer my question."

"I don't know what to suspect."

Jorge looked over the tube. "Why are you worried about this forgery?"

Alessandra smiled.

Jorge tore open the cap at the end of the tube and shook out *The Naked Maja Dancing.* He inspected the ring in the painting and then turned the painting over. The letters "BR" were plain to see, the sure sign the Nazi's had inventoried the painting. He threw his hands up, "How?"

"I'll tell you all about it on the way to dinner."

"How about a hint?"

She pecked him on the cheek. "I'll be ready at eight. Okay?"

"Okay, but this calls for a real fiesta. So, how about some Salsa after dinner."

"Sure. Why not."

He raised his arms and moved his hips as though to dance. "And don't worry about these." He flashed a full set of teeth and patted the tube. "Jorge Vieras will keep it safe."

#

A gaily attired band played Salsa at the La Coupole. The floor was crowded with hip Parisians of all ages and colors wearing everything from jeans to strapless evening dresses. Alessandra, attired in a black low-cut evening gown, and Jorge sat a small table near the band. Jorge wore a suit and tie which he constantly tugged at as if it was an unwanted noose.

"I think how you fooled those Nazi cops was brave. And brilliant."

Alessandra blushed. "Not all Germans are Nazis."

"You're right. Just the cops. I think it's in the blood."

"Did they treat you that badly?"

"It's over, so why don't we talk about something else," Jorge lifted a glass of Dom Perignon Champagne, "...like us."

She lifted hers. "I want to thank you for all your help. Without your contacts, we never would have been able to find the painting."

Jorge adjusted his tie. "You can thank me by showing me some of those Catalan moves."

Alessandra smiled demurely, rose, took his hand and led him to the dance floor. At first she was shy and slow to get into it, but soon she let loose. The past weeks of constant tension needed to be expunged. Her wild side poured out as she danced.

When the music stopped, Alessandra realized all eyes were on her. She flushed and started to leave the floor. But a slow dance started and Jorge held her close.

Jorge's Latin roots kicked in and he began to rhythmically move his body in synch with the music. Alessandra got caught up in his moves and soon was writhing with him in a snake-like erotic dance.

They danced for an entire hour, each trying to outdo the other with fancy footwork, spins and just pure sensuality. And although they both were exhausted, neither would give in. The band came to their rescue by playing Dave Brubeck's classic, *Take 5*.

Alessandra checked the time, midnight. "I'm exhausted. Time to grab a chariot home."

"Oh *chica*, I was just getting warmed up." He wiped beads of perspiration from his forehead.

"You can stay. I'll just grab a taxi back."

Jorge put his arm around her waist. "If you go, I go."

#

The desk clerk at the Ambassador peered down his glasses as Jorge and Alessandra skipped into the lobby. Alessandra toted her shoes in one hand and grasped Jorge's arm in the other. Jorge offered a glass of champagne to the clerk from the bottle he carried.

"Sorry, monsieur but I am on duty."

"I was led to understand the French thought it their civic duty to drink on the job."

The clerk put on a serious face. "Perhaps so, but as I am Algerian, I would not know."

Alessandra headed toward the elevator. Jorge followed her.

"Perhaps so, but as I am an Algerian, I would not know," Jorge mimicked in the elevator. She laughed. He took a swig from the bottle and offered one to Alessandra. She grinned and drained the remainder of the bottle. They laughed all the way to her room.

He kissed her passionately on her neck and started to move down toward her breasts. She gently pushed away.

"*Chica*, what's wrong? I thought—"

"You think too much."

"Didn't we have a great time?"

"Yes. And let's leave it at that."

"Baby, you don't know what you're missing."

Alessandra slipped her key into the door slot. *I know exactly what I am missing and you're not it.* Alessandra pecked him on the cheek. "Good night. I'll collect the painting in the morning." She closed the door behind him and moved into the bathroom. She turned on the tap. A long soak was in order.

Alessandra had dozed off. The water had turned lukewarm when she was awakened by a knock on the outer door. Then a louder knock. She quickly wrapped a robe tightly around herself and went to the door dripping wet. Jorge was in for a tongue lashing. She angrily flung open the suite door. David, soaked from the rain and looking forlorn, held the brown tube in his hand. For a moment neither spoke.

"I was hoping you'd invite me in," David finally managed, his voice filled with hope.

Alessandra stepped aside.

"How did you . . . Oh shit. I don't care how." David grabbed Alessandra and planted a long hard kiss. She fervently returned it. Her tongue delicately darted in and out of his mouth. He nibbled on her ear. A warm chill spilled down her spine.

David flung off his drenched jacket and worked his way down the nape of her neck. Her robe slipped from her shoulders and soon his tongue was dancing around her nipples. She inhaled his manly scent. Her hands tore at his shirt and caressed his muscled back. They fell onto the heavily carpeted floor, he on top of her. She pushed him to his side and ran her hands down his muscular shoulders, then onto his firm abdomen.

"Been working out?" Alessandra pushed away and lay on her back, all the while never removing her gaze from his body. *Why hadn't she noted his physique before when they were cuddled together in the van?*

"Not bad for a CPA, huh?"

"Especially a Jewish one."

David held her head in both of his hands. "Is that a racist remark?" He smiled.

"I'm sorry. I was trying to be funny."

"That's Jorge's job." He planted another kiss, this time more gently.

"And yours?"

David opened her robe completely and licked at her belly button. He worked his way down. "My job is to make a certain Spanish beauty scream for mercy." He nuzzled her thighs.

She pushed him away.

"What's wrong?"

Alessandra flicked off the lights, flung open the drapes and cracked the window. City lights and sounds flooded into the room. She wasn't sure where this would lead, but here in the City of Love, she didn't care. At this moment she was sure of one thing. She wanted him more than anything in the world. Her nipples hardened in the cold winter air. She touched her breasts and tingled with anticipation.

He ripped at his belt buckle.

"No, no. Let me, *mi amor.*" Alessandra knelt by his side. She took his index finger and sucked on it as she helped him wriggle out of his trousers and boxer shorts. Her hand stroked his manlihood. She could feel his body tense. He lifted his mouth to her nipples.

She felt herself wet with anticipation. She gazed into his eyes trying to read his thoughts. Was this as right for him as for her? His gentle touch told her it was. Once again their mouths locked as she eased onto him and swallowed him up.

#

As the light from the early morning sun drifted into the room, Alessandra sat on the corner of the bed and studied David. He lifted one eye.

"Mind if I open the curtains," Alessandra said, already halfway to the window.

David sat up and patted the bed next to him. "Hurry and come back here."

Alessandra pulled back the curtains and peeked outside. "It's snowing."

"I once told a friend of mine that if I could spend a week with a woman and felt the same way about her at the end of the week, as at the beginning, I'd marry her."

"Is that a proposal?"

"What would you like it to be?"

"Is that a serious question?"

They locked eyes. For a moment there was an awkward silence.

David picked up his clothes and dressed. "If I were ten years younger, it would have been."

"And if you were ten years younger," Alessandra smiled, "I would have said yes."

"And there's the Jewish-Catholic thing."

"Yes, there is that. So, it's good." Alessandra tried to keep her voice from quivering. "We are in agreement. It was a great night and we will leave it there."

David leaned over and kissed her forehead. He held her for a moment, then rose and grabbed the painting. "You know, I didn't just abandon the painting. I had a plan."

Alessandra smiled. "Remind Jorge to bring it back tomorrow."

"No. Really. I had a plan. I was—"

Alessandra held his face in her hands. "I know, my darling. I believe you." She pointed to the tube. "Just remember."

David gave her a quizzical look. "Why?"

"We still have to get the painting out of Europe and through American customs without it being confiscated. For that, we will need the help of someone I can trust. That man happens to be in Spain."

David hesitated for a moment and started to say something. She put her hand to his lips.

"We've said it all. I'm fine."

"I'll see you in New York," David said and closed the door after himself.

Alessandra stared at the door for a moment, then flung herself onto the bed. Her body quivered. She buried her head in the pillow and cried herself to sleep.

Chapter 28

Alessandra carried *The Naked Maja Dancing*, safely inside its brown tube, up the steps of the Prado Museum. Before leaving Paris she had emailed a message to Kleinermann. *I am going to stay in Europe for a few more days, but when I return, I hope to have good news for you. Regards, Alessandra.*

She wasn't ready to tell Kleinermann that she had the painting just yet. Too many things had already gone awry. This time she wanted to be sure she had the real painting securely in her possession when she came home. And she didn't want a welcoming committee like the Picasso fiasco just in case something went wrong.

It had been a year since she had left Madrid. She wished she had time to visit old haunts, but she had only a few days to both accomplish her mission and visit her father. She nodded to the guard, navigated past the information desk and marched into the bookstore.

Alessandra roamed the store searching for reproductions of Goya paintings. She spied some hanging on a rack. Nearby were tubes with small photos on the outside of the prints contained inside.

She found a tube with a photo of *The Naked Maja* on it. It was white and slightly smaller than the brown tube. She then searched for a copy of *The Clothed Maja* and took both to the counter, paid for them and headed for her old boss' office.

Sr. Ortega, the Prado curator greeted her warmly. "I was surprised when you called as I didn't expect to see you back so soon. It is a shame you won't have time to dine with me and fill me in on your adventures."

"I am grateful for your assistance, and when this is all over, I will tell you everything." Alessandra handed him all three tubes. "They need to be the same size." She took out a measuring tape and showed him the length of *The Naked Maja Dancing* tube, exactly 104 centimeters.

He wrote down the measurement. "How many do you need?"

"Just match these other two, so a total of three. But be sure the label you make of *The Naked Maja Dancing* is the same as the others."

Sr. Ortega clutched the brown tube. "Someday, I hope to see this painting hanging here."

"Perhaps one day, you will." Alessandra embraced him. "I'll be back in a few days."

"They will be ready."

#

The Santana Winery's limo picked Alessandra up at the airport. They rode silently toward Villafranca del Penedès. Alessandra always loved returning to her father's bodega, as much to see him as to roam the lush rolling hills of the Penedès wine region. The trip south from Barcelona took a little under an hour. As they approached the gate to the 3000 acre estate, she was surprised to see her father ride up on his stallion.

Manuel's white hair matched his horse's. He rode erect as though riding dressage. Alongside his own horse, he held the reins of a black horse. He dismounted and swung open the gate. Alessandra leapt out of the limo and threw her arms around him. He smiled broadly.

"Welcome, my daughter."

"I have so much to tell you."

"Yes, yes. All in due time." Manuel stepped back and looked at her admiringly. "You still look fit enough to ride."

"A lot has happened since we last spoke and - -"

"Spirit missed you." Manuel handed her the reins of the black stallion.

"I missed him also." Alessandra rubbed Spirit's nose. "I wish I could ride him now, but I don't have the proper clothes."

"Oh?" Manuel reached into his saddle bags and pulled out some chaps. "I thought you might want to ride back to the house, so I brought you chaparreras. Put them over your slacks and you'll be fine."

While she geared up, Manuel spoke to the limo driver who drove off toward the house. "Now my daughter, let us see if you can keep up with this old man." He mounted his horse, kicked it into a trot and headed into the hills.

Alessandra mounted her horse and galloped after him, her hair flying in the wind. She caught him at the hilltop. They trotted side by side along a ridge which looked over the vast vineyards. Slowly they worked their way down the hill toward some narrow rows of vines.

"Ready?" Manuel asked.

Without responding, Alessandra nudged Spirit and she was off at a full run.

Manuel raced to catch up. They turned into the vineyard, he took one row and she another. She slowed and he came alongside.

"Are *you* ready, my ancient papa?"

He nodded and kicked his horse hard. She did likewise. They stayed even through the first section of vines, then the second. As they approached the last section before reaching the house, Alessandra leaned over and chirped in Spirit's ear. He seemed to respond as they inched ahead of Manuel and came out of the section a neck ahead.

Posting now, Alessandra rose and fell rhythmically in the saddle. Male workers turned as she passed by. They tipped their hats. A woman worker applauded.

Alessandra mugged at her father in triumph as she halted her horse. She bounded out of the saddle and stood with her hands on her hips.

"I knew one day you would win." Manuel beamed.

"As did I."

"But not this soon."

"Are you disappointed?"

"To the contrary."

Alessandra placed her hands on his face, threw her arms around him and cried.

"This is no cause for tears."

"I think I'm in love."

"*That* is no cause for tears."

"He's Jewish."

"The young man you helped recover the painting? Mr. . . ?"

She nodded. "Edlestein. I knew you wouldn't approve."

"Is that what you think?"

"With priests in our family. Yes, that is what I think."

"You forgot the Cardinal."

"Papa, this is serious."

Manuel took her hand. "Then we should discuss this serious matter over dinner."

"Papa, how is Uncle Carlos?"

Manuel, took his daughter's hand in his, "We hope for the best."

"When can I see him?"

"Soon, my child."

Carlos was very dear to her, but Alessandra knew her father. Pushing him further at this point would gain her nothing. She would just have to wait, so she tried not to stress over it. She looked forward to luxuriating in the oversized bath her father had installed when she was a teen. She hurried into the house and pushed past a newly affixed mezuzah on her bedroom door.

Alessandra stripped off her clothes as she made her way to the bath. She passed a mirror and saw the key hanging on her necklace. With all the excitement, she almost had forgotten one of the reasons she was anxious to come home. She'd press her father about the key at dinner.

As she soaked in the tub, Alessandra was comforted by the large cross her grandmother had placed over the tub as a sort of Christening of the then new bathroom. Alessandra closed her eyes and conjured up visions of her grand mama teaching her religious tolerance. It was odd at the time, because in her school, there were no other religions to tolerate. Suddenly, she opened her eyes. "Ay, ay, ay."

She leapt out of the tub, nabbed a robe and dashed into the bedroom. She flung open the outer door and peered at the small silver mezuzah on the door jamb. She glanced down the corridor. Each door she passed had a newly mounted mezuzah on the jamb. Was this one of her father's pranks? She marched toward his chambers.

She was about to knock, when Manuel apparently anticipating her visit, suddenly appeared. Alessandra pointed to the mezuzahs all around the hallway on each room.

"Put on some clothes and meet me outside." Manuel headed downstairs. "I was going to tell you at dinner, but it seems it won't hold."

Alessandra found her father waiting outside the front door. He stooped at a figurine of the Madonna that adorned the side of the front steps. He kissed the statuette and then crossed himself. She followed suit.

Manuel glanced around. Two workers toiled nearby in the garden. He lifted up the foot of the Madonna to reveal an ornate miniature ceramic mezuzah. Alessandra was stunned and started to cry out. He put his fingers to his lips and pointed to the workers. She nodded.

"Come, my child, there is more." Manuel pointed to the cave built into the hills. It was the place where he stored his most prized wines.

When they entered the cave, Manuel hit a light switch. Wine barrels lined the walls and tunnels led everywhere. She followed her father deep into the cave. He stopped at what appeared to be a dead end and moved aside a few barrels on a wheeled pallet.

Manuel brushed off the ground underneath until she could see the outline of a square tile set into the concrete floor. Manuel took out a pocket knife, inserted it into one of the cracks around the tile and pried it loose. Underneath was a lever with a padlock attached to a metal loop anchored into the floor.

"I wanted Carlos to be here, but he will understand," Manuel eyed his daughter. "We will need your key."

Alessandra was stunned. She fumbled to unlatch her necklace. Her hands trembled as she removed the key and inserted it into the lock and slipped it out of the loop. She took a deep breath and pulled the lever.

The wall behind them opened revealing a small chapel. In an archway on one wall were crosses and a portrait of Mary holding Jesus. Along the walls were ledges adorned by menorahs. Her father lit some candles on a small table, on top of which lay a large ancient looking book.

Alessandra's eyes widened as she stepped into the chapel. She slowly turned and tried to absorb what she was seeing. A scroll that she recognized from movies as the Torah sat in an open cabinet. She was at loss for words.

Manuel lit the candles in the menorah and two candelabras on the table. He crossed himself, opened the book and flipped through it. He stopped at a particular page and placed it on the table. "Start here and when you are done, we will talk." He pointed to a button on the wall. "Push it and the door will open. Replace the lock when you leave."

Alessandra started to say something, but Manuel was gone. She heard the wall close behind her. She surveyed the room again and noticed a picture of her mother on another table. In the photo, her mother wore a Star of David.

Alessandra's head was spinning. What to make of all this? Trembling, she sat down and started to read the page her father had laid open on the table. She immediately recognized her mother's handwriting and that the book, written in Spanish, was a sort of family diary.

Her mother began: *My Dearest Daughter, I always assumed our family was and always had been Catholic. But on my thirteenth birthday I was told that in truth we were Jews at heart, but Catholic to the outside world.*

It was explained to me that in King Ferdinand's day, our family had the choice of leaving Spain and all our possessions or staying if we converted to the King's religion. Spain had been our ancestral home for four hundred years so we decided to convert. However, we secretly carried on our original faith in our own homes and eventually with others who had pretended to convert, such as your father's family.

When I was told our history I was given the choice of remaining in the Catholic religion or carrying on our ancient faith in Judaism while pretending to be Catholic as thousands before us had. But before I was told this, I was sworn to secrecy concerning the family's traditions. I decided to read the book you are now reading and came to understand that forced conversion was never Jesus' intention and so, I too became a crypto converso (a Marrano). Of sorts.

Through tear filled eyes, Alessandra turned the page.

Because I had been indoctrinated by nuns and priests, it was hard for me to feel Jewish. And I needed to experience the religion before I could embrace it. I therefore left Spain and studied under a rabbi in New York City. His name is Bernard Rosenbaum. He knows the whole family history and will welcome you should you decide to follow in my footsteps.

At this point you may ask, "Who am I?" The answer is whoever you want to be. As for me, I never fully embraced the Jewish faith, however I know in my soul that I am a Jew. I am writing this on your tenth birthday but, as I am already ill, I will not share the day our heritage is revealed to you. In fact, you are only reading this because something has occurred that caused your father (or uncle) to reveal our secret truth. Let me explain.

When I found out that I lived in two religious worlds, I became very confused. It caused me great anguish. I wanted to spare you the pain of being branded a Marrano. I therefore asked papa not to tell you unless he felt you had to know. I wish I could have been there to ease the shock, but alas, that is not to be. Please forgive us for not telling you earlier, but you will come to understand that it was out of love and concern for your own safety.

Alessandra closed the book and tried to keep her emotions in check. How could they not have told her earlier? Who would not want to know their own heritage? It didn't change who she was. Or did it? Was she a Jew? Certainly not. At least she didn't think so. She was Catholic to the core. Worse, as a student in an all Catholic school, she had been fed a litany of anti-Semitic propaganda and although over time she rejected such bigotry, she still harbored some negative views of Jews. And what was her father? And her priest uncle? Were they false converts also?

Regardless of her mother's wishes, she would have difficulty forgiving her parents for not telling her about their heritage. Anger welled up in her. And the more she thought about it, the more steamed she became.

She placed the photo of her mother under one arm and the family history in the other. She took one last look, blew out the candles and fled the hidden sanctuary.

Alessandra stormed into her father's library. Manuel glanced up from the guitar he was strumming.

"We're descendants of Jews?" Alessandra exclaimed. "All these years, you lied to me."

"Never." Manuel continued to play.

Alessandra thrust the photo of her mother at him. "When I asked you about lighting the candles on Friday night and you said it was only family tradition. Wasn't that a lie?"

"It was family tradition."

"Jewish Family tradition. Not ours."

"It was your mother's tradition."

"Was she Jewish?"

"She was Catholic."

"Then why is she wearing a Star of David in the photo?" Alessandra pointed outside. "And the Madonna. The mezuzah hidden in the foot all these years. If we were Catholic, why?"

Manuel put down the guitar and held his daughter at arm's length. "It was family tradition going back to the Inquisition. Our ancestors were Jews who converted, but kept some of the old ways. I'm sorry. I would have told you sooner, but your mother made me swear I wouldn't unless - - "

"Unless I wanted to marry a Jew?"

"Something like that."

"But you gave me the key before you knew about David."

"Yes. Carlos and I decided to give you the key after you sent us the pamphlet about 'Art and the Church.' We realized that your profession and religion were intimately related. If you were going to lecture about Spanish artists and their Jewish wives or mistresses, it would be unfair for us to keep your heritage from you."

"After mama died, I needed to be near you." Alessandra pushed away from her father. "Instead, you sent me away."

"To the best schools."

"And when regular school was not in session, you sent me off to learn horseback riding or ballet or scuba and even mountaineering. It was always something. Why didn't - -"

Her uncle Carlos, dressed in his priestly frock, peered in. "Am I interrupting?" He looked fit and not the slightest bit ill.

"Papa said you were ill."

"Do I look sick?" He hastened over to kiss Alessandra on both cheeks.

She avoided him. She glared at her father.

"I never said he was sick," Manuel said.

"You implied it."

"Once you told me about the painting and David, I thought it even more urgent that you know your heritage." Manuel smiled. "A ruse to get you home soon."

Alessandra looked at Carlos. "Why didn't *you* tell me about this before?"

Carlos adjusted his clerical collar. "If we could have anticipated you falling in love with a Jew, perhaps we would have."

Alessandra sensed herself losing control. She turned away from both men.

Carlos came to her side. "Have you ever heard of Marrano Jews?"

"Vaguely."

"After King Ferdinand issued his expulsion order, many Jews converted but secretly kept their old traditions. The Catholic Spaniards referred to them as Marranos, swine."

"We're Marranos?"

"Not exactly," Carlos continued. "Many families, such as ours, eventually embraced their new religion. But in your mother's case she insisted on keeping some of the Jewish rituals."

"Why would you keep this from me?"

"The tradition in Marrano families was not to tell the children until they were at least twelve years old. Families were afraid of being exposed and either brought before the inquisition or persecuted in some other way. Even until forty years ago it was still dangerous for Jews to live in Spain. Your mother wanted to spare you that. And you should be grateful to your father. He provided you with all the advantages of life."

"Except knowing who I was." Alessandra approached her father. "You were so busy building your wine empire. Didn't you think that I would have liked to know about my mother? And when you lit the candles, it was so beautiful, but you never told me why. It shouldn't have taken my falling in love with a Jewish man to find out about Jewish rituals that were part of our family heritage."

Manuel wrapped both of her hands in his. "Perhaps we both owe you an apology. But we cannot undo the past. The mezuzahs are our atonement. It was time to come out of the closet."

Alessandra pulled away from his grasp. "Am I a Catholic or a Jew?"

"There is only one God," Carlos said. "To him it doesn't matter."

"And you?" Alessandra pressed.

"For me it is easy." Carlos fingered his cross. "Whatever you choose, I will respect."

"As will I," Manuel echoed.

Alessandra glared at her uncle. "And what about the Church?"

"As for the Church," Carlos crossed himself, "they will have no choice. Besides, it will be difficult for the Church to complain about a person returning to her ancestors' original religion whose ancestors were forced to convert against their will. "

Alessandra let out an anguished groan. Tears flowed freely. Carlos approached, but she turned him away. "I need a few minutes." She gathered herself and wiped away her tears. She stared hard at her father who had a remorseful look on his face. He looked as sad as she ever remembered.

Manuel threw open his arms. "Come here, my child."

Alessandra hesitated but then rushed into her father's arms. She held him tight. "He says he cannot marry me because I am Catholic and he's Jewish," she sobbed.

Manuel raised her chin. "Are you sure?"

"He also says he is too old for me."

Manuel caressed Alessandra's face. "Perhaps he is afraid you will reject him."

Alessandra shook her head side to side. "Why would he be afraid of that?"

"How many years older is he?" Carlos asked.

"I'm not sure. Maybe ten, fifteen years."

"With a woman as beautiful as you, I would be afraid." Carlos smiled.

Manuel nodded. "As would I. Now go dry your eyes. Then we shall think this through together."

Alessandra wiped her tears and kissed both men. As she hastened toward her bedroom, she was sure her life had just taken a turn, but she couldn't decide if it was good or bad. Either way, she was determined to find out more about her history. She wondered if Rabbi Rosenbaum was still alive.

Chapter 29

Seigfried Kleinermann was pleased with himself. The Argentinean bank had confirmed the wire transfer to his friend Rutger Becker. Soon he'd be able to retire to Buenos Aires to join his many friends already there. Of course he'd have to wait an appropriate amount of time until the FBI completed its investigation into Alessandra's activities. Surely she'd be convicted. Such a nice girl and from such a fine family. Too bad it had to be her, but she was the perfect foil . . . and fool.

She was all too anxious to go off and find the missing Goya. But then how could she resist. It was the only way to clear her name and at the same time make herself famous for recovering a fellow countryman's work of art. And what a magnificent piece it was. Parting with it was difficult, but after all, twenty million was twenty million and that was only for the Goya. He had gotten another twenty for the other two paintings.

Kleinermann leaned back and dared to dream about the Paris of South America. And of course Mar del Plata, just 250 miles from Buenos Aires, with its ten miles of beaches and magnificent casino. Ah yes, the casino. By now Rutger should have transferred the money he owed to his sources in Germany and the remainder to the owners of the Casino. In return, Becker was to have received a one-third share of ownership in the Casino as trustee on behalf of one Seymour Klein, a.k.a. Seigfried Kleinermann.

As Klein, Kleinermann planned to play the role of gentleman host, have all the beautiful women he needed, and rub shoulders with the finest society people and politicians.

Kleinermann's reverie was broken when his office door burst open. Yoshiro, a burly Japanese bolted in. Yoshiro carried a large brown paper package under his arm.

"I told you never to come here," Kleinermann said as he started to rise.

Yoshiro pushed Kleinermann back into his chair. "Mr. Yokahama say you owe him forty million." He thrust the package at Kleinermann.

Kleinermann looked stunned.

"Mr. Yokahama say *Naked Woman Dancing* not Goya. You promise famous painting by Goya. He not stupid. He want money back."

Kleinermann ripped at the wrapping and stared at the painting. "What's wrong? It looks fine to me."

"You tell boss about letters on back." He turned over the painting and pointed. "No letters." He held out his hand. "You give back money now."

Kleinermann couldn't believe his braggadocio had backfired. He had indeed told Yokahama about the Nazi technique of marking the back of the painting with the victim's initials. Then he bragged about his bribe of the Kyritz security guards. "I can't give him his money back. I already paid my sources in Germany and Russia for those paintings. What about the others?"

"He not trust others either. He take them to expert. If say okay, then he keep. But you pay back all forty million."

"I am sure the Klimt and Van Gogh are genuine, so why should I give back all the money."

"Deal for all three. Goya not good. You pay back."

"Fine, then have him give me back the Klimt and Van Gogh."

Yoshiro glared at Kleinermann. "Boss not bargain."

"Give me some time. I can locate the real Goya."

Yoshiro wrapped one hand around Kleinermann's neck and squeezed. "Money now. You lucky you not dead already."

Kleinermann put both hands on Yoshiro's and tried to remove the death grip. "Look. I'm sure he would prefer the real painting," he gasped, "so why don't you call him now and ask."

The strongman loosened his grip, whipped out his cell phone and dialed. After a short wait, Yoshiro spoke into the phone. "He say he can get real painting." Another pause, then Yoshiro looked at Kleinermann. "How soon?"

Alessandra had told Kleinermann that on her return, she'd have a surprise. Kleinermann was sure he now knew what that surprise was. The real painting. Somehow she had switched the forgery for the true Goya. "I need a week."

Yoshiro repeated what Kleinermann had said. He closed the phone. "Boss say two days. No painting, then forty million." He grabbed Kleinermann's shirt and pulled him closer. "Understand?"

Kleinermann nodded.

Yoshiro looked ominously at Kleinermann and released him. "If find painting, only pay back ten." He grinned and strode out.

Kleinermann slumped into his chair. Even though the Hermitage painting was worthless, he had already laid out half of the forty million to the guards and Boris, and another ten to Becker for his share of the casino. If he had to pay ten back to his Jap client, that left no money to live on and certainly no dream house.

He couldn't believe he had been so careless. He had had his German cohorts deliver the paintings directly to the Yokahama Shipping Company. He thought that would make it difficult to trace it back to him in the event someone caught Yokahama with the stolen property. But by doing so, he hadn't checked the Goya to see if it was the real one. Now he was in deep *scheisse* and if Alessandra didn't come back soon with the real painting, his retirement plans would vanish. And worse, his life. He had no way of getting back the money he paid the guards or Becker. He cursed himself for not pressing her to come home earlier.

#

Alessandra hugged a large shopping bag of three identical white tubes as she made her way to a customs agent at JFK Airport. She was prepared to support her declaration that she had purchased "under $500," of goods overseas. She figured the value of the mezuzah, the matryoshka dolls and three prints of famous artists would easily total under that number.

When her turn came, Alessandra tried to look nonchalant as the agent studied her passport.

"You're Spanish?"

Alessandra, too nervous to speak, merely nodded.

The agent flipped through the pages.

"I have a green card," Alessandra stammered as she handed it to the agent, who glanced at the card and returned it.

"I see you've been to a number of countries. Did you purchase goods over five hundred dollars in value?"

Alessandra shook her head vigorously.

"Would you open your bags please?"

Alessandra fingered the ring. "Yes, yes. No problem." Her hands shook as she opened her two suitcases.

The agent deftly felt under inside the bag, under the clothes and along the edges of both cases. He lifted the suitcases and appeared to look for a false bottom. As the agent did his inspection, Alessandra twirled the ring on her finger.

"May I see that?" The agent pointed to the ring.

She had forgotten all about the ring as something that might have to be declared. Nervously, Alessandra slipped the ring from her finger and held it out toward the agent.

"Did you have this before you left the country?"

What to do? If she said no, she could be jailed for not declaring something this valuable. If she said yes and she was caught lying, it could be even worse. Maybe she could finesse it. "It was a family heirloom. My father gave it to me when I went home recently."

The agent turned the ring over and scrutinized Alessandra. "Anything else you might want to declare?"

Alessandra felt the tension in her neck subside. She had dodged a bullet. She confidently shook her head. "No."

The agent pointed to the tubes. "What's in those?"

She had to keep her composure. Without responding, Alessandra lifted the tube with the print of *The Naked Maja* inside and showed it to the agent.

"Open, please."

Alessandra struggled to pop the white cap at the end of the tube. The agent handed her a small screwdriver.

"Thank you." She tried to pry the end off with the tool, but decided it best to pretend she couldn't do it. She handed the tube to the agent. "Perhaps you could be of assistance."

The agent nodded toward one of the other tubes. "May I see that one?" He pointed to *The Clothed Maja*.

Alessandra smiled. She hefted the tube.

"No, not that one, the other."

Alessandra pointed to *The Naked Maja Dancing*. "This one?" Her heart raced. She smiled as sweetly as she could.

The agent nodded.

Alessandra thrust the tube at the agent. "Perhaps you will need this." She returned the screwdriver. Maybe her bravado would convince him there was nothing to hide.

"Not necessary." The agent signaled to another agent with a German shepherd. The other agent marched over with the dog who sniffed the tube but had no reaction.

"May I have the others please?" The first agent asked.

Alessandra handed over the other tubes.

The agent had the dog repeat the process. "Sorry about this, but we got word that a big drug shipment was on the way." He gave Alessandra back the bag with all three paintings. "Can't be too careful. Have a nice day Ms. Santana."

"Yes, I think I will." Alessandra could feel her heart beat return to normal.

Outside the terminal Alessandra waved down a taxi. She couldn't wait to see Kleinermann's expression when she turned up with *The Naked Maja Dancing.*

Chapter 30

Alessandra handed her luggage to the taxi driver. After he stowed the bags in the trunk, he reached for the posters. Alessandra snatched them back. He mumbled something in a language she didn't understand and dropped into the driver's seat without opening the door for her. Welcome to New York.

"The Metropolitan Museum," she said.

Alessandra spent part of the forty-five minute ride into Manhattan calling the Central Synagogue. She was assured by the operator that Rabbi Rosenbaum would be there all day.

When they arrived at the Museum, Alessandra climbed out clutching the tubes. The driver piled her bags on the sidewalk and waited for his money. She handed him the amount due plus a small tip. He glared at her and put out his hand as if to expect a larger tip. She pointedly took his hand and vigorously shook it. He launched into a rant, but stopped when a Museum guard hustled down the steps.

The guard glared at the driver. "He bothering you Ms. Santana?"

"Not anymore."

The driver flipped them off as he drove away. Alessandra merely smiled. The Big Apple never changed.

"Welcome back," the guard said as he hefted her bags and followed her into the building.

Bernard Von Herstellen, superintendent of the art restoration department met her as she exited the elevator to his basement workshop. After a perfunctory greeting, Alessandra handed him *The Naked Maja Dancing*. "Would you please mount and frame this? When you're done, call Mr. Kleinermann and tell him Alessandra's surprise is here."

She scribbled a note and handed it to Von Herstellen. "After he sees it, please deliver it to this address."

Von Herstellen turned to leave.

"And tell Mr. Kleinermann I'll be in tomorrow. I have some personal business to deal with today."

She left with her luggage and hailed another taxi. "Central Synagogue." The Pakistani driver looked puzzled.

"Lexington and 55th."

#

Alessandra carried her baggage up the steps of the Moresque style building and warily peered through the open outer doors of the Synagogue. A uniformed police officer stood near the entrance. He searched her luggage and then her handbag.

"Are you here to see the Rabbi?"

She nodded.

"Is he expecting you?"

"I don't think so."

"Please go on in and wait in the sanctuary." The guard called on his radio as she entered.

Inside the main sanctuary with its deep blue vaulted ceiling and arabesque arches, Alessandra felt she could easily have been in Spain. The stalls were empty so she knelt, crossed herself, then rose and wandered through the aisles admiring the architecture and ornate chandeliers. An elderly man in a wheel chair wearing a yarmulke and a prayer shawl suddenly appeared from the wings.

"You must be Alessandra," the man said in a heavy German accent.

She extended her hand. "And you must be Rabbi Rosenbaum."

"The same."

"My father called?"

The Rabbi warmly grasped both of his hands around hers. "Is he a priest?"

"That would be my uncle."

"A very interesting man. I'd like to meet him someday. We share many of the same views about religion. He wheeled around and headed toward a side door. "You can leave your things in my office."

The Rabbi's study was small and cluttered. Various plaques attesting to his scholarship hung on the wall behind his chair. On the wall away from the window, was a replica of an El Greco painting, *Lady with a Fur,* and next to it, Alessandra was shocked to see, was a painting of a Cardinal. "Is it common for rabbis to have pictures of Cardinals on their walls?"

The Rabbi's eyes crinkled. "Your parents never told you?"

"Tell me what?"

"That we are, in a way, relatives."

"How can we be relatives?"

Rabbi Rosenbaum gestured toward the painting of the Cardinal. "He is Cardinal Don Tomas de la Zaragosa, the great grandson of Jeronima de las Cuevas and El Greco."

The Rabbi gestured for her to sit. "The woman in fur," he pointed to the El Greco painting, "is believed to be Jeronima."

"I know."

"Then you also know she was a Jewess, but was forced to renounce her faith so El Greco wouldn't be brought before the Inquisition for living with a Jew. What you probably don't know is that Don Tomas had a brother Rafael who denounced his Catholicism. He later became the chief Rabbi of a small village in Italy where he had fled. My family traces its roots to Rafael. Yours traces theirs to Don Tomas."

"I'm related to El Greco?"

"I'm afraid so."

Alessandra turned away so the rabbi wouldn't see her tears. "I'm an art historian," she said in voice barely above a whisper. She stared out the window which looked out on a busy New York street but saw only visions of her father and uncle in their ancestral home. She turned toward the rabbi and continued in a normal voice.

"You'd think they would have realized what this would mean to me. A descendant of El Greco. How could they keep that from me?"

"Your parents grew up in perilous times. The Nazis in Spain might well have killed your grandparents just because they had some ancient Jewish blood. Discretion was always the way with any family who still observed the old Jewish traditions. They felt as though they had to protect you from your history until the time was right. I know your mother loved you and only had your best interests at heart. Your father merely honored her wishes."

"How do you know so much about us?"

"The descendants of El Greco have always stayed in touch. That book your father gave you lists every known branch and member of our family."

The Rabbi reached up for a binder on a bookcase. As he did so, the prayer shawl slipped from his arm, revealing a tattooed number. Alessandra blanched.

"We each keep our version of that book. This is mine."

He pushed the binder toward her.

Alessandra leafed through it. "I just learned about ours. Yours seems similar."

"You don't remember, but I visited your bodega when you were only a small child."

"Am I Jewish?"

"A tough question. According to Jewish law, if your mother was Jewish, you are."

"But I don't know if my mother ever practiced Judaism. My father says she was a Catholic."

"God doesn't take away your passport because you're not observant."

Alessandra teared up again. She grasped the Rabbi's hand and then embraced him.

"Your mother told me she felt Jewish but couldn't easily forget the teachings of her church. I think she left this world with one foot in Israel and one in Vatican City."

Alessandra looked around for a bathroom. Rosenbaum, apparently sensing her need, pointed to a room nearby.

In the bathroom, Alessandra rinsed her face. She took a tissue to wipe off her smudged mascara. As she did so, she spotted the mezuzah and the crucifix around her neck. She moved the cross to one side so the mezuzah could rest in the middle of her chest. Then she reversed the process. *One foot in Israel and one in Vatican City.* Yes. She understood her mother's dilemma completely. Oh, how she wished for her mother's counsel. She couldn't believe that ten years had passed since her death and until now hadn't realized how much she missed her.

In the ride back to her apartment, she pondered her mother's letter. If David had not come into her life bringing with him a story about a painting that was so intertwined with her own heritage, she would have gone on living her life contentedly believing she and her family were Catholics. And she would have died not knowing her family's true history. It saddened her to realize her father would have kept that secret if he hadn't been forced by recent circumstances to reveal the truth. It shouldn't have come to this. In her mind, she always had a right to know, at least since she was old to enough to understand. It would take a while for her to fully forgive both her father and her beloved uncle.

#

A frantic Kleinermann rushed into the bowels of the museum. Von Herstellen was busy framing a painting.

"Where is it?" Kleinermann demanded.

Von Herstellen pointed to a work table where *The Naked Maja Dancing* was laid out on a canvas stretcher.

"Remove it from the stretcher and bring it to my office right away."

"But I—"

"Now!"

#

Alone, in his office, Kleinermann inspected *The Naked Maja Dancing* with his magnifying glass. Satisfied, he retrieved the forged *Maja* from the closet and removed the canvas from its frame. He took out some thumb tacks and gently anchored the real *Naked Maja Dancing* to that frame. He would do a better job later after Von Herstellen was gone for the day when he could finish the job properly.

Kleinermann placed the real painting in the closet and called down to Von Herstellen. "Sorry to be so abrupt with you. I was just so anxious to see this important discovery, I couldn't wait. You can come back now and finish your work."

When Von Herstellen arrived, Kleinermann thrust the fake *Maja* at him. "Do as Ms. Santana requested." Kleinermann turned aside and stifled a broad grin. "Frame it and deliver it at once."

Von Herstellen looked puzzled, but took the fake painting and left.

Kleinermann immediately called Yoshiro. "I have that package I promised. I will deliver it later this evening."

#

When the doorbell rang at Devorah's apartment, it roused her from an afternoon nap. Devorah peered through the peephole. Two men, one in a uniform stood waiting. She cautiously opened her door, but kept the chain on. "I don't have any money."

"Madam, I'm not here to sell you anything." Von Herstellen said.

"What do you want?"

"I'm from the Metropolitan Museum." Von Herstellen slipped his card through the opening. "Ms. Santana sent me."

"Ms. Santana?"

"Alessandra Santana, our assistant curator."

"Oh, that nice *shiksa*." Devorah removed the chain and ushered the restorer into her home.

Von Herstellen handed Devorah a package wrapped in brown paper. "This is for you. Compliments of Miss Santana."

"What is it?"

"Why don't you open it? I want to make sure you're pleased with our efforts. I'll wait."

"That won't be necessary." It finally dawned on Devorah what it was. She needed to be alone. "Just set it down in the hallway," she said as she opened the door.

Von Herstellen handed her a form to sign. "I wouldn't advertise the fact you have that painting and I would get it insured at once."

"No one in this neighborhood will know," Devorah said, "but thanks for the advice." Without looking, she scribbled her name and ushered him out. Devorah turned the dead bolt lock, replaced the chain and leaned against the door.

She took a deep breath and placed the package onto her dining room table and cautiously peeled back the wrapping. Her hands trembled. She had to be careful not to damage the painting. With each layer she removed, her movements became slower until the frame appeared. She turned the painting over and gingerly lifted the last of the wrapping. "Oy, oy, oy!"

She began to cry, at first a sob and then large gulped cries of joy.

There was a knock. Suddenly, Devorah was transported to back to Germany. Fear engulfed her. The knock became more insistent. Then a loud bang. Her heart raced. The Gestapo! Where were her parents? And her brother? She had to find Arthur and hide.

"Mom. It's me. Come unlock the door."

Devorah looked out her window and saw the New York skyline. She cleared her head and wiped her eyes. "Yes, yes, I'm coming."

Devorah turned the dead bolt lock and smothered her son in her arms. "A mitzvah. A true mitzvah."

"They already delivered it?"

"Yes. Yes. Come look." Devorah led the way to the dining room and hoisted up the painting.

David at first appeared jubilant. Then slowly his smile evaporated. He came closer to the painting and sadness flowed into his eyes.

"What's wrong?"

David hugged his mother. "Nothing, mom." He clenched his teeth. "It's just too bad Alessandra's not here."

Chapter 31

Alessandra pressed "message" on her answering machine.

Hello, darling. It's me your Ukrainian madman. Just checking on your progress with our package. I'm still in Europe but please call me on my cell phone as soon as you get this.

The next message came on.

It's David. I just left my mother's apartment. I don't know who you thought you'd fool. I can't believe you'd pull the same stunt twice. I guess Paris was just a game to you. I was a fool to trust you.

Alessandra slumped in her chair. What was he talking about? She was about to call David back when the phone rang again. Instantly she picked it up.

"Welcome home." It was Kleinermann. "I hate to have to tell you this over the phone but I just received a disturbing call from your friend Mr. Edlestein."

"About what?"

"You don't know?"

"All I know is that he left and angry message. I have no idea why. "

"The Goya that was delivered to Mrs. Edlestein was a forgery and he swears you had the real one when he last saw you."

Alessandra sucked in her breath.

"Did you hear me?"

"And you believe I'm involved?"

"It doesn't matter what I believe. I had to inform the Board."

Alessandra sighed. "I think I know what's coming."

"I tried to talk them out of it. I asked them to at least wait until they heard your side of the story, but they were too worried about bad publicity. They insisted I fire you immediately."

Alessandra tried to keep her composure. She was on the verge of tears. This would surely ruin whatever career she had left in the art world. Or any world.

How had this happened? She thought back. This time the painting was never out of her sight, so how could it be a forgery?

"Surely there's been a mistake. I'll go see Mrs. Edlestein and check the painting."

"Mr. Edlestein told me to tell you not to bother them. He will bring by the painting in the morning to prove it's a forgery. He mentioned something about the ring. Do you know what he's talking about?"

Who would know about the ring? Without knowing about the ring, they'd have no way knowing about the forgery? After all, even the experts from the Hermitage thought their painting was a Goya. So either this was an inside job or there was some mistake.

"He gave me the ring we found in Palau and probably wants it back." She wasn't ready to share this secret with anyone, especially Kleinermann who would leak it to the press and then any chance of tripping up the thief would be gone. Too shaken to carry on the conversation further, she thanked him "for all your support. If I figure anything out, I'll call later."

She had to assume it wasn't a mistake. David would know how to count diamonds and of course would check the back of the painting. Assuming he wasn't the thief-he had no motive, who could be involved?

She quickly eliminated Jorge who had no access. What about Gregor? As with Jorge, he was in Europe with no access to the painting. Or was he really in Europe? His phone call said so, but why the message? To allay suspicion? He was one the few who knew about the switch she had made with the German Police, but he'd have to get the painting back from them. And then he'd need access to Metropolitan Museum and somehow monitor the painting's progress in the restoration department. But if he had someone in the museum as a partner, that would be easy enough. And he also was aware about her past. He knew she'd be suspected when it was discovered that the painting delivered to Mrs. Edlestein was a forgery. All the signs pointed to him.

But she knew Gregor, didn't she? After all, he worked for the U.N. No, it was all too preposterous. Nevertheless, Gregor's message bothered her. She replayed it. *I'm still in Europe, but please call me on my cell phone as soon as you get this.*

Calling Europe on a cell phone was expensive. Gregor surely knew he would have charges to his phone as well as the cost to her of the call. And he was known to be tight with money. So, was he in the U.S. and not Europe? Her suspicions grew. She wasn't sure how, but with his mysterious job at the U.N., all signs were pointing to Gregor as the prime suspect.

Gregor said to call him, but she was afraid she might say something that would alert him. If he was involved, she didn't want him fleeing.

Alessandra sank into her couch and closed her eyes. She was exhausted and needed to clear her mind. A little nap might help.

\#

Alessandra rubbed her eyes and checked the clock. It was only 6:00 am, but since she couldn't sleep anymore, she went to her the office early to clear things out. She wanted to beat the staff. Saying goodbye would be too difficult under the circumstances. She'd let Kleinermann tell them about her firing.

She opened her desk drawers, flipped through the contents of each and tossed them into a gym bag. When she got to the bottom drawer, it was locked. After some fiddling, she found the right key and unlocked it. There sat her most recent diary. She'd kept one since she'd been a teenager. There was lots to write about since her last entry which was shortly before she'd left for Palau with David. She decided to jot down her thoughts while they were fresh in her mind. Most of all she needed to say how she felt about David before events changed her mind.

She began. *Who could have predicted that a 200 year old painting of a nude Jewish woman could have such a profound effect on my life? That the painting would be responsible for introducing me to one of the woman's and possibly the artist's descendants. And that I would fall deeply in love with that man.*

Hours later she put down her pen and checked her watch. Workers would be coming in soon. She'd have to hurry if she was going to avoid them. She hastily tidied up and headed out. She'd arrange to have her books delivered later.

As she hurried down the outside steps of the Museum she spied a man who looked vaguely familiar. As she passed him, he tipped his hat and said with a heavy German accent *"Morgen."* She noticed a sly smile cross his face as though he knew something she didn't.

Where had she seen him before? That he spoke in German had to be a clue. She paused at the bottom of the steps and looked back just as he disappeared into the Museum. Then it hit her. The Castle. He was one of the guards. She dashed up the steps and flew into the entry hall just in time to spot Kleinermann shake the man's hand. Together they headed toward the private offices of the Museum.

What was going on? She started to follow when she was suddenly tapped on her shoulder.

"Sorry about your leaving Ms. Santana," Barney, the Metropolitan's guard said. "Can I help you with your things?"

The news got around fast. "That's very kind of you Barney, but I can manage." She couldn't very well spy on Kleinermann now, but wasn't about to let this pass. Alessandra quickly formulated a plan and would need Barney's help for it to work. "I'm going to get my car and come back later to get the rest of my things. Will that be alright?"

Barney nodded.

"Who's on the late shift?"

"Shawn and Mike. I'll fill them in."

She waited until Barney went back to his post and then whipped out her cell phone. It was obvious Kleinermann was somehow involved. It all fit. Now she had to know if Gregor was in with him. "*Hola*. It's me."

Chapter 32

"I need to see you right away," Alessandra said, trying to keep calm.

"What's going on?" Gregor asked.

"I was fired. I'll explain when I see you."

"Something happened to the painting again?"

"When will you be back?"

"I'm at the airport now, about to take off."

"What airport?"

"Heathrow."

"Call as soon as you land."

The conversation was equivocal. Why did he assume she was fired over the Goya? On the other hand, his voice sounded concerned about her and he didn't hesitate about the name of the airport. Before she could accuse him, she needed more information and to get that, she had some preparation to do.

She went home to gather what she needed, stuffed the items in her gym bag and prepared to leave. On her way out the door, she noticed the matryoshka doll sitting next to the phone and stopped. It had always bothered her how they were directed to a particular Russian merchant to buy the doll. At the time, she passed it off as the typical scam of directing tourists to a favored vendor who probably shared the profits with the person who directed them there. Now, that nagging feeling that something was fishy about the doll came back.

Alessandra had never been able to understand why David and Jorge were apprehended after the Castle break in. Who alerted the police and how did they know?

Gregor was the obvious choice, but seeing Kleinermann with the Kyritz guard now offered an explanation of the mystery. Was there some kind of conspiracy with their shadow in St. Petersburg and also the German Castle guards? Did Kleinermann alert the Germans and if so, why? She hoped to find that out soon, but meanwhile how could Kleinermann have tracked their every move? She never had told him about the impending break-in or he never would have approved. The doll seemed to be a clue of some kind.

She turned the doll over and removed all seventeen embedded dolls. She inspected each one. When she got to the smallest, after looking it over carefully, she shook it. Something seemed loose inside. She took her ice axe out of the gym bag and gently smashed the doll. A tiny small object popped out.

#

Hours after the Museum had closed to the public, Alessandra pulled her car into the garage, grabbed her gym bag and walked across the street. She checked her watch. 9:45. Most of the Museum workers had already left. In a few minutes, the cleaners would also be leaving. That would leave only the guards and her. She knew one of the guards would sit by a monitor and check the security cameras located all over the museum. The other would periodically patrol the exhibit rooms. What she had in mind would evade both the cameras and the patrol.

The last of the cleaning crew gathered at the door. She waited until one of the guards appeared and opened the door. It was Shawn. Alessandra quickly crossed the street and waved to him. He waved back and kept the door open for her.

"Barney told me you'd be coming back. Sorry about your leaving," Shawn said.

Alessandra stepped inside. "Me too."

"I have to finish my rounds. "Will you be long?"

"Can I have thirty minutes?"

Shawn checked his watch. "I'll meet you back here to let you out."

Alessandra rushed to the elevator. She got in and waved to the security camera. "Hi Mike."

Inside her office, she opened her bag, slipped into a black spandex outfit, and put on her climbing shoes. She took off her earrings, necklace and watch, and threw it in the bag. She didn't want anything to snag while she snooped around.

She stowed the bag under her desk and put on her fanny pack. She hit the light switch and bathed the office in black. She waited for her eyes to adjust, then opened a window and climbed out onto the narrow ledge.

Using only the lights from the city, Alessandra inched her way to Kleinermann's window only three offices over. She tried to open it, but it stuck. She pulled a small ice axe from her fanny pack and slid the edge of the axe under the window. Gently, she pried it open.

Flashlight in hand, Alessandra scanned the office. Kleinermann's desk was identical to her own. She wasn't sure what she was looking for, but the desk was a good place to start. She set the axe down and opened the top drawer. She rifled through the papers. Nothing. No surprise. He wouldn't be that careless.

She tried the bottom drawer. Locked. She started to check her watch and remembered she left it in the gym bag. Luckily Kleinermann had a clock on his desk. Ten minutes before she was supposed to meet Shawn. She slipped the blade of the axe into the crack above the drawer and tried to pry it open. It wouldn't budge.

She put down the axe and took off her fanny pack. She shined the light inside and searched for her keys. She found the one that opened her own locked desk drawer and tried it. No luck. She wiggled the key back and forth and turned again. No luck. She inserted it all the way and then slowly inched it out. With each notch she tried to turn the key. On the third try, the lock turned. She checked the clock again. Only four minutes left.

She spied an envelope from the Yokahama Overseas Shipping Company. Quickly she opened it.

THANK YOU FOR THE PACKAGE. OUR CLIENT IS MAKING ARRANGEMENTS TO PROVIDE A VERY GENEROUS DONATION. IT WILL BE DEPOSITED IN THE USUAL ACCOUNT. HE IS PREPARED TO PAY ANOTHER $10,000,000.00 IF A LIKE QUALITY PAINTING IS FOUND.

Bingo! Elated and frightened at the same time, Alessandra had no time to reflect on the import of the letter she had in her hand. She hastily stuffed the letter into her fanny pack and locked the drawer. Time to go. She cinched the fanny pack around her and bolted out the window.

Alessandra climbed back through the window of her own office just in time to hear a knock at her door. The handle to her office shook. "Are you alright?"

"Can I have five more minutes?" Alessandra asked.

"Why are your lights off?"

"I needed to change my sweater and was worried someone could see in." She hit the light switch.

"Okay. I'll wait right here," Shawn said.

Alessandra quickly changed clothes. She took a deep breath to calm herself and opened the door. "Sorry. I got distracted reading old documents." She pointed to the bookcases. "I'll arrange to have the books picked up tomorrow."

Shawn took a quick look around. He pointed to the fanny pack on her chair. "Did you forget that?" He started toward it.

Alessandra whisked by him. She snatched the pack and threw it into her gym bag. "Thanks."

Shawn stared at her sweater and started to say something, but stopped. He shrugged and led her to the exit doors. She was about to leave when he grabbed her gym bag. "Mind if I have a peek inside?" Without waiting for an answer he rummaged inside.

He pulled out the fanny pack and seem to weigh it. He unzipped it and pulled out the ice axe. "Planning to murder anyone?"

Alessandra smiled. "I ice climb and had left that in my office."

Shawn shined his flashlight inside the gym bag. "Sorry about this, but sometimes disgruntled employees try to steal stuff." He handed her back the bag. "Just doing my job."

She left the building trembling. At a safe distance she called David. "Please don't hang up. I know you don't want to talk to me, but I think I can explain what happened."

"There's nothing to explain. I should hang up."

"Please listen. Oh, I can't do this over the phone. Meet me outside the Museum in an hour."

"No way. It's too late."

"I still have your ring. And if you want it back, I'll be across the street in a black *Nissan Altima*."

Before he could answer, Alessandra hung up. If he didn't come, then she would be sad, but he at least owed her a chance to explain herself. If he couldn't do that, then he wasn't worth worrying about.

Alessandra tossed her gym bag in the trunk and drove out of the garage. She parked across the street from the Museum and pulled out Kleinermann's letter.

THANK YOU FOR THE PACKAGE. HE IS PREPARED TO PAY ANOTHER $10,000,000.00 IF A LIKE QUALITY PAINTING IS FOUND.

The "Package" had to be *The Naked Maja Dancing*. It was beginning to make sense now. Kleinermann's involvement explained everything; her hiring, the "missing" Picasso, even David and Jorge's arrest. No wonder Kleinermann had been so supportive of her. He used her to find the painting in order to steal it.

A tap on her window startled her. It was David. She rolled the window down. "Thank god it's you. Get in please."

David hesitated, but climbed in.

Alessandra reached into her purse and handed David the letter. "Read this."

He turned on the map light and began to read. She looked over his shoulder.

Alessandra glanced up in time to see Kleinermann enter the museum. If Sigi went to his office, would he notice the letter was missing? He disappeared into the building. Then the light in his office went on.

David looked at her. "You have anything more than this?"

"What more do I need?"

"This could be perfectly innocent."

"But you know it's not."

"Still I'd like something more," David said.

Alessandra searched her purse and pulled out the smashed matryoshka doll. Then she flashed the tiny object that had fallen out. "This was inside."

David turned the object over. "It looks like a transmitter of some kind."

"I think Kleinermann set this whole project up and enlisted the aid of his friend in the Hermitage. Then somehow, he made connections with the Kyritz guards and this is how he traced us."

"Let's say you're right. Then what?"

At the front door of the Museum, Kleinermann gestured to Shawn who pointed in the direction of Alessandra's car. Kleinermann put his cell phone to his ear.

"I think we're in trouble."

"Why?"

"I stole this letter from his desk." She pointed to the front door. "And I think he knows I took it."

"We should go to the police," David said. "I've done enough sleuthing for a lifetime."

"If we go to them now, he'll have time to move the Goya. We need to find it before it disappears."

"What do you mean we? *We* don't have to find anything."

"What if your painting is at the Yokahama offices waiting to be shipped out of the country?"

Suddenly, a hand reached into the open window and yanked the keys from the ignition. She turned toward the outside. Eckhard, the Castle guard pressed a gun at her temple. "Stay right there. Both of you."

He climbed in the back and handed her the keys. "Head across the Brooklyn Bridge. Your boss will be anxious to say goodbye one more time."

#

The Red Hook Container Terminal, with its natural 40-foot depths, ideally accommodated fully loaded ships with deep drafts, just the type of vessels sailed by The Yokahama Overseas Services, Ltd. company. Their offices took up an entire three story building on the docks of the terminal.

Alessandra drove her *Nissan* onto a freight elevator of the Company. It quickly whisked the vehicle up to the third floor on the outside of the building. Eckhard motioned for Alessandra and David to get out of the car. He searched them and removed a cell phone from David. He punched numbers into a security pad on the wall of the elevator.

Thick steel doors swung open into a high tech, modernistic loft space. Van Gogh's *Olive Trees*, Klimt's *Beechwood* and *The Naked Maja Dancing* hung unframed on the wall directly in front of them.

Eckhard shoved Alessandra and David forward. He stepped back into the elevator and the steel doors rumbled shut behind them.

Alessandra's stomach churned. "I'm sorry I got you into this," she said.

"It was me that you got you into it in the first place."

Alessandra inspected the paintings. "Ah, *mi dios.*"

"How the hell did they get here?" David asked.

Kleinermann, carrying Alessandra's ice axe, burst into the room. "Lovely, aren't they?"

"How could I have been so blind?" Alessandra said.

"I did try to protect you, but you got too nosy." Kleinermann waved the axe. "You also got careless. Even so, I have enjoyed our time together. You have been very useful, so don't take this personally."

David lunged at Kleinermann who dodged him and brandished the axe.

David backed off. "Well, *I* take it personally. That painting has been my in family's private possession for centuries."

"And because of that, it is so much more valuable."

"You won't get away with this," Alessandra snapped.

"How trite. You have been seeing too many bad American movies." Kleinermann waved a hand toward the paintings. "As you can plainly see, I am getting away with it. But I know how attached you've become to them . . .," he pointed at David "and to him, so you probably won't mind taking a little trip together. You'll even get to go diving with each other again."

Kleinermann nodded toward a security camera and the elevator doors opened again. "Yoshiro will take good care of you."

A Japanese man with an automatic weapon came forward and hustled Alessandra and David inside the *Nissan*. He popped the trunk and checked inside. He opened the gym bag and peered in. He looked at Kleinermann and shook his head. Kleinermann threw the ice axe in the trunk. Then, Yoshiro wrapped the car with four large nylon hoisting straps and directed a crane to lower a cable.

#

Alessandra peered out the window of their car. The *Nissan* swung from a crane three stories above the dock, hovering over a container ship.

David pointed toward two men who carried three large cartons, big enough to contain the stolen paintings, onto the ship. Yoshiro rushed over to the two men and guided them onto the bridge where the Captain waited.

"Your boss obviously had been planning this a long time. You had no way of knowing," David said.

The crane lowered the *Nissan* onto the ship's deck between two containers. Inside the car, they could hear another crate being lowered over the roof. Alessandra pulled back the moon roof cover and instinctively ducked as she saw a crate crash down on them.

The roof of the *Nissan* buckled and began to give way. The car was cast into darkness.

"Lower your seat back," David yelled as he lowered his. "Now!"

She frantically lowered the back of her seat. The crunching continued until the side air bags inflated shoving David and Alessandra together. She felt a sharp pain in her neck and became disoriented. The car seemed to spin.

She heard David ask, "Are you alright?" But she couldn't answer.

The crunching had stopped. She tried to move her mouth, but nothing came out. Her face was covered by the air bag. She was suffocating. She reached out to where David's voice was coming from. An arm. She squeezed.

"Can you speak?" David asked.

Alessandra couldn't breathe and was about to lose consciousness when she felt the air bag pulled aside. She could breathe again. She helped push the bag off of her. "Oh, *mi dios.*"

Alessandra tried to move her neck. It hurt but she could turn side to side. She reached for the light switch by the rear passenger seat. It worked. Blood dripped from David's nose. She wiped it with the side of her sleeve. "You look a mess."

"Well, you don't look so hot yourself."

Alessandra smiled.

"I apologize for suspecting you," David said.

"Apology accepted, but I should never have called you tonight."

"Wouldn't have missed it for the world." David pulled her to him. "Thank you."

"For what?"

"For Palau. For Berlin. For the Schloss. But most of all, thank you for Paris. We'll always have Paris."

"You've seen *Casablanca* once too often," Alessandra said. "And you make it sound like this is the end."

"Look around. Got any Great Escape plans?"

Alessandra surveyed the situation. "Yes. I do." She struggled to flip around so her feet faced the rear window which had partially given way from the pressure of the crate above. The glass in the window had shattered but there was still large pieces that stuck to the edges. She put her feet to the window and pushed. Most of the remaining glass burst onto the trunk of the car.

"Now what?" David asked.

"Now we see what's outside," Alessandra said. She slithered into the opening which creaked and began to close around her. Then the car light went out. She was trapped and couldn't see.

Chapter 33

As he watched the Kyoto Dragon steam off, Kleinermann felt a pang of remorse. Not for the Jew, the world was better off without them. Exterminating David was doing the world a service, but doing away with such a lovely specimen as Alessandra Santana was like burning a classic work of art. Unforgivable, but in this case, necessary. She knew too much.

Kleinermann congratulated himself. She had served her purpose well. It was brilliant to bring her to New York and had worked out better than even he imagined.

Contrary to popular myth, the art world was not populated by Indiana Jones types, but rather meek, bookish people who only took risks in their published papers, and even then cautiously.

So when his Japanese patron made him an offer he couldn't refuse, he needed someone with burning ambition and who would take risks most mortals, let alone artsy types, wouldn't. According to his sources, the Spanish beauty would fit the bill nicely. Indeed she had.

His initial plan was to blame her for the missing Picasso, perhaps she'd spend some time in jail, but that would have been the extent of it. He really hadn't expected her to discover *The Naked Maja Dancing.* That was a bonus, but unfortunately it also let her discover his scheme. If she only had accepted her role, but no, she had to meddle. Even so, for a brief moment he toyed with making her a deal, but his better judgment intervened. She knew too much and wasn't the kind to cut deals. She had to be eliminated.

If all went according to plan, and he had no doubt it would, the car, with Alessandra and David in it, would soon be dumped far out to sea. No trace would ever be found. There would be a brief and obligatory investigation. Perhaps the news media would nose around as well. He would express great concern for her welfare but drop the hint that she was despondent over being suspected for the missing paintings.

Eventually, everyone would come to the only logical conclusion. The shame of her "crimes" caused her to go into hiding or, better yet, commit suicide. As for David, obviously she was involved with his disappearance. Either she or her co-conspirators, and there were always co-conspirators, murdered him. The plan was perfect.

When the Kyoto Dragon became a speck on the horizon, he put Alessandra's fate out of his mind, and turned his attention to his upcoming meeting with the Board of Directors scheduled for the next afternoon. It was time to inform the Board of his retirement plans. He would say he felt responsible for the hire of Alessandra and would take the blame for the shame it brought on the Metropolitan Museum. Of course, in return for falling on his sword he expected a large severance package.

He would stay on until a suitable replacement had been found and trained. Then he'd head for South America where his friends were waiting. His friends had already purchased a magnificent villa in an exclusive compound for him. He had promised to pay them back when he could unload his interest in the casino. Fortunately, they were willing to wait.

From his point of view, all was well. Not as well as originally planned, but one had to be flexible in life and his idea for the severance package would help make up for the ten million he had to give back to Yokahama. He tried to quell his excitement of what the future was soon to bring.

#

Alessandra was in a frenzy. She was being crushed and couldn't move. She had to get out fast, but felt disoriented in the dark. She groped for a handhold. Shards of glass around the window frame ripped into her fingers. She ignored the pain, grabbed the frame and with all her strength, pulled herself free onto the trunk of the car. The crate continued to crush down onto the *Nissan*. Her stomach turned with each crunching sound.

"Alessandra?"

"Still here," Alessandra said.

"You okay?"

No, she was not okay. She was sealed inside a steel tomb on what she sensed was now a moving ship, going God knows where.

She reached up to see how much space there was between herself and the massive container pressing down onto the car. Perilously close. A few more inches and she was doomed. Was there space to fall off the trunk? She reached out and felt the adjacent container to the side. No room. She reached behind the trunk. Same result. She was trapped with nowhere to go.

Alessandra said a silent prayer while she quietly awaited her fate. And then, miraculously the crunching stopped. She felt above her and could touch the crate barely inches from her head. What had made it stop?

"Alessandra?" David shouted. "Are you hurt?"

She normally could control her claustrophobia but in a tight space like this without light, she was near panic. She needed light quickly. "Can you see if the other back seat light will work?"

"I already tried, but nothing happened. You keep a spare flashlight in the car?"

"Check the glove compartment." Alessandra took deep breaths to calm herself.

Moments later a faint light shone her way. "You need to change batteries more often," David said.

The faint light helped her fight off the sense of dread she felt. "Next time I anticipate a kidnapping, I'll be sure to check," Alessandra said.

David chuckled.

Good. Keep it light, she told herself. She reached her hand through the small opening in the rear window. "Can you hand me the torch?"

"What happened to your hand? There's blood all over it," David said.

"Just give me the light." She nabbed the proffered light and banged it against her palm. The light shone a bit brighter, enough to see her surroundings. She wiped her hand on her sweater and surveyed the damage.

The crate above had collapsed the roof about half the distance between the trunk and the top of the car before it snagged itself onto a protruding hinge of the rear adjoining crate. Hopefully it would hold. But the rear window opening of the *Nissan* was now too small for anyone to crawl through. She was cut off from David.

Alessandra shone the light around the car. The weight of the crate had buckled the frame of the car so the sides were touching the adjacent containers. As she had feared, they were sealed in. She struggled to calm her fear of tight places. Then she heard a faint ring. She put her ear to the trunk. "*Ai caramba.* It's my watch."

"Watch?"

"It's the cell phone on the watch. I forgot I left it in my gym bag. Push the trunk release."

"Where is it?"

Alessandra reached through the opening. "It's to the left of the steering wheel. Take the light."

Alessandra heard the trunk release but it didn't move. It couldn't. She was lying on top of it. "Drop down the rear seat and see if you can crawl into the trunk."

"Shit," David shouted. "The light burned out."

The phone stopped ringing.

"Great. Now, how am I going to find it?" David asked.

Alessandra squelched a sarcastic response. She had no time for this. At least before there was some light, now in the dark, the walls figuratively were closing around her. She took a deep breath. "Just reach into the trunk and see if you can locate my gym bag."

She could hear David push things around in the trunk. Hurry up.

The phone rang again.

Alessandra felt herself losing control. "It's in the side pocket," she shouted.

"Found it," David said. "Put out your hand."

"Just answer the phone."

"I don't know how."

"Push any button you can feel."

The ringing stopped again.

#

At JFK Airport, Jorge, cell phone to his ear, pushed his way past slow moving passengers in the baggage area. He knew it was late, but he was hoping she'd still be up. Before he could leave a message, he spied his luggage coming off the conveyer belt. He hurried over to nab it before it went around again. He'd call Alessandra back later.

He collected his bags and headed for the taxi line.

Outside JFK airport, Jorge was at the front of the line, about to get in a taxi when he heard someone shout, "Jorge!"

Jorge wheeled and searched for a familiar face.

Gregor broke out of line. "It's me. Gregor."

Jorge looked over the suit and tie Gregor wore.

"I didn't recognize you."

"Are you going to the city?"

Jorge opened the taxi door wide. "Get in."

"You look nice and tanned. Where are you coming from?" Gregor asked.

"Miami. Just saw a new client. Another Holocaust victim. I called Alessandra to see if she was interested in helping me locate the painting."

"Was she?"

"I don't know," Jorge said. "She didn't answer her phone. I assume she turned it off for the night."

"She never shuts it off," Gregor said. "Maybe she was in a meeting."

Jorge looked at his watch. "At midnight?" He redialed her number.

"Hello?" Alessandra's voice answered.

"*Chica*. How are you?"

"I don't have time to talk. I'm on a boat with . . and pretty soon we'll be . . . of range."

"You're fading out."

"Can you hear me now?"

Jorge could barely hear. Alessandra's voice kept cutting in and out.

"David . . . I . . . napped . . . Yokahama . . . hear me?

"Nap? What are you talking about?"

"Call . . . pol . . ."

"Alessandra. Are you there? Answer me."

Jorge looked at the screen. *Call ended.* He tried to call again. He heard it ring and then the voice mail message came on.

"You have reached the voice mail of Alessandra Santana. Leave a message and I'll call you back."

"It's Jorge again. I need to talk to you about a new client in Florida. Can you meet with them? And, oh, have a nice nap."

#

Alessandra rolled to her side along the edge of the car's trunk and squeezed as close to the adjacent container as she could. "Try to kick open the trunk now."

"Why?"

"What is it with Jewish men, can't you just—"

"Okay. Okay. "

The trunk lid opened enough for Alessandra to see its light. David's leg appeared holding up the trunk. She grabbed onto his limb, tumbled into the trunk and onto him.

Alessandra peered at her watch in the dim light and tried calling back. Nothing. She tried "911." Nothing. "I'm afraid we're out of range."

David wrapped his arms around her. "In case we don't make it, I need to tell you something."

She felt for his face. "Of course we'll make it. We have Kleinermann just where we want him."

David held her hand in his. "I've been thinking."

"About? "

David kissed her sweetly. "I wish we were back in Paris."

She fell onto her back. They laid there in silence until she glanced over at him. The shadows from the trunk light gave him a film noir glow.

Alessandra kissed him hard, her eyes wet with emotion. "We've got to find a way out of here."

"Do you think Jorge heard you?"

"I don't know. But we can't afford to do nothing in hopes the cavalry arrives." Alessandra pushed the trunk up higher so the light would illuminate more of their surroundings. She searched for some kind of opening between the crates. No luck. She fought off a sense of despair.

Chapter 34

In the taxi, Gregor asked what Alessandra had said.

"She said something about being on a ship with David, Jorge said. "I think she was going to Yokahama or something like that."

"You're sure they were on a ship?"

"I think so. But the connection was bad. "

Gregor grabbed his own cell phone and dialed.

"What's up?" Jorge asked.

Gregor lifted a finger as if to say, "Just a minute." He spoke into the phone. "Abi? It's me, Gregor. I think our man just made a mistake. Meet me at the Midtown Heliport. Tell the Coast Guard to check for any boats owned by the Yokahama Overseas Shipping Company that just left port."

Gregor tapped on the driver's window. He flashed his Interpol ID. "Midtown Heliport and hurry, please." He turned to Jorge. "We've been investigating the Yokahama Shipping Company for months."

"We?"

Gregor showed his ID to Jorge. "Sorry I couldn't tell you before, but I was undercover. At one time we suspected Alessandra might be involved. Recently, we tapped the shipping company's phones and heard some suspicious conversations with Alessandra's boss, Kleinermann. But he's been very clever. Until now."

"Mind if I tag along?"

"Sorry, too dangerous."

"Afghanistan was dangerous. Iraq was dangerous." Jorge grinned. "This. This is just a cruise."

Gregor looked at Jorge, smiled and patted him on the back. "Ah hell. Why not. You've been involved since the beginning. Consider yourself an embedded reporter. Welcome aboard."

#

Hours passed before the Coast Guard helicopter hovered over the Midtown Heliport. Gregor waved at Abigail Shimoro as she jumped down and zipped up her "FBI" jacket. He and Jorge made their way to the foot of the chopper.

"Sorry it took so long, but it was difficult to rouse the Coast Guard Commander at this time of night," Abigail said. "He wasn't at home and wasn't too pleased when I told him his wife suggested I call his cell. I think he was enjoying a night out with the boys and was hoping not to be disturbed. Now he's going to have to explain who 'Abi' was." She laughed. "He was reluctant to order this raid against the Shipping Company vessel. Apparently they have clout. So I told him the best agent at Interpol said it was a 'slam dunk.'" She gave Gregor a stern look, then smiled. "Anyway, my ass is on the line, so you better be right."

Gregor grinned and patted her on the butt. "Couldn't happen to a better ass."

She playfully waved his hand away. She looked at Jorge. "Who's he?"

"It's okay. He's a war correspondent I've worked with before."

Jorge showed a full set of teeth. His eyes betrayed his obvious lust for the young Japanese-American agent.

Abigail shook Jorge's hand. "Don't get any ideas." She pointed to her buttocks. "Only special agents get to touch that."

Jorge's eyes crinkled. "Where do I sign up?"

Abigail pointed to the pilot. "This is John O'Malley. He's with the Coast Guard."

Gregor and Jorge waved and squeezed into the tight back seats. Abigail sat in front.

O'Malley revved up the engines and lifted off. He raised his voice over the din of the chopper. "The Yokahama Overseas Shipping Company has two ships that left port within the last six hours. One is only just leaving the harbor now and is about to be boarded by the Guard. The other is thirty miles out and will be intercepted by our nearest ship in about twenty minutes or so."

"If Alessandra was on the one in the harbor, she would still have been in range of a cell tower," Gregor said. "I assume she would have called Jorge back. My guess is she's on the one thirty miles out."

O'Malley called on his headset. "Get me a fix on the Kyoto Dragon." He waited and a few moments later acknowledged the location. "Okay. Got it."

Gregor touched Abigail on the arm and shouted, "Can you get a warrant to search Kleinermann's apartment? And while you're at it, get a warrant to search the offices of our Yakuza friends. There's probably nothing there, but it can't hurt."

Abigail nodded and picked up the helicopter's radio. "Connect me to the assistant Attorney General on duty."

#

On board the Kyoto Dragon a crane lifted the container off the roof of the *Nissan*. Then it swung back and lifted the car over toward the port side of the ship.

Inside the trunk, Alessandra pulled on the emergency release and popped the trunk open. She grabbed the ice axe and peered out.

The sun was just beginning to sprinkle daylight on the water. More than one hundred feet down she could make out the waves of the Atlantic splashing against the side of the ship. "We have to jump."

David looked at the steel deck at least thirty feet below. "You crazy. This is not a movie and you're not Butch Cassidy. We jump we die."

"If we don't jump, we drown"

"I get your point." David grabbed her hand and just as the car started to swing out over the side, they jumped.

#

O'Malley pointed to his radar screen. "There are four ships in the area where the Kyoto Dragon should be. We'll have to check them all."

Gregor checked the magazine on his M9 Beretta semi-automatic pistol and snapped it back in place. Abigail adjusted the scope on her H-S Precision Pro-Series 2000 rifle.

Jorge squirmed in his seat. "Holy mother of god!" he exclaimed. "You guys are for real."

"You want in on the action?" Gregor reached behind his back and produced another Beretta.

Jorge eyes bulged. "The only thing this 'Rican shoots is craps. And I'm not very good at it." He waved the gun away.

A ship came into view. O'Malley took the helicopter down for a closer look.

#

Alessandra's ice axe skidded across the steel surface as she thudded onto the deck of the ship. A sharp bolt of pain rocketed from her leg throughout her body. She groaned.

David landed onto a canvas covered piece of cargo which softened his fall. Behind him the *Nissan* splashed into the sea.

He rolled to his side and off the cargo. "You okay?"

The crane hovered overhead. Its heavy metal hook plummeted toward Alessandra. She dove in agony toward the cargo David had landed on. The hook slammed against the deck a mere foot from where she had been. She grabbed her calf. "I think I've broken my leg."

David rushed toward Alessandra. The hook lifted up and swung toward him. Instantly it plunged downward and grazed his left shoulder as he jumped to one side. Blood splattered onto the deck and poured down his arm. His arm felt numb, but David felt no pain. He spied Yoshiro grinning as he operated the crane.

Again the hook swung back toward him. David ducked as it swung by. He needed to find cover fast. He looked for a safe place when he glimpsed the sheen of the ice axe. He picked it up and turned menacingly toward the crane. He started toward Yoshiro. David wasn't sure what he was going to do, but he'd had it.

Yoshiro smirked and jumped from the crane onto the deck with a gun aimed at David. He shouted what sounded like a Japanese expletive.

A huge wave crashed against the side of the boat causing Yoshiro to fall. David wobbled and tried to keep his balance. He saw Alessandra hurtling toward the edge. He lunged for her and grabbed her injured leg just before she slipped completely over the side. She dangled in the air upside down.

A bullet whizzed by David's head.

"*Mierda.* My leg."

David dropped the axe, reached for Alessandra's other leg and pulled her safely back on board. He hit the ground beside her as a second bullet clanged onto the deck beside them.

The ice axe lay inches away. David reached for it just as another wave hit. The axe skidded toward the side of the ship and teetered on the edge. With all his might David stretched his injured arm and managed to snag it before yet another bullet screamed by. His arm throbbed as he rose to his knees and turned to face Yoshiro, who was taking dead aim at him.

The chop, chop, chop of a helicopter suddenly roared into earshot. A distracted Yoshiro looked up as the copter closed in. David ignored the sound and with a motion that belied his inexperience, he flipped the ice axe toward Yoshiro. The pick end of the axe slammed into Yoshiro's shoulder and sent him sprawling to the deck.

Yoshiro's gun flew from his hand and landed yards away. With the axe still embedded in his shoulder, he battled to his feet and scrambled after his weapon.

David dove and tackled Yoshiro just as the henchman reached the gun. They hit the steel plated deck hard, driving the axe deeper into Yoshiro's shoulder who grimaced in pain. The gun went off.

David cried out. Blood gushed from his left foot.

Yoshiro pulled the axe free from his shoulder. He got to his knees, grabbed gun and leveled it inches from David's temple. "Sayonara."

Alessandra had watched horrified. She ignored her pain and crawled toward both men. She managed to sneak up behind Yoshiro and dug her nails deep into the shoulder where the axe had been.

Yoshiro threw her off. He turned toward her and aimed his pistol at her head.

#

In the helicopter, Abigail put the cross hairs of the scope on Yoshiro and pulled the trigger. The .306 shell ripped into Yoshiro's good shoulder and knocked him to the ground. He dropped the gun. Blood oozed from the bullet hole.

Jorge snapped photos of the scene.

Yoshiro reached for his pistol. On all fours, David scrambled toward him and snatched the gun before Yoshiro could reach it. David trembled and pointed the gun at Yoshiro. "I ought to blow your fucking brains out."

Abigail picked up a bull horn. "Drop all your weapons and tell the Captain to heave to." She shouted in Japanese.

A Coast Guard ship appeared on the horizon closing fast.

The Kyoto Dragon slowed. The helicopter hovered a few feet over the ship. Gregor jumped down with Jorge right behind. They headed for Alessandra. Abigail stayed in the chopper, her rifle poised.

Gregor rushed to Alessandra's side as she tried to get up. She put her arms on Gregor's shoulders and stood on one leg.

A smile of relief crossed Alessandra's face. "Glad you could join us, we were getting a little bit bored."

"If we had gotten here a few minutes later, you would have been a little bit dead," Jorge said as he snapped photos of the scene.

Alessandra glanced at the "Interpol" written on the back of Gregor's jacket.

"I should have guessed."

Jorge snapped some more photos, then helped David to his feet.

Alessandra pointed to the blood oozing from David's foot.

"I'll live." David gestured toward the Coast Guard ship which had pulled alongside. "Maybe they'll have a band aid aboard."

With machine guns trained on the Kyoto Dragon, crewmen from the Coast Guard cutter flung ropes onto the Japanese ship. Gregor secured them.

Soon the Kyoto Dragon was swarming with armed Coast Guard servicemen. Two medics rushed over to attend to David's foot.

Alessandra pointed toward the bridge. "They took some large cartons in there. I think that's where you'll find our paintings."

Gregor drew his gun and gestured for the Coast Guard servicemen to follow him up the gangway. Jorge chased after them, his camera ready.

Chapter 35

The board room of the Metropolitan Museum was lined with portraits of its ten former Directors. The most recent, Harold Portebello smiled down on the room. But it was Timothy Ravelle whom Kleinermann admired the most. For it was Ravelle whom he modeled himself after.

During Ravelle's term as Director, he had acquired many works of art with a questionable provenance. It was apparent to Kleinermann that Ravelle turned a blind eye to the true origins of any piece if it meant the Met could acquire it. And he usually did it with the full blessing of the Board of Directors, many of whom were the scions of New York society and politics. Of the thirty five Board members, most of the group had been handpicked by mega billionaire and noted philanthropist, Roger Masters, the unofficial king maker on the Board.

During his initial interview for the job, Kleinermann was bluntly asked about his plans for acquiring major new pieces for the Museum. At first, Kleinermann was wary. Was this a trick question? As the former Art Director for the Kunsthalle Museum, Kleinermann had acquired many questionable pieces and then traded them to American Museums, thereby adding a layer of protection to the works of art. In turn, the Kunsthalle would get a piece of equally valuable art with a pristine provenance. Both museums would benefit. Kleinermann intended to use this scheme if hired at the Met. But would the Board of the Met go along? Kleinermann had approached the subject delicately. "What if I know of an important work of art that has an unprovable provenance but comes from a reliable source?"

"How important is the piece?" Masters had responded.

Kleinermann knew then he had a kindred soul. Without saying it out loud, he had received permission to bend the rules and bend he did.

Kleinermann now sat at the head of a long table where a select group of five men and two women waited eagerly for him to begin. He already had informed Masters of his decision to retire and was indeed told he would receive a generous severance package.

He confidently strode to a lectern where he had placed his prepared notes. He welcomed each Board member personally, then cleared his throat and began.

"As you know, great shame has been cast upon this Institution by a person I hired, Alessandra Santana. Twice now she has been associated with stolen paintings. While there has as yet been no criminal trial to convict her, even the appearance of malfeasance such as this was too much for us to bear and therefore I was directed to terminate her employ. I take full responsibility for what has happened and therefore I hereby submit my resignation. It will do no good to try and convince me to stay. I'm not getting any younger and I think it's time for a new, fresh face to lead this great institution."

Suddenly the doors burst open. Alessandra, a cast on her right leg, swung through on crutches. David, with the aid of a cane, followed. He too wore a walking cast albeit on his left foot. Under his free arm, he carried *The Naked Maja Dancing*. Jorge came right behind carrying the Picasso Alessandra was originally suspected of stealing.

Alessandra stared into Kleinermann's widened icy blue eyes, eyes that had never before shown emotion. He prided himself in that. Now his face twitched like a rabbit's body when cornered by a fox.

She pointed to the paintings David and Jorge held upright. "Did you forget these when you left the ship?"

Kleinermann eyes darted around the room.

Obviously startled by the intrusion, the entire Board focused first on Alessandra and then Kleinermann. The room went silent as everyone waited for Kleinermann's response.

How had she escaped? It was impossible for her to be alive. Kleinermann was caught off guard. He had been so sure of her ultimate demise, he had no contingency plan. He struggled to formulate an answer but before he could, Masters broke the silence.

"Seigfreid," Masters said in a stern, paternal voice, "do you have anything to say?"

What could he say? *It was all a mistake.* Hardly. The evidence was right in front of them. Kleinermann's eyes cut from Masters to Alessandra and then to the door. He sneered at Alessandra and bolted for the door.

Alessandra jutted out a crutch. He stumbled over it and fell on his face.

"I hope you didn't mind taking a little trip," Jorge said.

Kleinermann scrambled to his feet and was confronted by Abigail and Gregor who blocked his way. A sense of dread overcame him. His knees buckled when he saw Abigail's weapon aimed squarely between his eyes.

Abigail spun Kleinermann around. "You're under arrest for kidnapping, dealing in stolen art and anything else we can throw at you. You have the right to remain silent." She cuffed Kleinermann and pushed him out the door.

Jorge blew Kleinermann a kiss and waved goodbye.

Alessandra motioned to Jorge and he displayed the Picasso on an easel. She faced the Board who collectively had sat wide-eyed while the melee took place.

"You can tell the French they can pick up their Picasso anytime. Tell them the airline finally located their luggage and is sorry for the delay." Inwardly she delighted in the upcoming embarrassment for the French when they tried to explain away the other "original" of *Nature Morte a la Charlotte* currently hanging in the Pompidou. She squelched a grin, turned and hobbled out.

David placed *The Naked Maja Dancing* on the table. "As you can see, I made a terrible mistake. But I apologized to Ms. Santana. Now, I believe it's your turn." He glanced at Jorge who smiled, put his arm around David and with the Goya in hand, they left as a stunned group of seven people looked on in puzzlement.

Alessandra was waiting outside. She helped David slip *The Naked Maja Dancing* into a velvet lined case.

"Now what?" David asked.

"Now we go pay a visit to David's mother."

Chapter 36

Alessandra called Ludwig to find out if he had time to remount the painting at Devorah's apartment. Assured he "would take the time," she turned to David. "We'll need an hour or so."

"Don't worry. It's my mom's day to play Mahjong."

An hour later David entered his mother's apartment. He wanted to make sure she wasn't home before he signaled Jorge, Ludwig and Alessandra to come on up.

"Mom, you home?" He checked the whole apartment. No sign of and her and no food cooking on the stove. Surely, she was gone. He went to the window and waved.

Minutes later Ludwig and Alessandra expertly removed the forged *Naked Maja Dancing* from its frame and replaced it with the real one. Jorge photographed everything. Alessandra stood back. "Do you think she'll notice the switch?"

"I never told her about the forgery so I doubt it," David said.

"Even I didn't spot it," Ludwig said. He tucked the forgery under his arm and left.

David turned to Jorge. "Please be discreet when you put this in your book."

"Perhaps you should tell her before the book is published," Alessandra offered.

"Yeah, I guess she'll be able to handle it," David said. "She's a tough woman."

"Can I photograph the apartment?" Jorge asked.

"Sure," David said, "but if you don't mind, I'd like to be here with just Alessandra and my mom when she comes home. You can interview her later."

Jorge looked disappointed.

"She's never met you and it's kind of a private moment. Please."

Alessandra motioned to David to join her in the kitchen. "Jorge wants me to go to Miami and meet with some clients about a new claim."

"Are you going?" David put on a pot of coffee.

"Does it matter to you?"

"Remember what I told you in Paris?"

"That you were too old?"

"Maybe I was too hasty."

Jorge popped his head in the door. "Señorita. He is too old for you. Now me—"

Alessandra gently pushed Jorge toward the door. "Now you, you will mind your own business and leave." She pecked him on the cheek. "*Por favor?*"

Jorge looked at David and then her. "A man has to try, no?" He grinned and left the apartment.

David carried some coffee cups into the livingroom. Alessandra followed and settled onto the couch next to David.

"And the Catholic/Jewish thing?"

"My mother won't like it,—"

"This is not about your mother. It's what you care about that's important. Is my being Catholic okay with you?"

"It's not that simple."

"I need to know."

David took her hand.

Alessandra pulled away. "I'm thinking of going back to Spain."

"I don't want to lose you."

Alessandra narrowed her eyes. "Then you'll have to decide."

"I'm all she has."

A key rattled in the door. Devorah shuffled into the kitchen, carrying grocery bags. David crept up and put his arms around her.

Devorah grabbed her heart. "You scared me. What are you doing here?"

Alessandra leaned on one crutch in the doorway

"Alessandra wanted to know if you were happy with the framing."

Devorah marched to the painting and turned her head to one side. "I'm happy." She looked back at Alessandra and then the painting as though she were comparing the two.

Alessandra's cell phone watch rang. She excused herself and hobbled into the kitchen. Devorah's gaze followed Alessandra until she was out of sight. "Nice *tsitskas.*"

"Mom!"

"Nice tush too."

"Mom!"

"What?" Devorah smiled mischievously.

Alessandra hopped back into the living room on one crutch and awkwardly carried a coffee pot in the free hand.

Devorah pointed to Alessandra's cast. "How's your foot?"

"Healing, but the crutches are a pain in the tush." She grinned, put the pot down and headed back to the kitchen. "And thanks for the compliment."

Devorah smiled as she filled the cups.

Alessandra removed the ring from her finger. "And I believe this belongs to you also."

Devorah hesitantly reached for it. She glanced at David.

"Yeah, mom. It's real." David put his arm around Alessandra. "We found Artie's plane and there it was."

Devorah touched the photo of the family in front of the Maja. She turned to hide her tears. Alessandra put an arm around her.

David looked at Alessandra. "Do you have any idea of what the painting's worth?"

"Priceless."

"The painting is not for sale. Ever," Devorah said.

David turned to his mother. "I think we should table this discussion until later."

Devorah wagged a finger at him. "And I'm not leaving this neighborhood either. Period!"

"Perhaps it's time to go," Alessandra said. She took Devorah's hand. "You will need to be careful with such a valuable painting hanging here."

Devorah nodded. "I will give it some thought. And thank you again."

David helped Alessandra off the couch. She hobbled toward the door.

Devorah sat staring at the ring. David embraced her. She tugged at David's ear and whispered. "A *shayna* maidel. Too bad she's not Jewish."

David smiled, "I know mom. I know."

He walked Alessandra to the elevator and started to kiss her, but she pulled away.

She took his hand in hers. "You're a good man, but I'm not the woman for you."

David watched the elevator doors close behind her and went back into the apartment. He couldn't let it end like this. He marched into the living room. "Mom, we need to talk."

Devorah's eyes were closed and her head lay against the top of the couch.

David waited for signs of life. He thought he saw her left eye flicker and just as suddenly close again. He was sure she was awake and knew what was going on. He'd seen this before and when she was in this mood, she was unshakeable. Maybe today was not the day to confront his mother. He tiptoed out the door and quietly shut it behind him.

Chapter 37

Alessandra went to her apartment distraught. She was sure he was the man she had long sought. He had transformed himself from a reserved CPA to a man of action. All he had needed was a little prodding and the inner cave man came out. Their love making in Paris showed he had a tender side. And in a crisis he proved to have the strength of character she needed in a man. He was the total package.

But she felt that if they were ever going to get together, she'd have to convert and she wasn't ready to do that. Even if someday she decided to change religions, or even stop believing, she wanted to do it on her own terms. For now, she needed David to accept her as a Catholic.

Sleep eluded her. Alessandra's emotions ranged from frustration to anger and then forgiveness. In the end, she couldn't be a hypocrite. After all, if she herself had not been prepared to offend her father by marrying a Jew then she had to respect the fact that he would honor his mother's wishes that he marry one. Moreover, it showed the importance of family to him, a character trait she demanded in a man.

In hindsight, this made him even more desirable. She wished somehow things could work out but was certain they wouldn't. He would never defy his mother.

The next morning, after she had finally been able to doze off, she was awakened by an early call. In her still dreamy state, she hoped it was David. She just wanted to hear his voice again.

Instead, Alessandra was surprised to hear Roger Masters' secretary Steve on the line. He wondered whether "his boss" could come calling that afternoon. Steve was sorry about the early call but "wanted to make certain to make contact" before she left the house.

Her initial instinct was to have Steve tell Masters not to bother. What could he possibly say that she'd be interested in hearing? The Board had acted abominably and she was in no mood to talk to any of them.

On second thought, Alessandra considered Masters' influence which extended far beyond New York. The art world was a small society of wealthy individuals. A negative recommendation from one could throttle her career. Besides, what did she have to lose?

"When did he have in mind?"

"Right after the lunch hour, say around 2:00. Will that be convenient?"

Promptly at 2:00 pm, the doorbell rang. The king maker himself stood there with a broad grin. He took off his hat and extended his hand.

A wary Alessandra ushered him into her living room. Leaning on one crutch, she quickly mixed his favorite late afternoon "pick me up," a dry martini made with Plymouth gin.

Alessandra waited for his reaction.

Masters took a sip, his pinky in the air. He lifted the glass. "It's good of you to remember." He picked up the Plymouth bottle. "You know before World War II, it was oldest working gin distillery in England."

Alessandra nodded. Of course she knew. Soon after she came to work at the Museum, she saw him reprimand a caterer for failing to have Plymouth gin on hand for a party. She had never heard of that brand before, so she researched it and found out it had a small following of savvy Americans. From then on, she had a bottle in her bar. But Masters wasn't there to discuss Martinis. She painted on a smile and waited for him to get to the point.

Masters tapped his glass. "Aren't you joining me?"

"Normally I would, but I'm on medication for this." She raised her casted leg.

"You did a magnificent job recovering *The Naked Maja Dancing*. The Board feels badly about how they handled the entire matter."

"From the Board's perspective, I can see how it looked as though I was guilty. They really had no choice." Alessandra plunked herself down and waited for whatever else he had in mind.

Masters began to pace. "I'm so glad you feel that way."

She wasn't sure she really felt that way, but no sense complaining at this juncture. "One has to be a realist in these matters. The museum had to protect itself."

"Yes, yes. But now we need to move on. We are anxious to replace Kleinermann as soon as possible."

Ah! He was there to ask her advice about a new Director.

"I am here unofficially, so what I'm about to say can go no further than this room."

Masters was never anyplace "unofficially." When he spoke, it was as good as the Board speaking. Alessandra was in no mood to play his game. "I may be from another country, but I do know how things work in New York," Alessandra said as blandly as she could.

Masters put down his glass. "If, and I say if, I could persuade the Board, would you be interested in replacing Kleinermann?"

Alessandra was stunned. Director of the entire museum. And not just any museum. She had come to New York in the first place because the Metropolitan Museum of New York was considered to be the finest in the world.

"You needn't answer right away. But consider this. You will be the youngest Director ever."

Alessandra was flattered. Thomas Ravelle was only thirty five when he was appointed to head the Museum. She'd be five years younger. But Ravelle had run the New York Department of City Planning before he was offered the job, so he had administrative experience. Other than the small staff assigned to her as European Art Curator, she had none. But if she turned it down, would such an opportunity ever come her way again? Probably not. "I'm flattered . . ." Alessandra paused.

"Great. Then it's done. I'll inform the Board right away."

"I didn't finish," Alessandra said.

"I thought— "

"It's a great honor, but I have some unfinished business to deal with," Alessandra said. No way was she prepared for such a grand position and Masters knew it. He was offering her the position so the Board would look good in the press. Inevitably she'd fail and then Masters would "reluctantly" terminate her and hire someone with real stature in the art world. Alessandra struggled to rise.

Masters rushed over to help.

Alessandra waved him off.

"If you need a leave of absence, it can be arranged."

"No. I just don't think I'm ready."

"Would you at least consider staying on as acting Director? If we are fortunate enough to be offered *The Naked Maja Dancing*, you should be the one to be in charge."

So that was the real reason for the job offer. He expected her to influence Devorah to either sell or "permanently loan" the painting to the Met. "It would make a wonderful exhibit, wouldn't it?"

Masters nodded vigorously.

"People would come from all over the world," Alessandra said.

Masters smiled. "It would be a great coup for the Museum and we'd love for you to be part of it."

Alessandra gave him a serious look. "I will not attempt to influence the Edlesteins in any way as to what to do with the painting. It's part of their history. But should they decide not to keep it, I believe *The Naked Maja Dancing* belongs in the Prado, not the Met. And if I'm ever asked, that's what I'd tell them."

Masters narrowed his eyes. "Perhaps you're not quite ready for the job." He tipped his hat. "I wish you the best." He made a slight bow and was gone.

It was now clear it was time to go home to Spain. Her life in New York was finished. No job and no lover. There was nothing to hold her here. But first she had some unfinished business to take care of.

She called Jorge and thanked him for the offer. "I'm not ready for another adventure. Maybe another time, *mi amigo*."

Jorge was disappointed but understood. "We make a good team, *Chica*. I would love to work with you again."

Next, she tried calling Gregor but as usual, he didn't answer his phone. She left a message thanking him for saving her life and told him where she was headed. She left a number where she could be reached. "If you're ever in Penedès, stop by and we'll pour you a glass of our reserve wine."

Finally, she called the airlines to book the evening flight. She still had the whole afternoon before she had to leave for the airport. Good. That left her time to do something she hadn't done in months, seek spiritual guidance.

#

As Alessandra entered the main hall, dusty shades of light filtered through the stained glass windows of St. Patrick's Cathedral. The church was the largest gothic-style Catholic Cathedral in the United States, a monument to the church's power and wealth, and the seat of the Archbishop of New York. She never failed to be awed at the sheer size of the building, one large enough to accommodate 2400 seated worshipers and house 18 altars and shrines.

She headed for the marble Lady Chapel set off from the main altar. It was a quiet place to reflect and worship. She knelt and bowed her head. Her world had changed in just a few short weeks. She glanced up at the ornate ceiling hundreds of feet above her. *Do you hear me God? Can you help me answer a question that has tormented me since my father revealed our family's past? Am I still a Catholic?*

A powerful surge went through her. For a moment she thought God had sent a message, but in reality it was her body reacting to what had been on her mind for some time. *Do I believe? Is there really a God?*

Learning about Devorah's experience with the Nazis and her own Jewish roots had caused Alessandra to question her long held beliefs. If there was a God, how could he have allowed the Jews to be evicted from Spain solely because of their religious practices? And the Holocaust? And Slovenia, Somalia and now Iraq? All this killing in the name of religion. And why so many religions? If there was only one God, why had so many different people claimed they knew God's will and established religions with opposing interpretations of that will? And then end up killing in His name?

She picked up a Bible and leafed through it. If this was the word of God, then what was the Old Testament? The Koran? And why did they need a new testament? If there was only one God, then why?

No answers came. Nor did she really expect one. She was beginning to realize she was questioning the very core of her beliefs and it made her feel uncomfortable. She leaned on her crutches, lit a candle and crossed herself. If she had offended God, perhaps he would forgive her. With a parting glance at the altar, she hobbled out.

Alessandra checked the time. Friday night dinner hour, Perfect. She hailed a taxi. "La Scala in Little Italy. And please wait while I go in. I'll only be a few minutes."

Alessandra came through the door of the restaurant and ambled over to the bar. David was seated next to the Master of Ceremonies. The diners slowly hushed.

"Good Evening Ladies and Gentlemen. I hope that you're sitting comfortably. At La Scala we don't need three tenors when we have one like David Edlestein. David's been around the world and in some deep water since last he was here. But he's back and ready to entertain you. So, a big round of applause, and a little kindness as he gets his lungs around Verdi."

The MC started to applaud. David limped with his walking cast to a stool and started to sing. At first he sang softly, but as the words became more loving, his voice became more passionate.

Alessandra was tempted to sing along with him, but a glance at her watch indicated she had to leave. She hastily scribbled a note with her home phone number in Penedès. *If you need anything more from me be sure to call this number as I will be getting a new cell phone number when I'm in Spain. If my father answers, he speaks fluent English so you can leave a message.*

She handed a five dollar bill to a waiter and told him to deliver the note after she had gone.

She hopped into the waiting taxi. "JFK. Iberian Airlines. I need to catch the 9:10 to Barcelona."

Chapter 38

Alessandra went home and reacquainted herself with her roots. She rode the hills surrounding the family estate. Sometimes she rode alone, sometimes with her father. As they rode, they talked. After days of conversations their relationship changed. She was no longer the child, but an equal. And he seemed to enjoy having a woman to share his thoughts with.

She reveled in her new found relationship with her father. They now had a bond that was unbreakable and it trickled over to her relationship with Uncle Carlos. But she still needed closure on the one issue that still troubled her. When the time was ripe, without rancor, she probed him again as to why he hadn't told her about her birthright earlier.

"I wanted to tell you about our past. It was clear to me you would have wanted to know, but your mother was adamant. What was I to do? Dishonor your mother whom I loved beyond life?"

After days of soul searching she came to realize that he had no choice. He had to honor her mother's wishes. All was forgiven.

During harvest, just as she had done as a child, Alessandra, her father and her uncle worked side by side with the workers picking the grapes. She enjoyed being a farmer again. It was hard work. Her nails broke, her hands were raw and lined with dirt. She came home every night exhausted but content.

Her skin turned dark from the sun and she felt an inner glow. She was happy to be away from all the politics of museum life. She even went into Barcelona and took up singing lessons again. Twice a week she'd make the trip into town. Life was rich and full, but there was a void. She tried not to think about it, but eventually she had to face up to it. She missed the action of the last few months of her life, but most of all, she missed David.

Three weeks had passed and every day she waited for the call that did not come. When she shared her feelings with her father, he gave her sage advice. "If it is meant to be it will happen. If not, then it wasn't meant to be." She decided it wasn't meant to be. She had to move on with her life and get David out of her mind. The way to do that was to go back to work.

Assuming it was still open, she was about ready to accept Jorge's offer, when Sr. Alvarez called from the Prado. Would she like to come to Madrid? He needed her assistance on a special project. "I guarantee you will be interested," he had said.

She wanted to press him on just what he had in mind but knew not to push him. He wouldn't have called unless he knew she'd be interested. Besides, life was getting a little boring in Penedès, and a break from her routine would be good. So, one week later she lunched with Pedro.

"I need you here to help me organize a new Goya exhibit. We have collected more than two hundred of his works. The Hermitage has agreed to lend us thirty of theirs, Wesleyan University also thirty, two museums in San Francisco fifty, even the Louvre has agreed to contribute."

"It sounds interesting," Alessandra said.

"*The Naked Maja Dancing* would finish the trilogy and be a great tribute to his life's work . . . and yours."

"Is that why you asked for my help?"

Sr. Alvarez frowned. "You owe me more respect than that. The offer is yours if you want it, with or without the *Dancing Maja*."

Alessandra took his hand. "I beg your forgiveness. You have been very kind to me. Without your help I would not have been able to get the *Maja* through customs. But I cannot impose on the Edlesteins. It would make it seem as though I helped them only to help myself."

Sr. Alvarez looked dejected. "I understand. Still it was worth a try."

"In your position I would have asked also. Can I have a few days to think it over?"

"Of course. By the way, your father called."

"About what?"

"He tells me you're singing again."

"What does this have to do with the Prado?"

"We are planning a special 'Opera at the Museum' evening to thank our donors who put up the money for the Goya exhibit. Your father asked Domingo if he'd be willing to donate his time. And of course his voice."

"And Placido agreed?"

"Actually no. He had a conflict. But he recommended Josh Groban with whom he once did a concert. Groban will be in

England performing with Sarah Brightman. And it so happens we have a common interest in the 'Find your light Foundation.' Our chairman who met him in Africa some years ago in connection with that NGO has already arranged it."

Alessandra looked suspiciously at Alvarez. "Did David have something to do with this?

"David? David who?"

Alessandra was not sure if Alvarez was lying. But she couldn't resist at least exploring the idea. "You know it's been a dream of mine to sing with Groban, but I didn't know he sang opera. "

"He doesn't. Will *Phantom of the Opera* do?"

Alessandra was stunned. This is not what she had in mind. She hadn't sung on stage in years. She was so stage struck the last time, she vowed never to do it again. And she doubted Groban would consent unless David was involved. But to have another opportunity to sing with one of the world's famous voices was intriguing. Nevertheless, she had to turn him down.

"Without proper training, my voice would drive away a goat."

Sr. Alvarez smiled. "I won't take no for an answer. I have already arranged for Dra. Caicedo to give you private voice lessons."

Caicedo was the best voice teacher in Spain. Alessandra embraced him. "Groban and Patricia Caicedo. It's too much."

"Then you'll do it?"

It was very tempting. "I'll think about it."

He nodded. "There is one thing."

Alessandra waited.

"We need to be ready in two months, by May 12."

"I'm sorry, it's too soon. I'm not going to make a fool of myself again." Her singing teacher had praised her "new" voice, but also said she needed another six months before she'd be ready to perform in front of an audience

"Why don't you at least visit Dra. Caicedo? Let her hear your voice and see what she says."

What could she lose? Alessandra shook Sr. Alvarez's hand. "It's an offer I can't afford to pass up."

#

Though David had gone back to work he couldn't get his mind off of Alessandra. He tried dating, but no one measured up.

Too bad she had left so abruptly. Maybe they could have worked things out.

He tried to put her out of his mind, but the news one morning made it impossible. Kleinermann had skipped bail. He wondered if Alessandra had heard. He located the number she had left and dialed.

#

Within the week, Alessandra had moved to Madrid. The Prado arranged for an apartment near the museum. Close enough to walk. The first morning, she worked on simple scales with Dra. Caicedo who seemed pleased with the quality of Alessandra's voice. They made arrangements for more serious work to follow.

Afterwards, since she was nearby, she dropped into the Museum to see how the plans were going for the exhibit. Before she knew it, she was deeply involved in both projects. She knew she had been manipulated, but silently thanked Sr. Alvarez and her father for doing so. She told Alvarez she was on board.

Every morning she studied with Dra. Caicedo and then hurried to her office in the Museum to spend the rest of the day making arrangements for the exhibit. She called museums, universities, shipping companies and insurance companies. She helped arrange insurance appraisers to visit the organizations which had agreed to lend their Goyas. She dispatched assistant curators around the world to assess the works and make final arrangements for shipping.

Invitations were ordered and sent to more than two thousand contributors and dignitaries. Five hundred accepted. The two months had almost elapsed before she realized it. The big date was only one week away and they still hadn't finished construction on the exhibition hall. The signs were ready, the art works had all arrived and were sitting in the bowels of the museum ready to be uncrated and hung, but nowhere to go. She barely slept and constantly exhorted the workers to hurry.

Four days before the big event, Sr. Alvarez asked her into his office. "Dra. Caicedo tells me you're coming along beautifully. Groban wants to sing three songs from the Phantom of the Opera. He wants to start with 'All I ask of you'."

Alessandra froze. Until now, it had all been a nice fantasy. She had envisioned the thrill of performing with a star like Josh Groban and the audience acclaim they would receive. But she had been foolish to accept.

She hadn't factored in the amount of effort it would take to put the exhibit together in so short a time. She was too exhausted to perform on stage and because of all the work left to do on the exhibit, it was only going to get worse. If she went on stage in such a state, she'd only embarrass herself and the Museum. "I'm sorry but I'm not going to be able to perform."

"But—"

Alessandra interrupted. "I'm going to call Dra. Caicedo and cancel any further lessons. You'll have to make other arrangements." She knew herself. If she let him speak, as guilty as she now felt, he'd convince her to do the concert. She had a hard time saying no, but she was determined. The exhibit came first.

"It will be difficult to replace you at this late date."

"I know, but I've thought of that. There are other sopranos on the program. You won't have any problem getting one of them to sing with Groban."

#

A special stage had been constructed for the concert which Alessandra had also supervised. She started to feel guilty about bowing out of her commitment to sing with Groban.

It was the first time in her life she had broken her word. Her father would be displeased and rightfully so. Besides, she always wanted to sing the melodies from Phantom. Coincidentally, she received a call from Groban that afternoon.

"I am calling to ask you to reconsider," Groban said.

She was shocked and excited. Too nervous to say anything. She waited for Josh to say more.

"Senora Santana. We have not been able to find a replacement for you. So, either you sing with this poor excuse for a singer or there is no Phantom."

"But I have no time to rehearse. I'll be an embarrassment."

"Then we will be an embarrassment together. I'm sure the patrons won't mind."

Before she could respond, he hung up. She started to dial but replaced the receiver. She realized she had no choice. She had made a commitment and should not have broken it. Somehow, she'd have to find the strength to perform. She'd do the best she could and with Groban there, she wouldn't be noticed anyway.

She came home to her apartment in Madrid. As always, the matryoshka doll welcomed her as it sat on the stand near the front door, next to the phone. She had placed the doll there so it would remind her of David. Tonight it made her realize she desperately wanted him to attend the performance, perhaps even agree to sing with her.

So, even though it was short notice, she wondered if he'd be interested in attending. Purely as a friend of course. She called David's home. When the answer machine came on, she panicked and hung up. Was she being too bold? Clearly this needed further thought.

#

David's call to Spain hadn't gone as planned. Alessandra's father had answered the phone. She was in Madrid, but he didn't want him to call her there. Upon hearing Manuel's reasoning, David agreed. But ever since, he had been awash in turmoil. Manuel had presented David with a dilemma and he didn't know if he could resolve it.

Weeks passed without resolution. Finally, on David's usual night to have dinner with his mother, he determined to address the issue.

Throughout dinner, David stared at *The Naked Maja Dancing*. He barely spoke. He was waiting for the appropriate time to bring it up. His mother beat him to it.

"What's wrong?" Devorah asked.

"Nothing." He was still trying to muster the courage to say what needed to be said.

"Forty five years I know you. A mother knows when something's wrong. Business?"

"No, mom."

"You're sick. You must have something and you are afraid to tell me."

He shook his head.

"A girl friend? You have a new girlfriend. *Mazeltov.*"

"No, mom. Nobody new."

"Old then. Someone I know?"

David looked at the painting. "Yes, mom. Someone you know."

"It's that *shiksa*, right?"

"Yeah mom, that *shiksa*." It was out in the open now.

"Is she back?"

"I have to see her."

"It's about Kleinermann isn't it?"

"You read about it?"

"You're surprised your mother reads?"

"I'm thinking of leaving this week."

Devorah looked hard at her son. "She's in Spain, right?"

David nodded. "And I won't ask her to convert."

Devorah raised an eyebrow.

"I want your approval."

"You're a big boy. You don't need my approval."

"But I want it."

"I think she's a wonderful person."

"But?"

"There is no 'but.'"

Devorah scooped up David's plates and headed for the kitchen.

David rose and blocked her way.

"It's not for me to decide," Devorah said. She looked sympathetically at him. "You must do what is right for you. I am not important."

David started to respond when his mother put up a hand. She pointed to *The Naked Maja Dancing*. "Reading about Kleinermann made me realize I need to make a decision about that. I'd like her advice."

Was this mother's way of finding common ground? Was she giving her approval without actually saying it out loud? He fished in his wallet for the note Alessandra had left at La Scala. "She's in Madrid now. Here's her father's number. He will tell you how to get in touch with her."

David kissed her goodbye and went home unsure of what to do. His mother's answers were too cryptic. The blinking light on the message machine resolved the issue for him. Caller Id indicated two overseas numbers had called but only one message was left. He hit the "message" button and listened. It made up his mind.

Chapter 39

On the evening of the fund raiser, everything was finally ready. Alessandra had arranged for one hundred twenty five of Goya's paintings, drawings, etchings and aquatints. *The Naked Maja* and *The Clothed Maja* were moved from their traditional place to the new exhibition hall. There they hung side by side drawing the eye of the visitor as they entered the room.

The exhibit, set to run for one month, had sold out. This evening was a special private reception hosted by the King and Queen of Spain, Juan Carlos and Sophia. One hundred patrons had put up ten thousand dollars each to attend.

The reception started promptly at 7:00pm. Alessandra was introduced to Juan Carlos and Sophia.

The King took Alessandra aside. "I wonder if you could give the Queen and me a private tour of the art before you open the doors to the public."

"After the concert, it would be my pleasure."

An hour later, the patrons filed into the concert area and took their seats. The Royal party took up the front row. Jorge, whom Alessandra had invited at the last minute, was seated right behind them.

In the back, a small elderly woman took her seat between a courtly gentleman and a priest. Devorah, Manuel and Father Carlos looked like they had been friends for a lifetime. They chatted amiably until the performance began.

After the lesser known singers warm up the audience, Alvarez comes on stage.

"And now for the moment you have all been waiting for. Senora Santana will perform a duet with a surprise guest."

Alessandra sauntered on stage dressed as Christine followed by the Phantom in a mask. Alessandra glowed with anticipation. Her dream of singing with Groban was about to come true.

The Phantom began to sing.

> *"No more talk of darkness,*
> *forget these wide-eyed fears;*

> *I'm here, nothing can harm you,*
> *my words will warm and calm you.*
> *Let me be your freedom,*
> *let daylight dry your tears;*
> *I'm here, with you, beside you,*
> *to guard you and to guide you."*

Alessandra took over.

> *"Say you'll love me ev'ry waking moment;*
> *turn my head with talk of summertime.*
> *Say you need me with you now and always;*
> *promise me that all you say is true,*
> *that's all I ask of you.*

The Phantom got on one knee and sang the final verse.

> *"Then say you'll share with me one love, one lifetime;*
> *let me lead you from your solitude."*

Alessandra was puzzled by the Phantom on his knees. The Phantom rose and took Alessandra in his arms as he continued singing.

> *"Say you need me with you, here beside you,*
> *anywhere you go, let me go too,*
> *that's all I ask of you."*

Alessandra was suspicious but kept up the act.

> *"Say you'll share with me one love, one lifetime.*
> *Say the word and I will follow you."*

The Phantom threw off his mask and swept her up in a long passionate kiss. At first she didn't recognize David but the kiss sealed it.

Alessandra embraced him and fervently returned the kiss. She gently pushed away so she could finish the duet. Her voice soared as she continued to sing.

> *"Say you love me..."*

David responded.

> *"You know I do."*

They were both caught up in the moment now as they sang together. Their voices cracked with emotion.

> *"Love me, that's all I ask of you.*
> *Anywhere you go let me go too*
> *Love me...*
> *that's all I ask of you."*

At the music faded out, the stage lovers appeared spent, fell into each other's arms and tumbled to the stage floor.

The audience seemed puzzled at first, but then applauded wildly. In the back of the room, Devorah, Manuel and Father Carlos stood and enthusiastically joined in the applause. Devorah then hugged Manuel and Carlos in turn.

Alessandra wiped a tear from her eye and turned to David. "How - -"

"Your father's quite the schemer. He plotted this from the very beginning. You almost blew it when you tried to withdraw."

As the applause grew louder, Alessandra and David, stood and took their bows.

"I never suspected," Alessandra said. She gently shoved David. "But how can I ever trust you?"

David looked puzzled. "You told me you could arrange for me to sing with Josh. Now I'll never get to sing with him."

David smiled slyly. "Well, at least I got him to call." He discreetly took the Goya ring out of his pocket. "And maybe this will restore your faith in me." He waved the ring at Alessandra and then placed it on her hand.

Alessandra was overwhelmed. She took a last bow and collected herself. "Come with me, I have to give the real King and Queen a private tour."

Alessandra escorted Juan Carlos and Sophia through a side door that led to the exhibit. David followed them into a dimly lit room.

Alessandra signaled to a workman. Lights flooded *The Naked Maja* and then *The Clothed Maja* while the rest of the room remained dim.

The King and Queen stood in front of the paintings. Suddenly light flooded *The Naked Maja Dancing* which hung gloriously alongside its siblings. A plaque next to it read:

> *Goya painted* The Naked Maja Dancing *shortly after he was warned by the Inquisitors never to paint another painting like* The Naked Maja. *It is of his mistress Leocadia Weiss-Zorillo and given to her as an expression of his love, but it came with an admonition that it was never to be exhibited in public. The painting was confiscated by the Nazis in return for which, Devorah Edlestein and her brother Arthur, proud descendants of*

Francisco Goya and Leocadia, were given passage on the Kindertransport to England. Arthur fought for the allies and gave his life so the Holocaust would never happen again. Devorah Edlestein donated this painting to honor all victims of prejudice and censorship.

Devorah's wish to have the painting hung side by side with the other *Majas* was not easy to arrange. Alessandra had to act fast and needed the Met's help to pack up the painting and ship it. It had arrived only that morning, but the staff had been alerted in advance and was prepared for its arrival.

King Juan Carlos gasped. He held the Queen close and stepped near the painting. "It takes one's breath away."

Queen Sophia stepped back from the paintings. "There is great similarity in the look of each model. Is it the same woman in all the paintings?"

"I was hoping they were, but the eyes are too different in all three paintings. It is possible of course that Goya disguised the face so the Inquisitors wouldn't discover the real model. I guess we'll never know. He left no notes."

She escorted the King and Queen out and asked David to join her after he changed his clothes. "I'll meet you in my dressing room." She pointed down a hall. "Third door on the right."

Alessandra went to her room and changed into an evening gown. The chain with the mezuzah, cross and key on it still hung on her neck as it had during the performance although it was hidden under her costume.

The jewelry she had set out for the evening sat on a dressing table. She had laid out two necklaces, on with diamonds and one with pearls. She was deciding what necklace went best with her black dress when there was a knock on the door. She hastened to open it.

Jorge stood there with a grin. He had a bottle of Champagne in one hand and a note in the other. "*Chica,* if I knew you could sing like that, I would have already proposed."

She smiled and welcomed him in.

He handed her the note. "A messenger gave this to me and asked me to pass it on to you."

She immediately recognized the writing and tore open the envelope.

Congratulations on a fine exhibit. If I couldn't have it, I admit The Naked Maja Dancing belongs here in the Prado, not the Met. And I think you have a marvelous voice. Sorry I couldn't stay for the whole performance.
Sigi

She couldn't believe Kleinermann had been there. It made her skin crawl. And what did he mean "If I couldn't have it?" She showed Jorge the note.

While Jorge read, David slipped in through the open door.

"I knew Abigail should have offed the Nazi when she had the chance," Jorge said. He handed David the note.

"We better check the painting," David said.

They hastily made their way to the exhibit room. Alessandra stepped close to *The Naked Maja Dancing* and studied the ring. Her heart pounded. *One, two, three, four, five, six diamonds!* She still wasn't satisfied. She asked a guard to help her remove the painting from the wall.

She took out her magnifying glass and inspected the ring again. She checked the symmetry of the diamonds. It still checked out. She turned the painting over. No "BR." Her heart stopped. Kleinermann must have had someone add another diamond to the forgery and somehow switched it again for the real Goya. She turned to David and pointed out the lack of letters on the back.

David grinned at her.

"Why are you grinning? This is serious."

"I had Von Herstellen remove the markings before he shipped the painting here. Those markings by the Nazis defiled the painting. I didn't want that stain permanently emblazoned on our family's treasure."

"I'm still worried. I better alert security." She signaled a guard who hurried over. She filled him in and handed him the note.

"We'll alert the Guardia Civil and call Interpol right away," the guard said and left.

"Maybe we should call Gregor," Alessandra said as she nervously fingered her necklace.

"He's already on it. He called just before I left and asked me to extend his apologies for not being able to make it here," David said. "I'm sure Gregor will catch him."

"Can we go and celebrate now," Jorge said. "The Champagne is getting warm."

They returned to her dressing room and popped the bottle. Jorge poured while Alessandra switched necklaces. She chose the pearls.

"That necklace is beautiful but I liked the other one better," David smiled.

She picked up the chain with the mezuzah, cross and key on it, and held it up to her neckline next to the pearls.

David pointed to the key. "I've been meaning to ask. Why the key? Is it a symbol of some kind?"

She pecked David on the cheek. "You two really must visit our winery soon." She removed the key from the chain and placed it in his hand. "When you come, I'll personally show you our very interesting cellar."

Both men looked puzzled.

She took a sip of the champagne and gave David a mischievous smile. "Now let's go visit our parents and see how they are doing. I don't trust my father with Jewish women. He ends up wanting to marry them." She turned and sauntered out leaving two very bewildered men in her wake.

ABOUT THE AUTHOR

Richard Katz is an attorney in Marin County, CA, who represented a family to recover a stolen Holocaust painting. His experience in that capacity drove him to write this book.

ACKNOWLEDGEMENTS

All of the people I list below played an important role in making this novel what it is. It takes a village and these people are its citizens. Thank you all.

Julie Oxendale, my screenwriting teacher and collaborator on the *Naked Maja Dancing* screenplay taught me how to think through a story. The hours we spent together sounding out the dialogue were invaluable. And the trip we took to visit the places we wrote about will forever be a source of wonderful memories.

Sid Israels, my cousin who alerted me to the history of Marrano Jews.

Kelly Baraka who spent the time reading through the novel and making pertinent suggestions to make the novel better.

Elizabeth Appel and Freddie Greene, my writing group buddies who helped edit the book. Thank you for the hours you spent reading my manuscript, suggesting changes and keeping me focused.

Raelynn Hillhouse studied with me at a course we took in Kauai and made suggestions to improve the novel.

Ana Hayes McCracken, a great friend who I met at one of the Maui writer's conferences and helped edit the book. Also, a great cheerleader.

Marimar Torres who arranged a trip and tour to her family's winery in Spain which helped Julie and me envision a scene we have in the story. Thank you for the wonderful treatment we received at the winery and restaurant after our tour.

Laurie Stein, the art historian who read the entire screenplay to ensure its accuracy about the protocol and laws regarding recovering a stolen piece of art. The authenticity in my novel about the protocols regarding recovering stolen art are a testament to her counsel.

Elisabeth Rottger, the owner of Schloss Karnzow, who was gracious in allowing Julie and me to tour the Castle and show us interesting details we use in the story.

And last but not least, Gary Kahn and Joanne Miller, my dear friends who read my book and constantly cajoled me to get the book published. Thank you for being such staunch supporters.

order at www.pegasusbooks.net

CPSIA information can be obtained at www.ICGtesting.com
Printed in the USA
LVOW10s2357181015

458789LV00001B/38/P